PARADISE CITY

PARADISE CITY

A Joe Gunther Novel

ARCHER MAYOR

Minotaur Books
New York

PARADISE CITY. Copyright © 2012 by Archer Mayor. All rights
reserved. Printed in the United States of America.
For information, address St. Martin's Press, 175 Fifth Avenue,
New York, N.Y. 10010.

www.minotaurbooks.com

ISBN 978-0-312-68195-1 (hardcover)
ISBN 978-1-250-01587-7 (e-book)

First Edition: October 2012

10 9 8 7 6 5 4 3 2 1

To Margot,

my oasis

ACKNOWLEDGMENTS

With all of my books, I am as much in debt to the kindness of others as I am to my imagination. Since in many ways, these novels are more stories of people in crisis than they are pure mysteries, I rely on those who know far more than I about certain places, situations, and circumstances to supply me with at least the impression that I know what I'm talking about. My thanks, therefore, to those listed below. You were invaluable—generous with your time and knowledge and understanding of my process. I will keep my fingers crossed that you find the end result worthy.

A small additional note for the sake of historical accuracy: I mention in the following pages the shopworn appearance of the Northampton Police Department's headquarters building. As of this publication, it has since been replaced by a beautiful, modern, highly functional two-story structure—a credit to Chief Sienkiewicz's vision, the good work of his officers and staff, and the support and hard work of the town's leadership and voting public. My hat is off to you all.

Margot Zalkind

Lisa Fusco

Russell Sienkiewicz

Sherry Young

Paul Gross

Maria Gross

Castle Freeman

Julie Lavorgna

John Martin

Ray Walker

Brent Dzilio

Pat Goggins

Jonathan Wright

Clare Higgins

Bryn Geffert

Don Siegel

Bill Dwight

Madeleine Kunin

Ruth Constantine

Jonathon Mayor

Amherst College

Smith College

Northampton PD

Brattleboro PD

and the City of Northampton, Massachusetts

PARADISE CITY

CHAPTER ONE

Mickey looked around for what felt like the hundredth time, so far from his comfort zone, he could barely stay put.

Beacon Hill. What was that? Might as well be standing bare-assed in the middle of Boston Common on a Sunday after church. Not on a roof in the city's fanciest neighborhood, waiting to be nailed by a cop, an alarm, an attack dog, a police helicopter, a motion detector, or who the hell knew what else. These people could buy anything they wanted to trap a guy like him.

He saw a silhouette gesture at him from a rooftop across the alley and waved back unhappily. His cell began buzzing and he flipped it open.

"You set?"

"Yeah," he whispered, trying to sound self-confident.

"Get down there and tell us what you see."

"Right," he said, and snapped the phone shut.

There were three of them—Tony, James, and him. He didn't know James at all. That was bad enough. Tony had vouched for him, but

Tony could be flaky, and Tony didn't know shit about this part of the world, either. This was all James's deal—the fence, the victim, the stuff to grab and how to grab it.

And that was the worst part—using a glass cutter, wearing hoods, going in with people inside the house. Like a bad movie. The man had been convincing, though: Forget about flat screens and laptops; James had a good-paying fence for jewelry, silverware, and collectibles. Old stuff, with no serial numbers or bar codes to trace. It was high-end, portable, easy to dump, and easy to steal if you knew where to go. And James knew where to go. A little old rich lady who lived alone. He knew a girl who'd cleaned the place once as a favor to her aunt, the regular maid. The usual guy-who-knows-a-guy trajectory that so often connects a target to the person seeking one out.

Mickey sidled up to the roof's edge and peered over. Less like a movie and more like a nightmare, he thought. He was a smash-and-grab man. Hit-'n'-run. In and out. No violence, no witnesses, no high-society pigeon. All this sneaking around in black clothes, with ropes and duct tape, ducking private security patrols . . . Gave him the creeps. This wasn't juvie time anymore. This was hard time. He *liked* laptops and flat screens and stereo equipment. He understood them and what they were worth. What the hell did he know about silver-ware?

He tested the rope he'd secured to a nearby chimney and hooked it to the carabiner on his harness.

This was why he'd been brought along, of course. He was the only one of them who knew about this mountaineering crap. Go figure that an outdoors course in climbing, rappelling, and rope work for inner-city kids would wind up coming in handy. That at least brought a smile to

Mickey's face as he imagined the do-gooders who'd trained him. If they could see him now.

Thanks, guys. 'Preciate the leg up.

Slightly bolstered by the thought, he stood on the roof's edge, feeling uncomfortably exposed, oblivious to the nineteenth-century vista surrounding him. In fact, it was a backdrop of operatic proportions, of ancient rooftops, clustered chimney pots, and softly glowing skylights, painted darkly against the spotlighted gold dome of the Massachusetts State House in the distance.

Testing the line with a final tug, he stiffened his legs and eased straight back, as if dropping in slow motion onto a bed.

Wishful thinking, of course. He was four stories up, gingerly walking backward down the wall toward a greenhouse roof far below. The plan was for him to alight there, gain access with a glass cutter, and open the back door for his two confederates. It wasn't actually a greenhouse—not way down there, overshadowed by neighboring brownstones. The owners had capped the near-useless backyard with a kitchen extension, complete with glass roof, to take advantage of the natural light.

To Mickey, though, as he looked over his shoulder to gauge his progress, the dark glass beneath him looked ominous and foreboding—crystalline panes of black water waiting to swallow him whole.

All of which suddenly transformed into blinding light, making him wonder for a split second if he wasn't about to be lifted high and away on a rising wave of lava.

"*Fuck*," he hissed between bared teeth, almost letting go of the rope paying out between his hands.

No longer simply exposed, but actually highlighted in the glare from below, he simultaneously felt the cell phone vibrate in his pocket and saw a person enter the kitchen below.

"Fucking moron," he murmured to himself, knowing Tony was on the other end of the ignored phone. "Like I'm up for a chitchat. 'Yo, bro. What's happenin'?' Jesus."

Mickey shifted his grip on the rope, locking it into the 'beener, and prepared himself to hang in the air for as long as it took.

Billie Hawthorn squinted slightly in the kitchen's bright light. Her granddaughter had told her to put in a rheostat here, so she wouldn't have to adjust her eyes every time she made a nightly visit. Perfectly reasonable, as were most of Mina's recommendations; and Billie did make a midnight cocoa raid every single night. But who could remember to do such things? She was nearing ninety, after all. Living alone in a huge place like this—stubbornly independent—she had a hard enough time remembering to pay the bills and take in the daily newspaper, much less start fussing with light fixtures.

She glanced up at the string of designer bulbs running the length of the ceiling's ridge board, reflecting attractively off the glass sheets of the roof. The entire room was very pretty—her late husband's last ambitious project before he died. Maybe that was one additional reason she so enjoyed these nocturnal visits.

Above her, frozen but unseen against the glare of those same lights, Mickey Roma watched the old woman seemingly staring right up at him. He prepared himself to see her transformed with alarm and running for the phone.

But all she did was look away and begin to boil water on the fancy stove, preparing herself something hot to drink and moving about slowly in a memorized ritual. Oddly, he found her actions comforting, although whether because they were so utterly domestic, or simply because they weren't what he'd been expecting, he wasn't sure.

In either case, he found himself considering the possibility that he'd survive a little longer. Even the phone in his pocket stopped buzzing against his leg.

Still, ten minutes later, he was stiff and sore and getting cold, hanging like a hunk of bait in the cool night air. It was late spring, which in New England could mean almost anything. He gratefully watched the old woman tidy up at last, lift her steaming mug carefully by its over-sized handle, approach the door linking the satellite kitchen to the main house, and finally kill the lights.

Mickey closed his eyes to regain his night vision, did a couple of bouncing horizontal squats against the wall to loosen up, and started slowly paying out the rope again, continuing his descent. Looking through the kitchen door below, he could see other, more distant interior lights getting turned off as the homeowner retreated into the house's embrace, encouraging him to hope for a little privacy and—more important—some sound insulation against his next move.

The phone started up again.

He ignored it for the rest of his short journey, settled carefully atop the crown of the glass roof, being sure to keep his sneakers on the metal crossbars, and, maintaining tension on the line in case he slipped, retrieved the phone.

"What the fuck you want?" he growled softly.

"You okay?" Tony asked, his voice high-pitched with fear.

I was the one dangling in midair like a pair of nuts in the breeze,

Mickey thought as he answered, "No, dipshit. She told me she was goin' for the cops, so I figured I'd wait."

He could sense Tony trying to figure that out.

"I'm fine," he said, relenting.

A second voice entered his ear. "Move it. We don't got all night."

James—Mr. Love and Support.

"Then stop calling," Mickey told him, and snapped the phone shut, feeling the anger warm him up. None of them would even be here without his skills. Son of a bitch.

He shook it off, refocusing on the job, and loosened his rope just enough that he could crouch over the greenhouse glass, apply a suction cup and a cutter, and quickly scratch a manhole-size circle by his feet. The noise seemed like a siren wail to him, even though he and Tony had actually tested the tool a few days ago at Tony's, just to make sure of its relative silence.

With a couple of solid taps from Mickey's gloved knuckles, the glass circle snapped free, still adhering to the suction cup. He placed it flat beside him, held it in place with his foot, tore off a long strip of duct tape from the roll at his waist, and stuck the circle to the glass surface so that it wouldn't slide off. He then straightened, retightened the rope, stepped over the narrow hole, and slid into the kitchen like a fireman down a brass pole.

Coming gently to rest on the floor at last, he stood stock-still for a moment, taking in the silence around him, incredulous that the whole operation had gone off with barely a hitch. He also discovered—now that he was inside—that the lady had killed only the primary lights as she'd left—the kitchen was dark, but he could see a soft glow in the next room, and another in the hallway beyond. They allowed him to see the interior of a house rich with paintings and elaborate old furniture, carpeted with thick, dark rugs and decorated with shelves of fancy porcelain, displays of artwork, and assorted expensive junk—the kind of stuff he associated with museums. He didn't much know what to make of it all, but he felt on the edge of a rarified world that he'd never visited in person.

With a quick, self-congratulatory fist pump, he unhooked from the rope, crossed over to the kitchen's heavily locked back door, and quietly opened it.

On the other side were James and Tony, also masked and black-clad, who'd climbed down the fire escape of the building across the alleyway.

"'Bout time," James said, pushing by.

Two flights up, at the far end of the narrow house, Billie Hawthorn took an appreciative sip of her cocoa and placed the mug on the nightstand by her bed. The television across the room filled the air with laughter as the pompadoured host introduced his latest guest. She knew these shows were nonsense; she even found much of the premise insulting—all those posturing fading stars or eager celebrity aspirants, saying whatever came into their heads as they wriggled on the couch, tossing their hair and discussing clothes or pets or their latest encounter with substance abuse. But at Billie's age, it was pretty harmless stuff, and she much preferred it over the white-knuckled, grim-faced fare that passed for news or commentary nowadays. She'd spent her years in the trenches of social welfare, putting in time, effort, and money, and standing up for her fellow human beings. She'd never asked for recognition then, and only wanted a little peace and quiet now.

She frowned suddenly at the screen and narrowed her eyes slightly. Patting alongside her leg, she located the TV's remote and hit the mute button.

In the abrupt silence, she heard it again—a sound from downstairs.

This had happened before, years ago, when a bird had gotten in and knocked something over.

But what was the likelihood of that happening twice?

And she hadn't opened any windows yet this year.

She rubbed her temple thoughtfully. Or had she?

Billie swept the thin blanket off and swung her legs over the edge of the bed. If it was a bird again, she didn't want it making the same mess as last time.

Downstairs, James crossed over to Tony in three fast steps, his fists balled, his eyes tight with rage behind his mask.

Tony looked up at him fearfully, half-crouched in the process of retrieving the book he'd just knocked off the coffee table.

"You stupid fuck," James snarled at him in the dim light, his arms trembling. "First you bump that chair, now this?"

Mickey stared at him, his own hands full of expensive crystal baubles from an antique sideboard. Having watched James for the past fifteen minutes, Mickey was convinced he was on something. He was jittery, pale, and sweaty, and as wired as a methhead. And that had been before Tony had pushed his buttons. Twice.

"It's okay," Tony said softly but urgently, offering a pleading smile. "She's probably deaf as a doorknob, right?"

Mickey wasn't so sure about Tony, either. For all the care that Mickey had used gaining them access, it seemed like his mastermind colleagues didn't have their act together. And Mickey hadn't wanted to come in the first place.

"*Guys*," he hissed across the room at them. "You wanna do this later?"

James clenched his jaw before telling Tony, "You screw up one more time, and I cut your throat. You got that?"

Tony was already nodding repeatedly. "I got it. I got it. I'm cool. I was nervous is all. Won't happen again."

James turned on Mickey. "And you keep your mouth *shut*. You wouldn't even be here without me. You're the bitch. You got that? You do what you're told." He focused on what Mickey was holding. "And that includes dumping that shit. We don't have a buyer for crystal, for Christ's sake. Steal stuff I can actually sell—silverware, old jewelry, crap like that. I got a guy for that."

Mickey let a two-second pause elapse before muttering, "Whatever, man," and quietly replaced the crystal.

You couldn't make this shit up, he thought.

And then it got worse. The room's overhead light suddenly froze them as in a flash photograph.

"Who *are* you people?"

The three men turned to face the small woman standing in the doorway.

With dread, Mickey saw James react precisely as programmed. He crossed the room quickly and simply clubbed the woman across the head with the back of his hand, sending her bouncing against the door frame and collapsing onto the floor.

"Ah, *man*," Mickey exclaimed, dropping the silverware he'd just picked up.

James pulled a gun out from under his shirt and pointed it at Mickey. "You *shut the fuck up*," he yelled, and then turned and kicked Billie Hawthorn in the head for good measure.

She didn't make a sound.

There was a momentary silence as they all stared at one another—Mickey stunned and a little resigned, Tony scared and confused, and James on the verge of opening fire, for lack of a better idea.

Mickey recognized that look in his eyes.

"You're the boss, man," he said soothingly. "What do you want us to do? We can make good on this—at least get enough to make it worthwhile. We might as well, right?" He didn't add, We're screwed anyhow, so we better make it count.

James blinked once, slowly. "Yeah," he said thoughtfully, as if considering a distant thought. "Sure. We'll do that." He lowered his gun.

Mickey gestured to the curled-up shape on the floor. "Let me take a quick look at her. Make sure she's breathing."

James glanced down, almost surprised, and stepped away. "Sure."

He placed the palm of his free hand against his ski-masked forehead, as if wondering what he might find. He then caught sight of Tony, who was still crouching with the dropped book in his hand.

"What're you looking at?" James demanded.

Tony released the book and stood up. "Nuthin."

"You got that right. Go through the upstairs, now that we got the place to ourselves. You can turn on the lights if you want, but stay clear of the windows or close the curtains. Find the broad's bedroom. Grab anything fancy and leave the rest. *Now.*"

Tony left, circling the woman and Mickey, who was crouched by her side, opening her airway. She was still breathing, and she didn't seem to be bleeding. Maybe she'd make it after all.

Things were bad enough. He could live without a murder rap.

Welcome to the major leagues.

CHAPTER TWO

Detective Jimmy McAuliffe studied the young woman a moment through the narrow gap of the waiting room's open door, watching how she handled herself when she thought she was alone.

She looked tired and drawn, with her unkempt hair pulled back into a sloppy ponytail. He'd been told that she hadn't left her grandmother's side since the old lady had been rolled out of the operating room. Even now, Jimmy was meeting her at the hospital, just down the hall from ICU. Wilhelmina Hawthorn was in a coma, as she had been since the beating.

McAuliffe entered the room and sat across from the young woman, a coffee table littered with out-of-date magazines between them. He'd directed a patrol officer in the hallway to make sure that they weren't disturbed—by anyone for any reason. He introduced himself. "I'm Detective McAuliffe, Ms. Carson. Boston PD. I'm sorry to be meeting under these circumstances."

Her eyes flicked up from the tabletop to his face. "Why?"

He hesitated. "Why what?"

"Why are you sorry?"

He'd heard this one before. He'd heard most of them before.

"I'm sorry when any innocent person gets attacked by a jerk with no conscience."

That seemed to catch her off guard, which was his intention. It was entirely cynical on his part, but he didn't know much about her, and he wanted quick access to her good graces. Mina Carson was twenty-six, a Brown graduate, employed by an architecture firm, although not an architect herself; she was also single, had no children, and lived alone in a fancy part of town—due in part, he suspected, to Hawthorn's generosity. Jimmy had learned that the old woman was worth a bundle and had only this one heir, which his hard-bitten view of reality could only see as having a potentially deeper meaning.

"I shouldn't have said that," she said softly.

"Sure you should've," McAuliffe countered. "You've been attacked, just like your grandmother. You're in pain, too."

He left it at that, not wanting to overplay, while also needing to judge her responses.

"Thank you."

Jimmy extracted a notepad from his inner pocket. "How's Mrs. Hawthorn doing?"

"No change," Carson said wearily. "And you can call her Billie. Everyone does."

He opened the pad and laid it before him, glancing quickly at its scribbled contents.

"You mind if I ask you a few questions?"

She shook her head, studying without focus the scattered magazines.

"You found her. Is that right?"

"Yes."

"Around eight this morning?"

"Yes."

"How was that?"

She looked up at him quickly, her eyes narrowed.

"I mean," he restated, "how was it that you went there so early? You don't live there, right?"

Her expression softened with understanding. "Oh. No, I don't. Billie and I had a ritual. She was my alarm clock. Called me every morning at seven. Never failed."

She stopped.

"Meaning," he suggested, "that her missing this morning was a cause for concern."

Mina nodded. "We both knew I could buy an alarm clock; that I was just checking on her. But it gave us a chance to chat every morning, sometimes for just a few minutes." Her voice caught a moment, and she swallowed before adding, "There's no one left in our family except us."

"So you went by," he suggested.

"I waited a little," Carson admitted. "I didn't want to embarrass her, in case it was just something personal. . . . You know, she's an old lady. Likes her privacy."

"Sure."

"But after fifteen minutes, I didn't care anymore. I was becoming too anxious. I called and got no answer, and that was it. There was no way I wasn't going to see if she was okay."

"Tell me what you found," Jimmy urged her. "And don't leave anything out."

Mina Carson was sitting forward. Now, for a moment only, she propped her elbows on her knees and placed her hands on her face as if she were splashing water on it.

He waited, not sure what might come next—a response to his question or an emotional breakdown.

It was the former. Mina rubbed her eyes finally and slid her hands back so that she ended up cupping her jaw. "Everything looked normal from the outside," she told him. "The door was locked, the windows facing the street were like they always are. I let myself in and called out her name; I always do that."

Jimmy had been to the house; had spent most of the day there. "As you stepped inside, did you sense anything?" he asked. "Any sound or odor? Anything at all?"

She sat back and dropped her hands in her lap. "Silence. I mean, she doesn't always hear me when I come by. She's a little hard of hearing, and if she's upstairs or listening to TV or the radio, she might not notice at all, especially if she's not expecting me. But that's the point, you see?" She gave him an expectant lift of her eyebrows. "That means there's usually noise of some sort. Billie loves to have something on to keep her company. This time, there was nothing. Nothing at all," she added in a slightly wondering tone.

"All right," he said. "Then what?"

"I went looking," she replied. "I found her almost immediately, lying on the floor, right by the door to the living room."

"Stop there for a second," he said. "If it's possible to make a snapshot of that very moment, tell me what you saw."

She seemed to understand the process, and kept the emotions that were stamped on her face under control. "I saw her, of course, but I know what you're asking. It was messy, and some of the lights were on."

"Explain that."

"There are always some lights on—night-lights, really, since she walks around at all hours, but not the overhead one in the living room—almost never. She doesn't like it. Too garish. It's a chandelier. I remember that. It stuck out."

"That it was lit, you mean?"

"Yeah."

"Okay. What else? You said it was messy."

She sighed. "Billie hates a mess. 'Sloppy place, sloppy mind' is like a mantra to her. But things had been thrown around—dropped and broken and ransacked. The whole place."

"You checked out the entire house?" Jimmy asked, surprised.

"After the ambulance took her away," she said. "At first, I went to her side and tried to wake her up. I saw she was breathing, but I didn't know what to do. She had that terrible bruise on her face. I didn't dare move her. I was worried I might make things worse."

Jimmy was nodding sympathetically, keeping her going.

"But after everyone left and they wouldn't let me ride with her," Mina continued, "I walked around, trying to figure out what had happened. That's when I called you—later. I saw that so much was missing. I'm sorry I took so long. I just wanted to take care of her first."

"Of course," he murmured, embarrassed at how things had in fact transpired. The police and the ambulance should have arrived simultaneously.

"Turns out you'd been called as well," she said. "I didn't realize that till later—the whole nine-one-one thing. But you were late." She smiled apologetically and added, "I mean, the police. Not you personally."

"Right," he said. "Mina, another officer asked you to write a list of everything you thought was missing."

"Yes," she confirmed.

"Have you thought of anything else since then?"

"No. I'm sorry. I didn't *look* at Billie's place like that. It was my home away from home, not like a store where you notice everything."

"I understand," he said supportively. "And when you went around the house, did you touch anything? Move anything?"

She shook her head. "I was in a haze, I guess. That's another reason I didn't do well with the list. I just couldn't figure out why this happened."

Jimmy lowered his voice for empathy. "Let me ask it a different way. Could you notice a pattern when you walked around? Things that were taken and others that weren't? I'm looking at types and/or categories, I guess you could say."

"Small," she said immediately. "Nothing big was gone. The paintings were left, and some of them are worth a fortune. The TV was still there, the big computer—the TV was on mute, by the way, as if she'd heard them and gone to investigate. But the laptop from the living room was gone. Jewelry, silverware, some fancier items. And crazy stuff, like the small clocks, her pens, a couple of CD players. She had a hunk of pyrite in a glass case—they broke the case and stole the rock."

"Pyrite?"

"Fool's gold," she clarified.

"You saw how they got in?" he asked after a pause.

"The hole in the kitchen skylight?"

"Right. How 'bout how they left?" he asked. "What do you think?"

"The back door into the alley. It was unlocked."

"You tested it?"

She'd been gazing around until then, lost in her recollections. But at that, she looked up. "Yes. Did I mess up?"

"No. I just need to know what you might have done, versus what the burglars did. You mentioned a laptop. You think she kept any records? A serial number or sales receipt? Or any accounts she might have used it for? Passwords, log-in names, favorite sites, things like that— something we could monitor or backtrack to a new user?"

Again, she was shaking her head. "No. Billie didn't buy anything online. She used it for e-mails, photographs. It was like a fancy type-writer to her. And I doubt if she kept a record of any serial numbers. She's tidy, but mostly because she throws things out a lot, like bills and instruction books and records. It drove me crazy until I got used to it."

After a short pause, Jimmy suggested, "You two are close, aren't you?"

Sorrow clouded the young woman's face, along with something he couldn't identify. "She's the only family I have. I love her so much. I'm named after her. Mina's short for Wilhelmina." She laughed suddenly, tears in her eyes. "We both hate that name. That's why she went by Billie."

"Tell me a little about her," Jimmy urged.

Mina seemed grateful for both the opportunity and the diversion. She brightened as she admitted, "There's actually a bunch I don't know. Rumors have it that she was a wild child when my grandfather Charles married her, and by 'child,' I don't mean that she was young at the time. She was well into her thirties when they met, but young at heart. She's still that. I heard that she traveled around Europe and South America and led quite the bohemian life in the early days. Her family had money, so she could afford it. For all I know, she married Charles 'cause she ran out of cash. I heard that, too. What I know for a fact is that they really loved each other. He was very quiet and kind of scholarly. Billie did a nice job of getting him out of the house more than he might have done otherwise."

"But she kept up the eccentric lifestyle?" Jimmy asked.

Her eyes widened. "Oh, no. That's why I wonder how much truth there is to all that. I mean, she was always lively and fun, but she and Charles were inseparable. They did the concert and museum thing, an occasional movie, and they had a house on the Vineyard they used every summer—something from his family. But basically they just hung out and read books and kept each other company. They were my safe haven growing up. Billie's supposed past always seemed a little fantastical to me."

"Charles died?"

"Yes," she replied sadly. "Ten years ago. It was quick and peaceful. He'd had a good life. Billie was heartbroken for a while, and then she got on with it, just like always. That's when I moved into a new slot in her life, and we became superclose."

"Your own family didn't supply that?"

"I don't have a family," Mina replied tersely. "My father was a drunk and killed everybody but me in a car crash, long ago."

"Ouch," Jimmy sympathized, recognizing at last the sense of emotional reserve that he'd been sensing. "What about Billie? She have any kids?"

Her voice retained a trace of hardness. "None who're alive. Like I said, it was just the two of us."

Jimmy glanced at his notes, having researched much of this

beforehand. The Internet and computerized databanks in general had made the foot slogging of old a comparative breeze. Mina's father had been Billie's only child.

Still, in the awkward silence following Mina's last comment, she added, "Carson was my mother's maiden name."

"Okay, Ms. Carson," he asked, "what do you think happened here? Why was your grandmother targeted?"

Mina looked hapless. "Wasn't it a robbery?"

"Then why her house?" he countered. "It's in the middle of the block. There are probably richer people all around."

"That's true enough," she admitted.

She paused, reflecting, before adding, "She didn't have an alarm. Could that have had anything to do with it?"

"That was a question I had for you," Jimmy conceded. "Who else might've known that? She had servants, didn't she? Or at least people who came in and helped out?"

"Pam—Pamela," Mina told him. "But she's been cleaning Billie's house for fifteen years or more. She's like family. She totally fell apart when I called her about the attack."

"What's Pam's last name?"

"Tosi." Without asking permission, Mina startled the detective by reaching across the table, grabbing his notepad, and flipping to a clean page, where she scribbled down a number with a pen from her rear blue jeans pocket.

Jimmy raised his eyebrows as she returned the pad, impressed by her reflexively imperious manner. There's attitude here, he thought. And perhaps as much anger as privilege.

"That's her number," Mina explained. "I don't know where she lives. I seriously doubt she had anything to do with this, though. She's only

about ten years younger than Billie. Very religious, ultraconservative. God knows what she thought of Billie's politics."

Jimmy glanced at the phone number to make sure he could read it, then added Pamela Tosi's name beside it.

"Anyone else?" he asked.

"Just the odd person, like an electrician or a plumber. No reason to think that they'd know if there was an alarm or not."

He didn't agree with her there. "I don't guess you have names," he said.

She gave him a slight smile. "I compensated for her record keeping. I do know most of that stuff. I keep a file at home. I'll get it to you."

"Thanks. What about friends or guests? Anyone you know about who may be hard up right now, or who showed an unusual interest in some of the things she had lying around?"

Her face showed surprise. "I can't think of anyone there. She didn't have many guests, and they're mostly wealthy old ladies like herself."

"Enemies?" he asked. "Even dating back to when Charles was alive?"

She was back to looking mournful again. "I know everybody says this about their grandparents, but these people were like saints. Everybody liked them."

"Not everybody says that," Jimmy couldn't resist telling her, adding, "Sad to say."

He slapped the notepad closed and returned it to his pocket. "That's about it for the time being, Ms. Carson. We did have the crime-scene people go over the place, and I haven't gotten their results yet, but I'm not holding my breath. The real deal is not like TV."

"I've heard that," she said.

"And of course," he continued, "we'll keep plugging away at this, interviewing people and checking pawnshops and whatever against that list you gave us. The Internet helps us there, too. And let's hope your grandmother gets better, so that she can tell us what she saw. I mean," he added awkwardly, "as well as just for everyone's sake."

He rose to his feet, feeling slightly stupid, and shook her hand. "You have any questions for me?"

"What do you think our chances are?" she asked simply.

He always hated that one. "I wouldn't get my hopes up too high. We get so many cases like this. . . ."

She finished the thought for him. "I know. Pretty much luck of the draw."

He backtracked a little, slightly defensive. "It's not that random. We do a thorough job, and these jerks generally talk when they get drunk or doped up or when we catch 'em for something else and they try to make a deal. It's amazing what can happen."

She smiled wanly and nodded, letting go of his hand. "Of course. I appreciate your help."

He moved toward the door. "My pleasure. I'll be back in touch as things progress. We might get lucky."

He stepped outside and began walking down the hallway.

When pigs fly, he thought.

CHAPTER THREE

Joe Gunther paused before reaching for the phone, blinking at the darkened ceiling of his bedroom, clearing his head of sleep. Increasingly these days, when he was jarred awake, he found himself wondering less about what lay behind a call, and more about how it might come back to haunt him. He'd been finding the toll of his profession to be mounting fast and costing him dearly as of late.

These had become hollowed-out times.

"Gunther."

"Joe, it's Sam. Sorry to wake you up, but I didn't want a reporter blindsiding you."

Joe pulled himself into a sitting position and rolled up the pillow behind him. His upstairs bedroom virtually qualified as a walled-in loft, complete with very low ceiling—a feature he rarely saw except by the diffused light from the outside streetlamp. It felt snug and rough-hewn and comfy, however, and not at all like the small rental it was, especially for a too-old cop who lived alone with no pets, no plants, no romantic life, and a fridge prominently stocked with Velveeta, bologna, and mayo.

"What've you got?" he asked her.

Samantha Martens, who also answered to Sammie, was his number two, and the one on call for the night.

"It's a little crazy, as usual. They had a break-in at Tucker Peak—one of the starter castles near the top. Place was cleaned out and then torched by the thieves. So far, nobody saw a thing—the place is buried at the end of a half-mile driveway. The PD and private security share a contract with the mountain. They called in the state police for support, not having the expertise or the manpower. So far so good. After that, it gets murkier and crankier real quick. It's hometown politics, involving the Tucker Peak brass, the local selectmen, the police chief, and the VSP barracks commander. Long story short, it was the VSP who decided it might be better if we get the honor of handling it, if we'd be so kind." Her voice dropped into a monotone, as if she were reciting a list of boring rules. "We are, after all, the by-invitation-only agency; it is a major crime, what with the arson and the value of what was stolen; and since everybody thinks we're a bunch of pain-in-the-ass headline grabbers anyhow, what've we got to lose?" She resumed her normal tone to add, "That last part is mine, but you get the idea."

Joe was laughing. "Are you done?"

"I am."

She had, in fact, put it succinctly enough. Their employer—the VBI, or Vermont Bureau of Investigation—was indeed a statewide major crimes unit, invited only when requested by a local agency—a face-saving mechanism that the legislature had cooked up as part of the Bureau's charter.

Unfortunately, the unit's elite nature was as often resented as it was relied upon, depending on the prevailing political wind. Cases like this were not as rare as Sammie would have liked.

"Okay," Joe said. "So what's the plan?"

"I've already started the crime lab, and Lester's coming in from Springfield. Willy and I have been on the road about ten minutes."

"You want company?"

"You want to sleep some more?"

He laughed again. "See you soon, Sammie."

He hung up the phone and swung out of bed. She knew him well.

As well she might. They went back years—she and Willy and Joe—to when he'd been their lieutenant on Brattleboro, Vermont's detective squad, before the VBI had been invented. They were all called special agents now that they constituted the VBI's southeastern office—a title few of them used—and they'd been joined by Lester Spinney, who'd transferred from the state police, but the original detective squad's informal pecking order had remained.

Joe began dressing in the dark, so used to such callouts that he always draped his clothes where he could find them easily and in sequential order, down to the gun and badge. Over the decades, he'd made a few small adjustments—accommodating a couple of girlfriends and even a wife, who'd been taken by cancer in her twenties—but the fundamentals had remained.

As a cop, Joe was one of the lifers.

He carefully worked his way down the narrow, steep staircase to the small apartment he called home—actually an ex-carriage house tacked onto the rear of a huge and ancient Victorian pile on Green Street in Brattleboro, Vermont—and quickly nuked himself a cup of instant coffee for the road.

With that, he was ready to go to work.

. . .

Some ski mountains in Vermont developed haphazardly, near preexisting roads, largely due to neighborhood interest and the need for returning World War II vets to blow off steam. Tucker Peak had been planned as a resort straight out of the box by urban financiers in the sixties—complete with stockholders, a base village, and a brand-new access road green-lighted by the state legislature. It had been built by money, and been sustained by it ever since.

As some of its more ostentatious homes made clear.

The address Joe received while en route led him to such a place—or what had been one before an entire wing had been blackened by fire.

It hadn't been difficult to find, despite the driveway that Sam had described. He merely followed the pulsing glow of some twenty emergency vehicles—fire, rescue, and police—all flashing their strobes up into the night sky like an earth-tethered fireworks display.

Fortunately for him, most of these units were shutting down, rolling hose or actually leaving, as he worked his car slowly uphill, hugging the edge of the far ditch for most of the way. The cool air through his open window was thick with lingering damp smoke.

At the top of the drive, near the remains of the mansion, the vehicles became less utilitarian and more representative of the next phase of such a scene: unmarked cruisers, equipment-laden SUVs, and the state's lumbering forensics truck.

He parked in their midst and stepped out onto the glistening, water-soaked tarmac.

"Took you long enough. You bring breakfast?"

Joe smiled to himself. The familiar shadow of Willy Kunkle emerged from amid a small forest of blinding portable halogen lights. Wiry and short, Willy sported the extra distinction of a crippled left arm—a memento of being shot by a sniper many years ago while on the job. The disturbing visual effect of this was enhanced by his perpetually keeping the useless hand buried in his left pants pocket.

Also, to say that Willy tended toward irascibility was like describing Einstein as above average. The emotional scars of a troubled and violent past were flaunted as if on a dare, utterly disguising a man of integrity, ruthless honesty, and even a jarring, if only occasionally visible, artistic sensibility.

Sadly, as Joe saw it, these last few winning traits were for but a select few to admire. Joe was Willy's champion when others wanted him fired; Sam lived with him and was the mother of his baby daughter; and even Lester had eventually come to terms with Willy's bluntness.

But that was virtually it, barring a thick-skinned handful of others who'd learned to take the guy in stride—some of the time at least.

"I figured I'd let you do all the dirty work first," Joe told him as he drew near. "I hope you haven't been dawdling."

"Up yours." Willy turned to stand beside his boss and gaze at the huge wounded structure before them.

"Some mess," Joe said softly. "The owners here?"

"Nah. Probably busy padding their insurance claim. No one was here when it was hit."

"Why the fire?"

Willy paused before answering. "There's the question. The arson dick's here." He gestured with his right hand. "In there, poking around with the others. Haven't heard what they've found yet."

"Hey, boss."

They turned as a startlingly tall and skinny man approached—Lester Spinney, whose desk at the office was appropriately festooned with stork iconography, given to him by people who all thought they alone had been struck by the similarity.

"Any word from your old trooper playmates?" Joe asked as he drew near.

"Not much," Lester admitted. "The owners are supposedly sending a staffer with an inventory list and insurance information. He should be here pretty soon."

Willy snorted.

Les ignored him. "They found a pillowcase filled with silverware in the driveway, which makes it look like whoever did this left in a hurry. That could mean the fire moved faster than they thought it would."

"Which is one of a half dozen other theories," Willy said.

"True," Les agreed pleasantly.

"Witnesses?" Joe asked, watching people entering and leaving the building, all of them wearing either coveralls or Tyvek suits.

"Nope," Lester said. "The fire triggered a central alarm—"

"Ask the owners," Willy interrupted.

Joe looked at him. "Meaning?"

Willy indicated the huge house with an upward tilt of his chin. "Sam's in there, too. She told me there's a shitload of security cameras but—so far—no recording equipment. That tells me it's wireless and probably sending images directly to some receiver in Connecticut or somewhere."

"I read about those," Lester said. "You can control the lights, heating, run system checks, and even pan the grounds from anywhere in the world. Amazing stuff."

"Yeah. If you've run out of yachts to buy," Willy grumbled.

"Do we know if the cameras got anything?" Joe asked.

"I bet that's the person to ask," Willy replied, pointing into the night sky, whose edges were just now paling with the coming dawn.

His two companions looked up, seeing nothing, and certainly hearing nothing over the accumulated rumbling of diesel engines around them.

They knew better than to question him, however. Willy had been a sniper in the military, with an ominously impressive confirmed kill list. His senses could approach the supernatural.

Sure enough, moments later, a pinpoint of light appeared over the tops of the nearest trees, along with the familiar *chop-chop* of a helicopter's blades.

"God, I love the rich," Willy said, and headed toward the rear of the house, where an enormous lawn was about to serve as a landing pad.

The young man who emerged from the aircraft was medium in all things—height, weight, appearance, and affect. His name was Tom Smith.

"You're kidding, right?" Willy asked him, ignoring the man's proffered hand. "They couldn't just beam you here?"

Joe grabbed it instead. "Joe Gunther. Vermont Bureau of Investigation. You represent the home owner?"

They were walking away from the noisy helicopter as they spoke.

"Yes," Smith acknowledged. "I'm one of Robert Hampton's assistants, charged with maintaining his estates and property."

"Mine mows my lawn," Willy said. "You do that?"

Joe stopped and took hold of Smith's elbow. The younger man was staring at Willy with his mouth half-open. "May I call you Tom?"

Smith blinked and shifted his gaze to Joe. "Sure."

"Then why don't we get out of all this and sit in my car, Tom?" Joe motioned to Spinney. "Les? You want to join us?"

Willy laughed and walked off, point taken.

A couple of moments later, the three of them slid into Gunther's car and shut the doors. In the resulting quiet, Joe said, "There. That's a little better. Tom, I know you're here to get an idea of what happened and report back to Mr. Hampton, but I hope you're receptive to our asking a few questions, okay?"

"Of course," Smith said, balancing his briefcase on his knees. "That's one of the reasons I'm here."

"Great. Special Agent Spinney will be running you through all that in a minute, but I wanted to ask you one thing first: Do you have a recording system that monitors what goes on inside the house?"

Smith was precise in his response. He snapped open both clasps of his case, flipped back the lid, and reached inside to extract an envelope containing a DVD. "Mr. Hampton authorized me to give you this. It's a recording of the break-in, both inside and out."

Joe took hold of it daintily and handed it to Lester, who was in the backseat. "Impressive," he said. "That may be the fastest service we've ever gotten."

"Mr. Hampton has five properties," Smith said officiously. "All of them are wirelessly connected to a central office that monitors what happens in them, twenty-four/seven."

Joe had never liked that expression. "I'm sure. And yet it was the fire alarm that got everybody running."

Smith's mouth tightened briefly before he conceded, "We're looking into that."

"Yeahhhh," Les said, his voice barely audible. "We will be, too,"

"You look at the disc's contents?" Joe asked their guest.

"I did."

"And?"

"You can see two masked men going from room to room, stealing Mr. and Mrs. Hampton's belongings."

"They look like they know what they're doing? Like they're familiar with the house?" Joe asked.

"No," Smith said flatly. "Several times, you can see them getting lost. It's a big place." He looked out the windshield briefly and added, "Or was."

"What're they stealing?" Spinney asked.

"Portable things. Electronics, like all the TV sets, except the really big one in the den, which takes a whole crew to move. Stereo equipment, portable computers, guns, silverware, jewelry . . . I'm also here to take inventory, so I don't know for sure, but that's a general idea."

"What kind of guns?" Spinney asked.

"Shotguns, rifles, a few handguns. You can see them tearing apart the gun case to get at them. We definitely have serial numbers for all that."

"Any safes?" Joe asked.

"There are two, but they didn't mess with them. One they didn't even find. The other they ignored."

Joe shifted slightly in his seat to make better eye contact with the young man. "Tom, with all the high-tech gadgetry, how did they get in without triggering anything? I mean, I got it that the people watching the monitors were asleep at the wheel. Special Agent Spinney will get what we need about them. But surely there's an automatic alarm if a window's broken or a door's forced. What did you see at the very beginning of the video?"

Smith pointed outside. "See that second-floor window? The small one right near the corner of the wall there? It belongs to a guest bathroom. They put up a ladder and broke through there. What we don't know yet is if it was never wired, or if somehow it got bypassed. We've scheduled a major meeting with the security firm for later this morning."

"I bet you have. Can you see the vehicle they used?"

"Yes. It's an old van, but you can't make out the registration—too dirty."

"And what about why the fire was set?" Joe asked. "What can you tell us there?"

"Personally?" Smith said. "I think they hoped to destroy the evidence collected by the cameras by burning the house down—not knowing about the wireless aspect. But I'm just basing that on body language. You'll see what I mean on the video." He hesitated and then added, "I know that sounds a little pathetic, but it doesn't make much sense otherwise. Not to me anyhow."

Lester was laughing. "Hey, we're used to pathetic. That bumper sticker that says 'It seemed like a good idea at the time' was designed for some of these people."

But Joe was less amused. "Let's not count our chickens prematurely. Didn't I overhear that this place has a sprinkler system?"

The smile that had barely touched Smith's face faded. "Yes. That's correct."

"So, given the damage, either it was a crummy system or the bad guys really put some effort into the fire."

"Gasoline," Smith admitted plainly. "They poured it all over the place—well, one wing at least—hoping it would spread, I guess."

"So they came prepared," Joe suggested. He didn't wait for the rich man's assistant to weigh in, opening his door instead and sticking one leg out in preparation for departure.

"Thank you, Tom. We appreciate the help—and the video. Special Agent Spinney will continue the interview, which we'll share with the others, so that you can get back to work. For what it's worth," he said, indicating the house, "the arson investigators wouldn't have let you in anyhow right now. We work a little slower up here—with hopes that it makes us more thorough."

They shook hands, and Joe stepped out, leaving the door open for Les to circle around and continue the conversation side by side.

Joe stretched as he walked toward the yellow crime-scene tape isolating the house from its environs. A very young local police officer was standing by a gap in the line, controlling access. He had a clipboard in his hand.

"Yes, sir?" he asked Joe.

Joe showed him his identification. "Busy night, huh?" he said conversationally.

"Yes, sir," the officer replied, recording his name. He looked up, impressed. "You're Joe Gunther? You're like a legend."

Joe laughed. "So is the brontosaurus. What's your name?"

The officer swung slightly into the light, so Joe could read the metal name tag pinned to his uniform shirt. "Tim Knowles, sir, and it's a real honor."

Joe shook his hand. "Don't get carried away, Tim. I just outlived everyone else. Doesn't show great creativity. Is Samantha Martens still inside the perimeter?"

"Yes, she is, sir."

Joe aimed for the yawning front door—a double wooden arched affair big enough for a garage. As he approached the marble steps leading up, a diminutive woman exuding energy appeared in the door frame, clothed entirely in a Tyvek suit that looked as if it had been used to sweep a chimney. Her bright smile radiated white in contrast. "Hey, Joe. Come to join the fun?"

"Like you thought I wouldn't."

She countered, "Like you wouldn't've given me hell later if I hadn't called, right?"

He waited at the bottom of the steps as she joined him, pulling off her soiled latex gloves. "Fair enough," he said. "Just so you know, the owners choppered in one of their people with a recording from the security cameras. Tom Smith by name."

She pulled back the hood of her suit and shook her short hair loose. "That fast?"

"That was my reaction. We haven't looked at it yet, but Smith said it showed two masked men who didn't seem overly familiar with the layout."

She raised her eyebrows. "I can believe that. You realize this place has a swimming pool in the basement? Big one, too. I bet the *owners* get lost." She partially unzipped the front of her suit to let in the cool air, adding, "Whoever they were, they knew how to spread gas around. The place reeks of it."

"Smith thinks they were trying to torch the camera system."

Sammie frowned at the idea. "That doesn't make much sense. Did he say if you can see them touching it off?"

"Apparently."

"Well," she said, "they had to have brought the gas with them, then. Who in their right mind burns a place down *after* being recorded robbing it? It's stupid. And you say they were masked?"

"That's what he said, and in his defense, they probably didn't know the images were being transmitted off-site."

Joe led her a few dozen feet off to one side and played his pocket flashlight across the surface of the dirt near the wall.

"There," he finally said. "Impressions of the ladder they supposedly used to gain entrance."

Sam tilted her head back to see the second-floor window above them, her face reflecting the colorful strobe lights nearby. "I wondered about that. The window's alarmed from the inside, but it's not connected."

Joe nodded thoughtfully. "That ought to make backtracking this easier. We'll have to get a list of employees and regular service people from Mr. Smith."

"Yeah," she agreed. "And then pick out the really pissed-off one, 'cause to my mind, *that's* why you burn a place down."

CHAPTER FOUR

Mina lingered out of sight beyond the checkout counter, pretending to scan the contents of the magazine rack while watching the reflection in the large plate-glass window beside it. She was tracking a small woman in a head scarf at the checkout counter. The woman was placing her few groceries carefully into a worn but sturdy L.L.Bean canvas bag—a gift, Mina knew, from Billie.

Mina waited until the woman had added the sales receipt to her purchases and shouldered the bag before she turned away from the rack and approached with a broad smile.

"Pam," she said, feigning surprise. "How wonderful to see you."

Pamela Tosi, Billie's maid of many years, opened her eyes wide. "Miss Mina!" she exclaimed. "What are you doing here?"

"Oh, I wander all over, and this is such a neat neighborhood. Have you lived here for ages? Can I help carry your bag?"

Pam's expression bordered on the suspicious, and she subtly shifted her load to just beyond Mina's reach. It had been two weeks since the attack on Beacon Hill, and Billie Hawthorn was still lying unconscious in the hospital. "No, no. I'm all right. This is not a nice neighborhood."

Mina laughed and indicated the exit. "Oh, goodness. It's not *that* bad. I'll walk with you."

Hesitantly, out of options, Pam began heading outside. "Miss Mina, this is confusing."

"I know," Mina conceded, patting her back. "I'm a little upset because of what happened to Billie."

That changed Pam's demeanor. Just outside the store, she turned and gripped Mina's forearm, her expression anguished. "Of course. I'm so sorry. I was just surprised to see you. What a terrible thing. I went to the hospital, but of course . . ."

"I know, I know," Mina sympathized. "They only allow family. I saw the lovely card you left. Very sweet."

Pam was shaking her head, moving slightly to get out of the doorway. "Such a nice lady. It had to be druggies. That stuff is ruining everything."

"It's true," Mina said, not having the slightest idea what had stimulated the robbery. "Did Billie tell you that she's been having problems with anyone?"

Pam considered the question thoughtfully, shuffling along the sidewalk with Mina. "No," she said eventually. "I don't think so."

"How 'bout a delivery person who looked around too much or asked too many questions?"

Pam shook her head. "I'm only there once a week, Miss Mina. She didn't say anything like that to me. But like I told the police, there *might* have been somebody when I wasn't around."

She then paused to give her companion a direct look. "There aren't too many people who go there, you know? She has her old friends, of course, but . . ."

She didn't bother finishing, and Mina understood. "No, I'm not saying it was any of them."

They walked along for a few more paces before Mina asked, "Pam, when did the police talk to you?"

The cleaning woman was surprised. "Oh. Right after it happened. Why?"

"I just wondered what that had been like. Were they okay with you?"

"Oh, sure." Pam's voice was conversational. "They asked questions like they do on TV. Kind of like what you're doing, Miss Mina." She then raised an eyebrow. "Aren't they doing a good job? Is that why you're here?"

Mina waved that away. "I'm sure they are, but they told me how swamped they were with cases. They almost flat out told me that it's dumb luck that usually solves these things. Were you able to tell them anything interesting?"

Pam looked slightly uncomfortable. "No, no," she said, and resumed walking.

Mina pondered that a moment, struck by Pam's apparent evasiveness. On impulse, she laid her hand on the older woman's back again and said, "Pam, it's okay. Billie and I love you. You're like part of our family." She struggled to come up with what she hoped would be the right words, unsure of her sudden suspicion. "Sometimes, things come up that we just can't do anything about. We understand that."

Pam kept trudging along, silent but visibly struggling.

Mina moved ahead slightly and ducked down to make eye contact, forcing Pam to stop in her tracks.

"Tell me," she urged. "Was there something you couldn't say to the police?"

Pam looked away and teared up. "I didn't mean to do any harm."

Mina felt a lurch in her chest. But the source of it surprised her. It went beyond the "aha" moment of a plot thickening. That was part of it, of course, but the feeling was closer to when she'd been told that her father had died, after killing everyone but her in that car crash. He'd lingered for days, perhaps compounding her survivor's guilt at having walked away without a scratch. When the docs told her that he'd finally "passed," in their words, she'd felt a confusing maelstrom of fury, relief, joy, and disgust.

Billie was the only love Mina had left in this life, and now—in some way—this tiny bent woman beside her was about to reveal how that love had been placed in harm's way.

"Tell me," she said with gentle encouragement, stuffing all other feelings back down into their hole.

"Jill Dean, my niece. About a month ago. She came in and did Mrs. Hawthorn's for me."

"Why? What happened?"

Pam kept studying the sidewalk, now sniffing and wiping her nose on the back of her hand. "I told your grandmother I was sick, but I wasn't. I wanted to see my grandson before he was shipped off overseas."

"You could have told her that," Mina protested, stunned by the revelation's banality. "She would have totally understood."

"I didn't know. I didn't know."

Mina was rubbing Pam's back, wrestling harder against a growing anger. "It's okay. It's fine. So, Jill went instead, and then what?"

Finally, Pam looked up, her eyes wide and red-rimmed. "Nothing.

She said Mrs. Hawthorn was there after all—she wasn't supposed to be, which is why I thought she wouldn't know. But Jill said she was fine with what I'd done, and Jill did what I told her and left. And when I went the next week, I found everything okay and Mrs. Hawthorn very happy. Jill had done a good job."

Mina straightened and looked up the block for a moment, collecting her thoughts, still absentmindedly caressing Pam's shoulder blade. Billie had told her none of this, presumably because it had mattered so little.

Mina's rage let off another ripple. Billie should have been right—it shouldn't have mattered that Jill had taken Pam's place one time.

So why did it weigh so heavily on Pam?

She dropped her hand and turned to the cleaning lady one last time, her expression grim. "Pam. Look at me."

Reluctantly, the older woman lifted her face silently.

"You are more upset about this than you should be. I know you're not telling me everything. Billie's in a coma. We've never done you any harm. Tell me the truth. Please, Pam. She's all I have left." She stopped, breathless, the words having poured out in a cold torrent.

Pam's words were hard to distinguish from the sound of passing traffic. "I'm worried what Jill might've done, Miss Mina."

Mina took a breath before saying, "Give me her address, Pam, and don't tell her I'm coming to see her."

Willy Kunkle sat in his car, the windows down, the police radio on low, and a sketch pad strapped to the steering wheel before him. He was on stakeout—alone as usual; not having told anyone—again, as usual. Although by now he didn't doubt that both Sam and Joe had at least a vague idea of what he might be up to, albeit with none of the details.

He knew intellectually that this was not a great way to function inside an organization—or even how to treat the few friends and colleagues he had within it. And he *was* getting better, if impressively slowly. But he'd been driven his entire life to both question authority and to represent it, to embrace the idea of order and to undermine it, and to respect true humanity while holding most of humankind in contempt.

Having a conflict-based job was a natural for a man whose very soul was conflicted.

Willy glanced down at the pad and the elegant portrait he'd half-penciled from memory so far, and he smiled at how he was parked here to intercept and subsequently interview a low-life informant. Even here, he liked to juxtapose opposites, for the portrait was of the baby daughter he shared with Sammie—a sweet and beautiful girl named Emma.

With that, however, he quickly stopped his ruminating, pocketed his pencil, and smoothly removed the pad from its jury-rigged easel. The purpose for his being here had arrived at last. Several hundred feet away, wobbling uncertainly atop a beaten bicycle, was a scraggly bearded man, working his way along Brattleboro's Canal Street. This had once been a neighborhood of nineteenth-century factory workers assigned to live in a tidy parade of repetitive triple deckers. It now housed the town's highest concentration of those euphemistically referred to as underprivileged, and the housing had predictably suffered.

Not surprisingly for a man trained to hunt humans, Willy, who lived in a secluded middle-class nook on the far side of town, knew these rough streets as well or better than most of their inhabitants. Just as some cops made forensics or computer crime or DUIs their specialties, Willy long ago had chosen the anthropology of the down-and-out. He spent far beyond his paid hours walking their sidewalks, eating at their fast-food counters, and hanging out in their bars with a glass of water spiked with a slice of lemon. Most of all, he spent time among them, looking like one of them, despite the fact that in a town of a mere twelve thousand people—of whom maybe two hundred were routinely on the law-enforcement menu—everyone knew who he was.

But unlike most other cops who might try the same thing, Willy didn't find this a disadvantage—in large part because he wasn't like most other cops.

That was something they instinctively knew about him down here. Word was out about this one-armed cripple with the lousy attitude, who worked by a different code. Like some knight of old who'd been banned from the Round Table, he wandered their world, alone and aloof, and yet still as a knight, demanding the respect of his station.

Despite his flaws and eccentricities, his physically reduced appearance, Kunkle was someone others knew to heed, for the law he upheld was different from the Law paying his salary—at times more severe and unyielding, at others more nuanced and less rigid. But he lived by its code, and showed little mercy to those who violated it.

Willy waited until the subject of his interest unsteadily steered his bike off Canal and into an alleyway before he swung out of his car and headed in the same direction.

Locally, Don Packer was almost as well known a crook as Willy was a cop. He was riding a bike now, for example, only because he'd lost his license due to too many drunk-driving convictions. He'd also been involved in bar fights, domestics, shoplifting, drug dealing, car thefts, disorderlies, and—most pertinent to Willy at the moment—home invasions. This was a man who, at the age of thirty-eight, was nine-tenths of the way to spending the rest of his life in prison as a habitual offender—and who didn't find the prospect remotely daunting.

The alleyway was dark even in the middle of the day, crowded in by two rows of dilapidated apartment buildings. All grass had been transformed into dirt, no trees were in sight except for on the side of the hill marking the dead end, and even the pavement was cracked and potholed. To either side, the one-hundred-year-old-plus wooden walls were peeling at best—if all their paint hadn't been replaced by mildew—and most of the balconies clinging to them were misshapen, precarious, and gap-toothed due to missing railings.

The only hint of vitality was implied by a scattering of abused and abandoned skateboards, Big Wheels, balls, and assorted toys.

Aside from the muted chatter of several unseen television sets, the alleyway was still and silent. It was that time of morning when little motion was seen in a neighborhood like this, either because people were out and about or because they were sleeping off the excesses of the night before. Windham County, of which Brattleboro was the dominant town, called itself "the Gateway to Vermont." Cops invoked a doormat instead. All to be expected, given their specialized view of the world.

Willy knew where he was going without having seen where Packer had disappeared. People like Don were permanent fixtures on Willy's mental radar, making their current whereabouts worthy of constant updating, regardless of how many times they changed addresses.

He nevertheless paused at the entrance of the proper building, standing beside a broken chair that was propped up on an upended log on the porch. He listened to the structure's inner and outer heartbeat, attentive to anything unusual, present or absent—as attuned to this environment as an owl to the night woods. Cops, by protocol, were not to make such visits by themselves. And any incursion to a high-risk address was to be done tactically, which at least included routine backup.

But even in combat, in the old days, Willy had often dumped his spotter, preferring to wander the countryside alone. It was a part of his character—even more than his acerbic personality—that made it difficult for colleagues to now imagine him as a father and live-in companion.

Satisfied, he eased into the apartment building as silently as a breeze and slowly glided up the stairs to the top floor.

Again, he listened, motionless in the hall, before placing one hand on the doorknob and giving it a cautious twist. It turned without trouble, and the door opened a fraction.

Extracting his pistol, Willy barely pushed on the door with his toe, slowly expanding his view of the apartment's interior. He could see most of it when he was done—a living room and a kitchenette, with an open door to the balcony at the rear. He heard the sound of a man urinating into a toilet.

Moving faster now, if just as quietly, he entered the place, taking it in, checking for other people, for booby traps, for weapons lying about, for anything illicit—drugs, child pornography, stacks of clearly stolen goods. He saw only some marijuana and a few pills on a table—amid a pile of junk befitting a tornado's aftermath. To call Packer's apartment a mess was to shortchange the effect. EPA Superfund site rang truer.

Satisfied, Willy sidled up to the bathroom door just as the noise abated. Peering in, he saw the shoulders of his quarry shift slightly, heard the sound of a zipper working, and then smiled at Don Packer's astonished face as the man turned to leave the room.

"What the fuck?"

"Not gonna flush?"

Packer shut his mouth. The two had known each other for over twenty years, from when Don routinely misbehaved as an adolescent. Willy had arrested him more times than either man could recall, and used him as an informant more frequently than that, albeit a reluctant one more responsive to threats, bribes, and/or blackmail than to any calls upon his conscience.

"What?" Packer asked, already adjusted to Willy's presence.

Willy nodded slightly. "Flush. It's unsanitary."

Don scowled, but he turned and gave the toilet's lever a halfhearted push. The water filled the bowl with an anemic swirl and gurgled unhealthily.

Packer faced him again. "Happy?"

Willy holstered his gun. "Gonna wash up?"

"Gonna shake hands?"

Willy stepped aside from the bathroom doorway. "Good point."

Packer emerged into the living room and looked around. "You alone?"

"What do you think?"

Don crossed to what passed for a couch, sat on a combination of dirty clothing, torn pillows, and what might have once been a bedsheet, and set to work constructing a roach from the strewn marijuana Willy had noticed earlier. He didn't offer his guest a seat.

Willy nevertheless chose a chair near the kitchenette, first having to remove a pizza box half-filled with something moldy and stiff. It was one of a half dozen paradoxes ruling him that he took no umbrage at this, despite the fact that he kept his own home in a near-surgical state of cleanliness.

"What d'ya want?" Don asked without looking up.

"Tell me about the Tucker Peak job," Willy replied.

Don didn't look up, carefully sprinkling a line of weed along the axis of some rolling paper. "You think I know about that?"

"Yeah."

Packer ran the edge of the paper by his tongue and folded it over onto itself, finishing with a quick twist at both ends to form an imperfect but functional joint. He picked up a lighter and ignited his creation, then leaned back against the couch's cushions with a smile.

"Why would I?" he asked, and immediately inhaled a long, self-indulgent toke.

"You didn't ask me what I meant," Willy told him.

"I might've read about it in the paper."

"You don't get the paper," Willy said without pause, although he knew no such thing.

But Packer chuckled. "That's good. Why would I tell you what I know?"

"Not for your sake," Willy told him. "I know that."

Packer inhaled again and held the smoke for several long seconds. The apartment was already pungent with the odor.

"Right on," he said in a slightly strangled tone.

"But you might for Wendy."

A blue cloud rushed out of the man as his eyes widened. "Wendy? What's she got to do with it?"

Willy tilted his head like someone appraising a purchase. "She's about to lose custody of her kid. I know a few things that could influence DCF to cut her some slack."

"What?"

Willy merely smiled. Wendy was Don's daughter, and probably the only person on earth he was inclined to protect.

Defeated, Don's shoulders drooped, the joint dangling between his fingers. "I wasn't in on that job."

"Didn't say you were."

"Well, I don't know who was, either."

Without further ado, Willy rose and headed for the door. "Cool."

"Whoa," Don protested, sitting upright. "What's the fucking rush?"

Willy looked down at him. "You don't know 'em, we're done. And so's Wendy."

Frowning, Don crushed out the joint. "Jesus H. Christ. What's got you so friggin' worked up? It's not like you give a fuck about some rich bastard's third mansion."

"Fifth."

Packer stared at him. "No shit?"

"Really."

"Huh."

Willy glanced at the front door. "So?"

Packer impatiently waved at the chair Willy had abandoned. "You're making me nervous."

Willy didn't move. "Tragic."

The other man swore inaudibly and asked, "How do I know you'll come through for Wendy?"

"Name me once when I haven't delivered."

Kunkle had him there. Willy made very sure of his ground in these conversations. In fact, he'd already looked into Wendy's case, and knew that DCF had decided to cut her slack one last time. He'd asked them to hold off notifying her for twenty-four hours.

"Talk to Russ Kinney," Packer said in a monotone.

"He in on it?"

"He's been a real happy camper ever since it happened."

Willy knew Kinney, of course. "With who else? He's the village idiot."

"I can't say for sure. He's been hanging with Richie Geno."

That was different. Geno was a careerist like Packer, but more focused and better organized. None of these bad guys were like the ones in the movies, with their polished manners, fancy clothes, and hired henchmen. At least not in these northern, rural climes. But even among the deadbeat, shiftless, chronic offenders, there were some who knew how to run an operation, as long as it wasn't too complicated and could happen on the fly.

Alpha dogs of a dysfunctional pack, they were above average at keeping their people loyal and in avoiding the authorities. All of which meant that if this lead resulted in the arrest of Richie Geno, it would be unusual. Willy had met him, investigated him, even harassed him on occasion to see if he could get a rise, but to no avail. Geno had actually learned as he'd aged, and while his rap sheet portrayed a seasoned and versatile crook, none of it contained anything recent. Richie had either been lucky over the last few years or he'd finally figured out how to protect his back.

Whatever the reality, Willy knew that to confront Geno now would be fruitless. Better to work at the situation from the edges, identifying and unraveling the weakest connective fabric of the man's organization.

"Where's Russ Kinney hanging his hat nowadays?" he asked Don Packer.

CHAPTER FIVE

Lǐ Anming tried to ignore the huge man's grip on her upper arm as he escorted her along the passageway. He kept flexing his hand every so often, as if to readjust his hold, but she knew it was so he could brush the backs of his fingers against her breast.

She was used to it. In fact, she was used to far worse. And it no longer mattered, not to her, despite the anger she felt every time. She'd learned to absorb emotions that used to control her early in her odyssey.

And it certainly helped that she was approaching her ultimate goal.

She was in Northampton, Massachusetts, after all. In the United States—not just Canada, as for the past two years. She was even in the very state where the American Revolution had begun.

Given the price she'd paid to get this far, some man fondling her breast—a coward ruled by others—was a small insult.

"What's your name, sweet cake?" he asked, his heavy boots resounding off the bare wooden walls of the building's central corridor.

She recited her name formally, knowing from experience what little impact it would have. "Lǐ Anming."

"What?" he glanced down at her. His shoulders were like a weight lifter's, making his bald head look unnaturally small.

She remained silent.

"Sounded like Amy to me. Remember that. From now on, you're Amy. *Capisce?*"

Lǐ Anming had heard similar variations. None of them had any relevance. She knew who she was. "Yes," she replied, although without understanding the last word he'd uttered.

"My name's Ed." He laughed, adding, "People call me other things, but you don't get to do that."

Ahead, an odd light began to stand out from the diffused glow at the end of the long walkway. When she'd been pulled from the windowless van, she'd caught a quick glimpse only of an enormous factory building—wooden, sagging, weather-beaten, virtually eroded of all paint except for a faded sign advertising BOBBINS. It was shaped like a giant's pencil box, two stories tall, mostly long and narrow.

The big man had steered her through a small side door into a central windowless tunnel—dark, dusty, and echoing with their footsteps—patterned with doors on both sides and a line of several large trapdoors overhead. She presumed that many years ago wagons had lined up here to receive whatever this place had produced from the square holes above, some of which were open, and through which she could just see some ghostly equipment and perhaps a conveyor belt. But she wasn't familiar with what *bobbin* meant until she saw a scattering of them on the floor—forgotten memories of a textile-rich past once dependent upon the workers, machinery, and raw material that had made this place a crucial supplier to a major industry.

Now it made sense to her, including the bobbins, since she'd seen similar operations back in the very same China that had worked so hard to put plants like this out of business.

The light ahead distinguished itself at last as a large, square, raised dais, illuminated by two spotlights high above in a tower reaching up to the roof. The platform was littered with old tree trunk shards and wooden splinters, and above it dangled a device as devilish as any she'd ever seen.

It stopped her in her tracks, displacing her world-weary aplomb with a sudden, chilling fear.

Her guide tugged at her impatiently. "What?"

Her wide eyes gave her away. He glanced at the device above them. "It's like a guillotine," he explained, speaking slowly, as if she didn't understand English, which, in fact, she did very well. She'd attended school in China and had lived in several English-speaking locations over the years, during her journey here.

Not that she was going to admit to her fluency, however.

"A big knife," he went on, filling in her silence. "It drops from the sky—BAM," he yelled, making her jump. "To cut logs into small pieces. That's what they used to make the bobbins. Before OSHA, of course. Thing could cut both your hands off if you weren't lookin' out." He laughed again and muscled her closer to the menacing setup, forcing her to feel the presence of the now dull and rusty blades, hanging from some arcane chain and pulley arrangement that shot straight up into the blackness beyond the spotlights.

"Two guys used to throw the wood on and off the platform, just like that crazy thing was nuthin', flying up and down within inches of them. They were from Canada, from what I was told as a kid. No American was stupid enough to get near it."

He dragged her toward a rickety staircase lining the wall of this towering, empty, and now utterly silent space. Looking over her shoulder, Lǐ Anming could see how the operation worked, with a nearby conveyor belt positioned to take the chopped wood up a ramp for further processing upstairs.

One floor up, Ed, who by now was letting his hand stray to her bottom, as if in an effort to move her along, pushed her in the direction from which they'd come, into a large, low-ceilinged, rectangular room filled with a row of lathes running alongside the central conveyor belt. She could imagine the noise that had once pulsated here, thrumming against unprotected eardrums, not to mention the raw threat of so much exposed high-speed machinery, snarling within a hairsbreadth of tired, overworked, fast-moving limbs.

Ed didn't have anything to say about all of this as he herded her down the length of the room. She noted, however, what the procedure must have once been, with the lathe operators throwing their bobbins, one after another, into holding bins, which, in turn, were emptied through the trapdoors to fill the waiting wagons below.

Lǐ Anming could sympathize with the ghosts of these workers, given her own experience in sweatshops, where she'd daily balanced her drive and ambition against a cultural stoicism inbred to absorb all hardship.

She even considered herself lucky. Her skill as a jeweler had spared her the life of a sex slave, for example, prostituted to retire the debt incurred to pay for this voyage toward independence. There had been occasions of that, of course, given her gender, the circumstances, and men like Ed. But the jewel-smithing had been her salvation.

Daily, she thanked her grandfather for having taught her that skill.

"Here we go," Ed announced. "Home away from home."

He opened a door at the long room's far end and ushered her into an area so bright she had to blink to regain her sight. Not that it was truly blinding, really—more that, so far, they'd been walking in virtual darkness.

She stood in place for a moment, studying a double row of rough-hewn wooden work cubicles, each equipped with a lamp and a large magnifier, and most filled with silent artisans hunched over their creations of gold and silver. Among them walked another man like Ed, hard-looking, much smaller, and grim, making sure that none of the workers talked or slacked off or did anything other than what they'd been ordered to do.

With a small sigh of resignation, Lǐ Anming settled into her own cubicle.

Joe pushed away from the conference table to cross his legs while he studied the long whiteboard hanging on the opposite wall.

"I agree," he said. "Let's try to keep Richie Geno in the dark for as long as we can."

Covering the whiteboard was a standard case-flow array—photographs of the burned mansion, typed lists of missing items, copies of mug shots, and multiple stills extracted from the security camera footage. A number of color-coded lines ran from one item to another.

Lester Spinney, standing by the board, tapped on the picture of an unsavory bearded man. "How 'bout Kinney?"

"He's a moron," Willy said from his seat. He pointed at another shot. "Who's that?"

Sammie answered. "Bobby Schultz. Joe came up with him. No prior record, but a Spillman check on the computer came up with a bunch of local dirtbag associates. The man likes bad company."

Joe filled in. "I think he's the key. He's an electrician's assistant, and until yesterday, he worked for the company that put in the alarm system at the house on Tucker Peak. We find him, we find who brought him on to the break-in crew. That's my bet. Unfortunately, he quit yesterday, claiming personal reasons. Whatever those are, though, I doubt it was a death in the family. My contact said he was downright upbeat."

Willy asked Sam, "Did Geno come up as one of Schultz's bad company?"

"No, but Kinney did. It's looking like Kinney might've heard about the house from Schultz over a beer and then contacted Geno to plan the rip-off by using Schultz's inside knowledge of the security setup."

"All based on one person's employment record and another being described as a 'happy camper' after the robbery by Willy's dope-smoking snitch," Lester said.

"So?" Willy asked.

"So nothing," Lester replied. "Doesn't mean it's not true, just that we have to prove it."

"Schultz's personal van matches the one this crew used for transportation," Sam threw in. "The one with the plate that was too dirty for the camera to read."

"He have any family in the area?" Willy asked.

"Not that I could find," Joe admitted. "I checked all the standard sources, starting with his employment record, but whatever I found was out-of-date. Seems like he moved around without telling anyone."

"Great," Willy murmured. "You calling this guy the key?"

Lester was undaunted. "What about Russ Kinney? If we can't get a line on Schultz, since he's not a regular on our radar, and we don't want to ruffle Richie Geno's feathers until we can get some hard evidence, we do know where Russ hangs out and who with, right?"

This time, it was Willy who applied the dampener. "I wasn't kidding, what I said about Russ." He touched the side of his head. "He really is scrambled inside. If Packer was right about his hanging with Richie nowadays, then he'll be like a tick on a dog—you poke him any way at all, you'll end up poking Richie."

He abruptly got up and crossed to the whiteboard, as if seeing some detail everyone had missed. "The way you laid it out, boss," he said, addressing Gunther without looking at him, "makes it look like Geno's the brains." He gently thumped on Schultz's photograph with his large fist. "What about ol' Bobby here? He had to have seen the house first. I could see how a mope like that—who likes to hang with losers, has no life, and has a dead-end job—might be dreaming about all those goodies, ready for the plucking. Two plus two equals four, right? Why couldn't he be the one who got the ball rolling? He might've even gotten Geno to sign up Kinney, instead of the other way around."

"Okay," Lester agreed. "Does that change how we chase 'em down?"

"It means we let all the sleeping dogs lie and focus only on Bobby Schultz for the time being," said Joe, interpreting Willy's line of thought. "He's the wild card, the unknown amateur, *and* the one who's disappeared. We put most of our resources on finding him, since we'll have to do that anyhow, and only keep an eye on the other two, in case they do something interesting."

"Like what?" Sammie asked.

Willy filled that in. "Leave town, start living high."

"What kind of money are we talking about here?" Lester asked suddenly.

Willy answered that, too. "We got an insurance quote from Hampton's slave unit, Tom Smith. It came to two hundred grand for the stolen items alone, but I bet they padded the losses, like I was saying, and you know the thieves'll get ten cents on the dollar, if they're lucky."

"Split three ways?" Lester asked incredulously. "How the hell do you live high on that?"

"These losers live high on twenty bucks." Willy spoke from experience. "But I see your point. What I like about Schultz is that he quit his job. It's one thing to do a smash-'n'-grab now and then, to feed your drug habit, but what he did implies a life changer. Something beyond this job got him thinking bigger. That's what I'm seeing here." He waved his hand at the whiteboard.

"I'm guessing Schultz's van vanished with him?" Lester asked, sounding mournful.

"Yeah," Sam said. "Why?"

"We could've at least gotten a search warrant for it and run it by forensics."

"If Willy's right about Bobby's ambitions," Joe said, "then we might have the next-best thing. We should check every house he ever helped rig with alarms, 'cause if I were him, that would be my new career path."

Sam burst out laughing. "Oh my God—*of course*. The son of a gun has a hit list. No wonder he was happy when he handed in his papers. He thinks he's looking at the big time."

"We just have to figure out a ghost's next target and be there when he hits it," Willy said, downplaying the very notion he'd set in motion. "Cinchy."

"May I help you?"

Mickey Roma instinctively held up the cheap bouquet he was holding like a badge of legitimacy before even focusing on the small, elderly candy striper standing before him.

"Flowers," he said, instantly feeling like a fool.

But the woman merely smiled at him. "Very pretty, too. Who are they for?"

"Mrs. Hawthorn. Wilhelmina Hawthorn."

The woman's face saddened. "Oh my."

Mickey felt his face turn red and the sweat prickling his spine. "Did she die?" he blurted out.

The hospital aide laid her hand on his forearm reassuringly and said in a low voice, "Technically, I'm not supposed to say, but so many people have shown such concern. You should see the flowers she already has." She suddenly smiled again, adding, "None so sweet as yours, though."

Spare me, Mickey thought. But he just looked at her expectantly.

She leaned in closer and whispered, "She's still with us, thank the Lord. Still in a coma, but her vitals are strong. I heard one of the doctors say that the coma can actually be a good thing. It allows the body to heal naturally."

Swell, Mickey thought. So she can still nail us to the wall.

He thrust the flowers toward the candy striper. "Would you see that she gets these?"

"Of course, young man." She hesitated, studying the bouquet more closely. "Who shall I say they're from. There's no note."

"Musta fallen off," Mickey stalled, before saying, "She'll know. With love."

That did it, of course. Yet another toothy ear-to-ear grin and a quick squeeze of his hand before he was able to turn on his heel and get away. All he needed now was for some cop to catch wind of this and corner him for a chat. He was half-surprised that he'd gotten as close to the old bag as he had. He figured they'd have a guard on her, in case anybody came back to finish her off.

Mickey had no idea how low Billie Hawthorn had slipped on the police priorities list.

He did know how low he rated with that bastard James, though. After all he'd done for him and that jerk Tony—totally getting them into the house—James had not only put the owner on the critical list for no reason but had gotten all technical when it came time to pay out. Complications with the buyer; the items were too unique to turn around; the market ain't what it was a year ago. That's the one that really got to Mickey. *This is stolen shit, fer crissakes.* It's not pork bellies. We gonna stand in the welfare line now, explaining that we just got laid off from the burglary business?

Mickey was fuming as he hit the hospital parking lot. A few days ago, he'd been just a loser making ends meet; now he was either an accessory to murder or—if Pam's employer woke up—the eyewitnessed perpetrator of an aggravated assault, guilty at least by association, masks or no masks. Felonies either way, and with only a few hundred bucks in his pocket to show for it.

It was becoming clear what he had to do. First, it wouldn't hurt to either lay low or get out of town. Second, or maybe he had the order mixed up, but he wanted to find out what James was up to. That idiot Tony could be all impressed by James and his swagger, but Mickey knew a two-timer when he saw one, and he was sure James was cooking the books and getting a lot richer from this deal than he and Tony.

And that crap was gonna stop.

It was late when Joe returned home. He'd become ambivalent about the place lately, struggling with how much he liked it, while regretting how it revived painful memories. He'd moved here after splitting up with his longtime companion, Gail Zigman, and had put more energy into it than he had any previous home. For decades, as a younger man, he'd lived in a third-floor apartment on the corner of Oak and High, in Brattleboro—book-filled, comfortable, but pretty innocuous. This Green Street address was more of a freestanding structure, however, and he'd gotten the landlord's permission to tack on a small addition to hold his late father's woodworking tools. He was no master craftsman, but he'd been steadily improving with a string of modest projects, which he liberally handed out to friends and colleagues. As Willy had commented upon accepting a birdhouse, "Well, at least it's not a fucking clay ashtray." High praise.

The wood shop hadn't seen much use lately.

He wasn't morose because of Gail. That parting had been reasonably accepted by both of them. She'd been the driving force behind it, but he'd come to accept her rationale and they'd become close friends.

The lead weight in his chest was from a young woman named Lyn Silva, with whom, much to his surprise, he'd fallen in love after being left by Gail. He'd alternately enjoyed this house and her apartment across town during the intense and passionately shared moments when he was off work and she was free of the popular bar that she'd owned on Elliot Street. He'd been amazed by this romance, coming late in life, and at how revitalized it had made him. But just as Lyn had come to him serendipitously, so was she violently snatched away by a sniper's bullet.

It had compounded his mourning that he felt responsible for her death. In fact, Joe hadn't even been in the same county as Lyn when that trigger was squeezed, but the shot would not have been taken if the shooter hadn't wanted Joe alive to suffer the loss. As Joe had come to see it, there'd been two killings as a result—one physical, the other emotional. He had never felt so empty within, and despite therapy and returning to work and the passage of time, he'd felt only a modest dulling of the pain.

Coming home every night, therefore, had become a tangle of mixed feelings.

He walked to the wood shop's door and flicked on the lights, surveying the ancient cast-iron monsters that were once his father's lathe, table saw, shaper, and drill press. Heavy, black, and faintly gleaming, they'd traditionally inspired him with their stalwart sense of purpose, reminding him of how he wished to be viewed in the long run—not fast or flashy, but dependable and solid.

But he wasn't feeling that way now, and hearing the phone ring, he was relieved for the excuse to kill the lights and not embark on any new project.

"Gunther," he answered.

"You sound tired, Joe," Gail told him.

He smiled thinly, but he was pleasantly surprised by the lift he experienced from hearing her voice. "Hi to you, too."

"Seriously," she pressed. "How are you?"

"A bit in the dumps," he conceded. "Long day. Started early with a new case that is looking a little cranky right now. We'll get it settled, though."

"A murder?" she asked.

"No," Joe responded instinctively, but then he suddenly considered the oddness of their present standing with each other. Not the fact that they'd once been a couple, but that he was second in command of a statewide major crimes unit, and she was the newly minted governor of that state.

It didn't have any relevance to her question or his willingness to respond, but it was something that he realized he'd have to keep in mind from now on, which only added to the weirdness of their current relationship.

"You probably heard about it in a briefing or the news," he explained. "A major house fire and burglary on Tucker Peak—one of the mini-palaces. I think we mostly got pulled in 'cause of the guy's high profile. It's not something we'd usually handle, but it's still got some interesting wrinkles."

She laughed in recognition. "Robert Hampton. I did hear about that."

"You know him?" he asked, surprised. Where else but in Vermont would the report of a single-structure fire, with no casualties, be a news flash from one border to the other? Sometimes, he felt the entire state behaved more like an extended village.

"He's a major financial backer of almost everyone I hold in contempt," she explained. "He's a little right of Attila the Hun. I think he spends about three weekends a year in Vermont, but he loves to throw his cash around, and his opinions. I hope the place was a wreck."

Joe chuckled, his mood lightening. "Jeezum, Governor. You better hope I don't have this line bugged."

"It wouldn't surprise me if it was," she said sourly.

"Ouch."

"No, no," she quickly added. "I didn't mean you'd do that. I just feel like I'm so exposed all the time. When I was a selectman in Brattleboro, I had to mind my manners when I was around town—always smile, try not to hit any kids or kick any puppies. But then I could leave town and be a nobody again. Now, I get nervous when I fart in the bathroom. Who's going to overhear it? How's it going to be reported and interpreted? Will the legislature order a subcommittee to discuss its implications?"

He was laughing by now. "At least the legislature's wrapped things up for the year, haven't they? I thought they'd all gone home."

Vermont's was a so-called citizen legislature, in session for a two-year span, but for only four or five months per year. The design was antique, catering to when quasi-volunteer politicians had to return to their fields and livestock to make a living.

"Times have changed, Joe," Gail said, echoing his thoughts. "The session may end, but these guys have so many extra meetings and hearings scheduled for the rest of the year that it doesn't make much difference to me."

"You're liking it, though," he half-asked. "Being governor."

"I love it," she said flatly, her voice betraying that she wasn't merely speaking to be quoted. "It's the best job I've ever had. Even with all the wrangling with lobbyists and special interests and everyone else, I still feel I've gotten to a place where I can finally get things done."

"And not even a half year into your first term," he commented. "Pretty good."

"Yeah." She sounded happy. "It is cool."

There was a slight break in the conversation before she added, "I am sorry you're feeling down."

"It'll pass," he said quickly, feigning confidence.

"I don't think it will, Joe," she told him quietly.

He straightened and looked at the phone, surprised. She'd never lacked in honesty, but the directness now was something newly honed— perhaps from becoming a head of state.

She softened the remark immediately, adding with more spirit, "I'm sorry if that sounds hard, but you're always being so stoical, and I don't think you should be this time. I barely knew the poor girl, and I feel guilty that she's dead and you've been devastated. She wouldn't even have been there if she hadn't wanted to ask me about you—she was working so hard to get closer to you. She loved you, Joe, and you loved her. It's bound to hurt for a long time."

He bit back another self-diminishing one-liner and stayed silent instead.

"You okay?" she asked.

"Some days're better than others," he replied more honestly. He reflected a moment before asking, "Why did you call, by the way? Was there something you wanted?"

"I was just checking in," she said. "You're often on my mind, especially lately. I wanted to hear your voice. Too much mindless chatter in this job, and not enough reason. I needed a break. We were always good at being each other's best sounding board. I guess I miss that most."

He wasn't sure how to take that, laden as it could be with possible coding. He knew that Gail felt isolated, and possibly even lonely. Her job meant that she lived in a fishbowl, and he knew that it had cost her

her latest boyfriend. But the territory she and Joe occupied nowadays had become uneven and strewn with potential pitfalls.

"Well, I am fine. Honestly," he assured her, keeping with a topic he could easily track. "I am sad. I won't deny it. But it's kind of like when Ellen died. Time'll help out."

"Ellen was decades ago," she reminded him, referring to his late wife. "You were both in your twenties. And it was a disease. You got to say your good-byes."

That stopped him, his head full of the sight of Lyn's bloody body lying in the ER of the hospital near where she'd been shot.

No good-byes, just longing.

"It still takes time," he repeated lamely.

"I know it does."

The politician in her seemed to sense the time had come to retreat. She suddenly laughed and said, "My cell phone's collected about ten messages while we've been talking, so I better put out some fires. I'll call again soon, okay?"

"Sure, Gail. Thanks."

"I love you, Joe. Take care."

"Love you, too."

He stood in place for half a minute, holding the phone, after the line had gone dead.

CHAPTER SIX

Mina took a breath and exhaled slowly, hoping to calm herself. She was far from home, from Billie's neighborhood, from her life as she'd led it so far. She was surrounded by a Dorchester apartment building, overwhelmed with smells, sights, and sounds that threw her off balance, her fist poised to knock on a scarred and flimsy door whose frame looked as if it had been shouldered open half a dozen times. She'd made sure to dress down, wearing old jeans and a sweatshirt, but she knew she stuck out like an American Express billboard down here. Every look she'd received since getting off the T had told her that much.

She knocked with an authority she wished she had.

After a pause, she heard a woman's harsh voice come through the door. "*What.*" It was demand, not a question.

"Is that Jill Dean?" she asked.

A slow count of three was followed by "Who wants to know?"

"I'm Mina Carson, Billie Hawthorn's granddaughter."

A muffled and unintelligable curse was followed by a series of turned locks and dropped chains. The door half-opened, revealing a young woman dressed in a tank top and sequined jeans that looked spray-painted on.

Dean's eyes were narrow with suspicion. "What d'you want?"

Mina tried for disarming. She smiled apologetically. "I just need to talk about Billie. You heard she'd been hurt?"

"I heard nothing but. It's all Pam talks about. She die?"

Mina blinked. The bluntness was like a poker, stirring up a bed of hot coals. Just keep going, she told herself. The woman was probably scared, defensive, and fatalistic about tough breaks. Stay cool, she told herself.

"No, no. She's hanging in there."

Dean's face became harder still. "Then what're you doing here?"

A door slammed down the hallway, and a child began to cry. "May I come in?" Mina asked. "It's kind of awkward out here."

"That's not my problem. I had nuthin' to do with that lady getting hurt."

"No, of course not. But you substituted there for Pam once, and so I . . ."

Dean flushed. "Is that what the old cow told you?"

"Just that you helped her out. One time."

"And that's a crime?"

Mina took a breath. She couldn't gain any footing, and the frustration was fueling her resentment, given what she thought this girl might have done. "Jill, please. We're getting off on the wrong track. I'm not here to—"

"That is such bullshit," Jill shot back. "You didn't come down here to share old news. You came to jam me up. Fucking rich bitch figures trash like me is just about right to carry the load. Am I wrong?"

"Stop it," Mina said loudly, holding up her hands. "I have a grand-mother in a coma, for crying out loud. Wouldn't you want to know what happened if Pam got hurt?"

Jill's hand appeared on the door's edge, clearly preparing to slam it shut. "After siccing you on me, she probably *deserves* a little pain. You want to talk to me, girl, you can do it through a lawyer."

The door had begun to swing to when Mina's rage exploded and propelled her forward like a linebacker, surprising them both and shoving Jill backward. Mina staggered into the room, only catching her balance by pushing against Jill's chest and completing her collapse. Jill landed on her back, with Mina dropping to her knees, pressing one on either side of the girl's torso, and pinning Jill's hands to the floor.

"Listen, you little shit," she heard herself say. "Tell me what you did, or I'll make sure the cops are the next ones to pound on your door. I'm the rich bitch, remember? I can make that happen. Any lawyer of yours will be fucked when I'm through with him. Now *talk* to me. You tell me what I want to know, and I go away."

It was a split-second watershed: a blink of time in which Jill Dean could have easily thrown her off and drawn on her own abilities to beat Mina senseless—all legally, given the latter's mode of entry.

But something else had been feeding Jill's attitude—the guilt of a young woman who, by helping her aunt, had only betrayed them both in the end. It was a case of no good deed going unpunished—given that Jill had then divulged where she'd been and what she'd seen to the wrong person. It turned out that her aggression had been as manu-factured as Mina's posture of self-assurance.

She burst into tears.

Mina looked at her with astonishment and released her wrists. "What?" she asked, dumbfounded.

"I told Kenny about Mrs. Hawthorn's," Jill confessed. "My boy-friend. I couldn't believe all the beautiful things she had. It was like a museum." Her crying increased. "I didn't know what he'd do. I just told him to share what I'd seen—like what you do with friends. I didn't want to set her up for a robbery."

"She got worse than that," Mina said bitterly, once again angered by the stupidity of it all.

"I know," Jill wailed. "I asked him not to do anything dumb—that it would get me in trouble. But he couldn't let it go. Kept asking me for more details."

"Which you kept giving him," Mina suggested, impressed by the girl's narcissism.

Jill did a double take. "What would *you* do? These guys *kill* people. You wanna tell 'em to get stuffed? I sure as hell don't."

Mina softened her tone, hoping to match the sudden change of mood. "I understand. I do. Did Kenny assemble a team, or what?"

Jill shook her head. "That's not his action. He took it to James for a cut."

"Like a finder's fee?"

A furrow appeared on Jill's forehead. "Whatever."

"What's James's full name?"

She shrugged, still on her back. "Who knows? He's just James."

"How do I find him?"

"Tony Leto hangs with him. Tony's ma owns a market; he works there most of the time. James comes by." She gave Mina the address. It wasn't far away. "I figure it was James and Tony that did the job," she added.

"Just the two of them?"

"Maybe. I don't know. I don't ask. But that's what got me almost feelin' sick about it—that they did that to the old lady. She didn't know me from nobody, and she still treated me good—even fixed me lunch."

Mina got up and offered Jill a hand. The two of them moved to the nearby sofa.

"What do they do with what they steal?" she asked.

"That's James's thing," Jill explained. "That's why he's the boss. He's got connections."

"You know how that works?"

"I hear stuff when they think I'm not listening, or maybe when one of them's on the phone or somethin'."

Mina tried leading her. "And?"

"Me and Kenny were at Tony's a couple of nights ago. That's where I figured out why Kenny was so interested in your grandmother when I told him about her, back when."

"Why was that?"

"Her jewelry and silverware," Jill said, by now almost conversational, as if they were exchanging shopping tips. "That's not normal. The money's in electronic stuff—popular, hard to trace, easy to sell. Jewelry's tougher. It's a specialty market. But Kenny was real interested, and I think it was because of James."

"James has a conduit for jewelry?"

Jill stared at her. "A what?"

"A pipeline."

"That's what I think. And it's out of town. Tony was talkin' on the phone and kept saying, 'West,' making it sound like a car drive."

Mina was silent for a moment, mulling this over. "Has this happened yet? The selling of my grandmother's things?"

"I think so," Jill conceded. "They don't hang on to it long. You know, it's hot."

Mina was disappointed. It wasn't so much the return of the items that she wanted, but more the closing of a circle, as if locating everything and replacing it might help make Billie whole again, too.

She knew it wasn't rational, but it was something that she could do, which was more than she could say about bringing Billie out of her coma.

She pressed Jill again. "But this thing with jewelry and James, it's ongoing, right? Something he'll probably repeat? That's why Kenny thought of him in the first place."

"Yeah, yeah," Jill agreed.

"Well. That's something," Mina murmured.

"What is?" Jill asked.

"One way of catching him—if he's still doing it."

Recovered by now, Jill rose and glared down at her uninvited guest. "Catching him? Who the hell do you think you are anyhow? Barging in here and talking about busting my friends. You're no cop, and you don't know jack about who we are and what we deal with. You go poking into all this, all it'll do is get everybody fucked-up."

She crossed to the door. "I'm sorry about your grandma. She treated me okay. And if James and the others ripped her off, then they deserve what they get. But I don't appreciate you doin' a Wonder Woman on my head and acting like something you're not. Plus, I don't even know for sure they did this job."

She opened the door. "Get the hell out of here and leave me alone. Now."

Mina considered her options, balancing staying friendly against the likelihood that she'd get nothing more from this source.

She rose slowly and came right up to Jill's face, hoping the girl's earlier sense of responsibility would stop her from punching Mina in the mouth.

"What I do know, Jill, is that you didn't just tell your boyfriend about seeing a house full of nice things. You also told him it had no alarm system. I don't need to be a cop or a lawyer to know that's enough to make you an accessory to burglary."

Jill barely whispered, "Kenny made me tell him."

Mina ignored her, adding, "And if my grandmother dies, guess what that does to you?"

She brushed by the girl and left.

Burlington detective Kemp Wagenbach pressed his throat mic to whisper, "All units in place?"

He received a chorus of "ten-four" responses before switching to a channel connecting him to the unmarked vehicle across from the Elmwood Avenue apartment building they'd quietly surrounded during the past half hour.

"All set, John?"

"Roger that."

"Send him in."

Kemp adjusted his night-vision goggles and watched as a heavyset man emerged from the car and shambled over to the apartment building, a bag slung over his shoulder. This was Reuben Witham, a longtime local thief, given the choice by the authorities to either compromise his fence or go to jail as a habitual criminal, based on the latest charge against him. This was fine with Wagenbach; Witham was a harmless deadbeat whom he'd known for years. The fence, on the other hand, was Brooks McCandlish, a sleazy, high-born societal dropout and suspected sex offender who'd recently beaten back two charges of receiving stolen goods and who raised Kemp's righteous hackles as a result. There was an odd form of working relationship between many cops and crooks, occasionally bordering on camaraderie. Kemp, a history buff, recalled stories about trench combatants in World War I who'd sometimes emerged from the mud and filth to share meals or an impromptu soccer game before returning to the slaughter.

Reuben he considered as one of those combatants—the respected foe; McCandlish was just a shithead in need of jailing.

Kemp adjusted his radio, simultaneously eavesdropping on Reuben's conversation and maintaining an open line to the members of his team, who were hiding around the neighborhood.

The clarity wasn't great; it rarely was. He always supposed that the feds had better equipment than any local department could afford, but he actually wasn't sure. It would have made as much sense to him to discover that they all shopped at Radio Shack.

Reuben and McCandlish knew each other, which was the whole point of this sting. And Reuben was an old and trusted player of the game. He'd been a crook since he could walk, and had played tonight's role more than once in his ongoing—and increasingly tricky— negotiations to avoid spending the rest of his life behind bars. Kemp expected no opening-night jitters from him, and from what he could catch behind the microphone's scratchy reception, he was getting none. What he did hear were the usual exchanges, the noise of Reuben's stolen goods being poured out for inspection, and the resulting haggling over their value and worth.

This was no one's inauguration, in fact. Kemp's bosses had made it clear that they wanted a solid case, and they'd insisted that several buys be recorded and witnessed before McCandlish was arrested. This was the third such outing for them all, therefore, which is what made Kemp wonder later if they might not have all become too complacent as a result.

In any case, he found himself sitting up in startled dread as he overheard McCandlish say, almost offhandedly, "Tell you what, Reuben. For shits and giggles, take off your shirt so I can admire that fat gut of yours, and see if you ain't got a wire. I heard rumors the cops have been putting the squeeze on you."

Kemp keyed his mic. "Heads up, everybody. Our guy's about to be made. Get ready to move on command."

He was listening as Reuben protested, invoking the usual stack of Bibles and his mother's grave. To no effect. McCandlish's voice gained a dangerous edge.

"Go, go, go," Kemp ordered, jumping from the command post trailer himself and running toward the building. There wasn't too much chatter yet—this team trained together all the time. Burlington had the state's largest PD, and even if that didn't mean much in global terms, it still dictated that it got more action than any other agency in Vermont, barring perhaps the state police. As he ran, Kemp could hear the command post folks speaking calmly, along with the now slightly breathless responses of the various team members.

Still, he knew the fighter-pilot cool wouldn't last. The excitement would get the better of them. It always did.

He hit the door with several others; they burst in and spread out, crouching low, weapons at the ready. Being a fence in a liberal state like Vermont was hardly a hanging offense, but McCandlish had money, was an addict, had been violent before, and was fond of guns.

Because of the jabbering in his ear and his own past experience,

Kemp could hear or imagine the forced entries through all portals, the explosions of flashbang grenades, the shouted reports from people who thought they were speaking calmly.

But then he heard an all too familiar sharp, metallic, rhythmic snapping noise over the radio.

"Shots fired. Shots fired."

Wagenbach stormed down a hallway, leaped over a prostrate Reuben Witham—who was wide-eyed and calling out, "I'm okay, I'm okay" as he curled up into a ball—and continued up a flight of stairs. They knew where they were going. They'd gotten a detailed description of the place from Reuben, and a set of plans from the city building inspector. There was a roof access, with a possible escape route across the top of the building. Nevertheless, at each of the three floors, team members spread out to make sure McCandlish hadn't stepped out of the race to double back out the front door.

He hadn't.

"On the ground, you son of a bitch" was immediately followed by the formalized report: "Subject secure, roof location."

It didn't end quite then. Any and all other potential threats had to be ruled out, from armed associates to booby traps. But some thirty minutes later, Kemp found himself on the second floor, facing a room as filled with goods as Filene's Basement in its heyday.

Except that everything he saw was stolen.

All shots had gone wide of their mark, and everyone was safe and sound. The brass would criticize how things had gone down. That was their job. And partly, they'd be right. Kemp himself wasn't thrilled with every detail of the evening.

Still, not too bad, he thought.

"He lawyer up?" he asked a colleague as she stepped into the room.

"Of course," she replied. "He even said, 'I know my rights.' I hate it when they say that." She whistled, taking in the room's contents. "I didn't know he was this big."

Kemp nodded. "Me, neither." He stepped farther inside, looking more carefully at the stacks of loot.

"It's interesting," he finally said. "It looks like he has a system, kind of. He piles the stuff up on this side, like it was the receiving dock at a warehouse, while over here, you can see him starting to divvy it up into categories. It's anyone's guess what kind of network he must have." He straightened and gave it all an appreciative scan. "Amazing."

He stopped and leaned over, scrutinizing one heap of especially fancy items. "Wow. Nice." He smiled before adding, "And looking familiar." He turned to his partner. "You read that list of stolen goods circulated by the VBI a few days ago?"

"I saw it," she admitted. "I can't say I read it. Too long."

"Long and upscale," he agreed. "I read it because I wanted half the things on it." He picked up a fancy engraved hunting knife and held it up for her to see. "We'd better call Joe Gunther and tell him we found some of his missing trinkets."

CHAPTER SEVEN

Jimmy McAuliffe entered the reception area smiling and stuck his hand out in greeting. "Miss Carson. Nice to see you again. How's your grandmother?"

"Unchanged," Mina replied tersely.

His eye contact sharpened momentarily as he assessed the response. He trimmed his smile accordingly, gestured to a far door, and suggested, "Would you like to chat privately?"

"Thank you," she said, and let him open the door to a small conference room.

"How have you been?" he asked as they sat opposite each other at a wobbly round table in need of replacement.

She ignored the polite opener. "I'd like to know how the investigation's going."

He nodded understandingly. "I did say at the beginning that results in these situations are often disappointing."

Her expression tightened. "I interviewed Pam Tosi's niece, Jill. She substituted for her aunt once as a favor and then told her boyfriend about everything she saw, including the fact that the house had no alarm."

Jimmy stared at her for a couple of seconds, organizing his thoughts. Sadly, in addition to feeling ambushed and not wanting to show it, he was struggling to remember the relevant details of a case that he hadn't considered in several days. He had over thirty others on his desk at that moment, and while he hadn't assigned Billie Hawthorn's a ranking, he couldn't deny that he'd been putting more effort into the ones he hoped would be easier to solve.

"That's good, Miss Carson. Take me through what you learned step by step, so I don't miss anything."

Mina looked at him questioningly, not having expected that. A stone wall, anger, forgetting her name—all had crossed her mind as possible reactions. But this bland neutrality was odd, and, she hoped, promising.

"I worried that I might cause problems by getting in your way," she began diplomatically. "But then I figured that, a, it couldn't hurt and, b, you were probably used to it anyhow."

Jimmy nodded encouragingly, finding the second comment all too accurate, in fact. "True enough."

"So I started by asking Pam, Billie's cleaning lady, if she knew anything about why the house had been targeted, and I got her to admit that she'd used Jill as a substitute once, when she knew she couldn't make the usual appointment. I told her she should've just been up front and asked for the day off, but she was too embarrassed." Mina shook her head. "So much of this is just so dumb."

Jimmy stayed quiet, listening. He might have been struggling initially to recall the details of the investigation, but he knew for a fact that he'd never heard of any niece named Jill, much less talked to her. Pam, he had interviewed, which only compounded his embarrassment, considering what he'd missed.

"Anyhow," Mina continued, "I found out where Jill lived, dropped by her place, and got her to admit that she'd told her boyfriend about what she'd seen at Billie's, including that it didn't have an alarm system."

Jimmy decided to reveal a bit of his ignorance. "The boyfriend have a name?"

"Kenny. That's all she said, and I didn't think to ask for more—mostly because she said he had nothing to do with it."

"Okay."

"She told me that Kenny probably gave what she'd told him to two guys named James and Tony Leto."

"Brothers?"

Mina stopped, her mouth half-open. "What?"

"James and Tony are brothers? Leto?"

She smiled, her confusion cleared. "Oh. No, no. James, I don't know his last name. Tony's named Leto." She slid a piece of paper across the tabletop to him. "That's the address where he works with his mother, at her store. It's also where he and James usually get together—to plan their jobs, I guess. The niece, Jill, has heard them doing that, although not Billie's specifically. She made it sound like James was the ring-leader."

Jimmy held up his hand. "Let me ask a couple of questions here. Is that okay?"

"Of course."

"Is Jill saying for a fact that she knows who robbed Billie's place and beat her up? Tony, James, and Kenny?"

"Not Kenny, but yes . . . sort of."

Jimmy couldn't stop a tiny flinch of irritation, which he hoped she wouldn't notice. "Okay. Not Kenny. What do you mean by 'sort of'?"

She had noticed it, of course. "Look, Detective, it's a lead, and I *do* know for a fact that neither you nor any other cop has spoken to these people. I realize you're all busy and maybe I also got lucky. Who gives a shit, right? The question is, Are you going to do anything about it?"

Jimmy swallowed hard. Beneath it all, she was right, which pissed him off even more. "Of course we are, Miss Carson, and I want to thank you personally for doing this. We dropped the ball. *I* dropped the ball, and I'm sorry. No excuses."

"That's not why I'm here."

His jaw tightened in the face of her hostility, and he worked to stay focused, concentrating on the pressure she was under—and on how she was merely trying to be helpful, however clumsily.

He pulled out his notepad and cleared his throat. "Understood. Let's start from the top. Give me what names you've got, addresses, dates and times you spoke to whoever. The works."

Mina read his body language, took a breath, and began doing as he'd asked. It took her about twenty minutes, including answering his questions.

"Do any of those people or places ring a bell with you?" she asked once she was done.

He shook his head. "Not me personally, but that doesn't mean anything." He indicated the page before him. "There's no way that this James character or the Leto store haven't come onto the radar. I'll look into it—*today*," he emphasized, "and run it all by the cops covering that area. They're the ones with local knowledge."

Mina sat back, at last slightly mollified. "There was one other thing that Jill told me about James," she said.

He raised his eyebrows inquiringly.

"She said that one of the reasons Billie was interesting to them was because of her jewelry. She said that was unusual—that mostly, they went after TVs and computers and electronics. But James had a buyer that made it worth the effort . . . or something to that effect. Anyhow, she said that when he talked about unloading the jewelry, he mentioned someplace out of town, west."

"West?" Jimmy asked, "As in California or somewhere?"

"It sounded more like a car drive. It didn't feel that far away to her."

"But she didn't know exactly?"

"No. It was just something she overheard. She said they sometimes talk together as if she isn't even in the room, so that she picks things up."

"West," Jimmy murmured, half in exasperation, as he rose and crossed to the door with his guest, opening it for her. "Thanks for coming in, Miss Carson."

He shook her hand but then held on to it to make a point. He looked at her carefully as he said, "Do me a favor, though, okay? Stop the private eye routine. You did good work—I thank you for that, and I promise that I'll move on it—but no more. You said yourself that you got lucky. You're right. You could've gotten hurt out there. So stop now, please? And in exchange, I swear I'll keep you informed, even if I get nowhere."

He squeezed her hand again for emphasis. "Do we have a deal?"

She returned the shake and said, "Yes, we do."

But as they parted ways, neither one of them had much faith in the other's credibility.

Lǐ Anming glanced down the row of workstations and saw Ed rounding the corner. She tensed as he approached, already prepared for the caress he'd inevitably administer between her shoulder blades. He did this every time he patrolled the line. She'd been brutalized by others, of course. But in an odd way, perhaps because of his seeming ineffectualness, she'd come to loathe his slimy, repetitively presumptive manner as much as the worst of them, despite having met him only a few hours earlier.

She returned to studying the piece in her hands—an unusual antique ring featuring a gold oval supporting a pink-and-ivory cameo of a woman's profile. She flipped it over to analyze its structure and to see how to disassemble it without causing damage, all while sensing Ed's approach. She'd already noticed that in most cases, the worst he did with the other women was lay a hand on a shoulder or look down their shirt-fronts as they bent over their work.

"How's my girl doin'?" she heard him say, feeling the heat of his body as he lightly pressed his stomach against the small of her back. Involuntarily, she straightened, pulling away, her eyes on her work and her mouth pressed shut.

He leaned in closer, pretending to glance over her shoulder. "Pretty piece. You should do something catchy with that."

His right hand slid under her arm, took the ring from her, turned it over a couple of times, and then retreated, fondling her breast. She stayed utterly still as the hand, like a disembodied entity, then wandered down across her stomach before finally retreating with a final stroke along her flank.

"Nice work, Amy. I'm real happy you joined our little crew."

He chuckled and moved on to her neighbor, an older woman with graying hair, whom he all but ignored.

Lǐ Anming exhaled quietly and forced her fingers to move again, nurturing her pulsing anger. She'd experienced this frustrated impotence for most of her adult life, starting as mere confusion and resentment when she was a child, then blossoming into the fury that had pushed her at last to abandon her family, her province, and her country and to pay any amount and suffer any humiliation to reach this country about which she'd heard so much.

She therefore looked forward to being able—someday—to confront Ed or his ilk with some gesture of retribution, even if just symbolically. It would be her way of applying the tiniest bit of her own weight toward the leveling of the scales.

But for the moment, that would have to wait.

Ed circled to the front of the large room—in fact, it encompassed the entire end of the building—and clapped his heavy hands together.

"Okay, listen up. Put your tools down, leave your work on your benches, and line up over here for inspection." He pointed to his left.

Lǐ Anming let out a tiny puff of air as she complied, knowing what to expect next.

She'd been laboring as an enslaved artisan for four years, working her way across the globe—in camps, factories, abandoned buildings, basements, and urban tenements. She was always part of a group, its membership changing; always isolated from whatever culture she was dropped into; and always held to practice her particular skill of jewelry making, whether by creating original work according to furnished designs or by commingling raw materials from other, older pieces that she'd initially disassembled. She was supposed to be paid for this— which money would then be applied against her passage. But those were merely the terms of the agreement. She had no knowledge or proof that the contract was being honored. And, of course, she'd never actually seen a dime.

The one thing she and the others had been able to count on throughout had been men like Ed, who'd treated them at best like stock to be herded and at worst as if they were a traveling harem.

Based on her unfortunately expanding experience, Lǐ Anming placed Ed in the middle of this spectrum—as fitting neither one extreme nor the other, while practicing habits from both. She lined up as ordered with the rest—men and women from a cross-section of cultures and ages—and awaited her turn to lean spread-eagled against the wall and be pawed yet again—this time with a thoroughness leaving nothing to subtlety—as Ed purportedly made sure that none of them were hiding any of the precious metal or stones they'd been handling all day. He either did this quickly and efficiently, searching for anything hard or lumpy that could represent contraband, or—as with Lǐ Anming and several other young women—languorously, combining the poking and probing with caresses, pats, and invasive gropings.

Through it all, not a word was said, nor a protest murmured.

When Ed was finished, he and the silent, resentful assistant he called Miguel guided the entire flock down the long passageway to the spindly, uncertain staircase, past the wood-chopping guillotine, and out toward where a van stood waiting to take them away. They were unceremoniously packed into the darkened back of the vehicle, told to sit down on the floorboards, and locked inside. Lǐ Anming found herself wedged between the front wall of the compartment and a young woman with a kind face.

She nodded carefully to the girl, unsure of the results. In the past, she had found fellow travelers in this underworld to run the gamut from the sullenly near-catatonic to the stubbornly optimistic, with an endless variety in between.

In this case, the young woman pressed against her smiled and nodded back, timidly introducing herself in English as Wú Méi.

Lǐ Anming returned the courtesy and spent the next minute determining that their differing dialects dictated that they should stick to English, which, fortunately, they spoke with enough rough ease to communicate.

"You are new?" Wú Méi asked.

"I am. You?"

She shook her head. "Here many months."

Lǐ Anming wrinkled her nose. "With Ed?"

Wú Méi laughed a little and made a similar face. "Not too, too bad. When not drinking."

"That is good," Lǐ Anming agreed. "We are going where?"

"Northampton," her new friend said, albeit with some difficulty.

Lǐ Anming had never heard of the place, and she tried to confirm that it was in Massachusetts.

"Yes," Wú Méi assured her.

The van started up and began rocking violently as the tires skidded and bumped across the chopped-up surface of the abandoned parking lot. Wú Méi indicated the pinpoint constellation of rusty holes in the vehicle's metal skin and said, "Look. See," twisting around to squint through one of them. Lǐ Anming immediately joined her.

It was nearly dark. Although daylight lasted longer now that winter was past, it was a given that their handlers would always demand more of them than any standard eight-hour day.

Still, streetlamps soon became part of the blurring landscape, and with them enough light that Lĭ Anming could sense her surroundings, starting with the occasional house, then morphing into a rural neighborhood and, finally, a village street. After only ten minutes, they were surrounded by cars, pedestrians, businesses, and restaurants, until downtown traffic brought them to a halt.

At that point, Lĭ Anming turned wide-eyed to her companion and asked, "Is it real?"

"Yes," Wú Méi replied. "Crazy place."

If not quite that, the center of Northampton struck Lĭ Anming as the most unusual spot that she'd been to so far. Flashing signs, street musicians, eccentric-looking people, and an assortment of odd offerings behind hundreds of shop windows amounted to a near-theatrical experience. Crowded streets, she was used to; streets sporting the odd unicyclist, or panhandler/street artist, or group of cheering and laughing women, all sporting T-shirts with lesbian slogans, that was very different.

She liked it.

It struck her as chaotic, undisciplined, even reckless—characteristics that she'd been brought up to avoid—while being simultaneously freewheeling, energetic, and attractive. It reminded her, she realized suddenly, of the contrast that she addressed in her jewelry-making. While traditionally trained in the old methods and styles, she'd often yearned to be free of such constraints. She longed to give open expression to her imagination and release the true potential inside so many of the objects that she handled daily. So often, she'd been given a piece to reshape or raw materials to craft and had struggled not to form something utterly different from what she'd been assigned.

Squinting through the rusty hole in this creaking, stuffy, bad-smelling van, she sensed that she might have finally reached a place that met her needs.

It was just as she'd always imagined America to be.

Quickly, the downtown area slid away as their van turned the corner onto King Street and headed north. The wondrous show of moments earlier yielded to fast-food outlets, concrete-clad businesses, few pedestrians, and of empty, weed-choked parking lots stretching out before cast-aside shopping outlets.

This was more the setting she was used to. From the beginning of her long trip, begun in wonder and rebellion, she'd seen virtually every slum and ghetto imaginable.

Yet, even in this context, it was better here—cleaner, less oppressive, and fresher-smelling, a fact she discovered when the rear doors were finally thrown open.

"Everybody out, out, out," Ed chanted, gesturing to them to hurry up.

They stumbled onto the darkened driveway of an exhausted three-story building wrapped in peeling wooden clapboards, scalloped siding, and unpainted plywood, then were ushered through its open front door at a run, Ed and Miguel actually slapping the slowest of them as if they were dawdling cattle. Here again, Lǐ Anming was not surprised, even noting as she ran that the nearest overhead sidewalk light had been either extinguished or broken to obscure their arrival.

No need for passersby to wonder who all these people piling out of the back of an unmarked, windowless van were.

Similarly, the lobby of the shabby building was dark. Ed herded them up a narrow staircase, through a doorway at the top, and into a small bare room on the second floor. There, he turned on a single light and addressed them from the entrance.

"That's it. You know what to do and how to do it." He looked directly at Lǐ Anming and added, "You newbies, figure it out. Old-timers, help them do it."

With that, he stepped back and slammed the door. They all heard the lock snap to before his feet went thumping downstairs.

Lǐ Anming looked at her new companion and shrugged. "Newbie?" She pronounced it New-bee.

Wú Méi laughed, tried for the Chinese name, got nowhere, and then said, "Newcomer." She touched her chest. "I am old-timer. I will help."

The others were already filing out a rear door, heading toward the rest of the second floor. Lǐ Anming discovered that it led to a hallway lined with bunk rooms, with a communal room to the rear. There were also two bathrooms. It was rudimentary, smelled bad, allowed for no privacy or space, and all the windows were boarded up, but there was food laid out on the far room's table, and for once, they were alone without supervision. As they spread out and used the bathrooms, sought out their bunks, or pawed through the packaged fast food, there was a palpable sense of relief in the air, along with— for the first time—noise as they all began speaking in normal tones.

Wú Méi tugged her charge by the hand toward one of the bunk rooms and showed her an empty spot, smiling and saying, "Your new home."

"Thank you," Lǐ Anming said, touching the bed tentatively and looking forward to a little rest. She hadn't slept in two days, ever since being smuggled across the Canadian border.

Wú Méi studied her expression for a moment. "You are happy?" She seemed genuinely curious, seeing something unexpected in Lǐ Anming's face.

The newcomer looked up and considered the question, thinking back to what she'd seen through the tiny hole in the van's side. "Yes," she admitted. "I think I am close."

Wú Méi looked quizzical. "I hope you are right."

CHAPTER EIGHT

The man they were seeking was short, bearded, and built like a boy of twelve—an odd combination that made him look computer-generated. Joe and Lester found him sitting at the back of one of the alarm company's trucks, his feet dangling just above the pavement, like a kid about to hitch a ride. He was smoking a cigarette, something he did frequently enough to have stained both his forefinger and thumb, and one lopsided portion of his otherwise-gray mustache.

They were located north of Brattleboro, in Putney, at the construction site of what Willy might have called a McMansion. The view to the east was spectacular, taking in the Connecticut River Valley and the New Hampshire hills beyond. The immediate acreage just below them was being shaped by a dusty crisscrossing of bulldozers, so that eventually, the oversized home would dominate a perfectly configured setting Mother Nature could only envy.

"You Euclid Washburn?" Lester asked as he and Joe rounded the end of the truck.

Washburn continued pulling on his cigarette, eyeing them both, one at a time.

"Could be."

They pulled out their credentials and introduced themselves. Washburn merely nodded. Joe was reminded of his own equally taciturn father, once a farmer and now long gone, with whom he'd exchanged perhaps five conversations in a lifetime.

"You used to work with Bobby Schultz," he stated as a matter of fact.

Washburn extracted another puff of smoke from his hand-rolled cigarette.

"Is that correct?" Lester asked, already showing his impatience.

The little man examined one of his nails as he said, "You seem to know that already."

Joe smiled, by contrast enjoying the encounter. "We do know some things, don't know others."

Euclid shifted his gaze to Joe's face. "Gunther. From up around Thetford?"

"Yup," Joe told him. "Father was Arvid. People called him Al, the way they do."

Euclid thought a moment. "Any relation to Leo?"

"My brother."

He nodded silently, paused, and finally said softly, "Heard of him."

Joe commented, "Not through a female relative, I hope."

Euclid laughed briefly, almost despite himself. "Don't know where Bobby is," he said, as if out of the blue.

By this point, Lester had relaxed, having yielded to an older, more time-tested pattern of conversation.

"You have family up north?" Joe asked, in turn ignoring Washburn's reference to why they were there.

"Some," Washburn acknowledged, adding after another puff of smoke. "Thought I recognized the name."

Joe now felt free to share a perch on the back of the truck, albeit near the other corner. "Your people called Washburn, too? Doesn't ring a bell."

"Higgins."

Joe's eyes widened. "Don Higgins? No kidding."

"My cousin. Dead now."

"I heard that."

Washburn studied what was left of his cigarette, which Lester estimated to be about an eighth of an inch, and carefully ground it out on the sole of his work boot.

"What d'you need to know about Bobby?"

"You worked on a lot of houses together, especially lately," Joe explained. "For starters, I'm looking for your impression of the man."

"Lazy," came the unhurried but immediate response. "And dumb as a box of rocks. He could do what I told him, but that was about it."

"What else?"

"Talked too much."

Joe chuckled. "Just what we want. What about?"

Washburn stared out over the scenery, taking in a landscape second only to West Virginia in its hilliness. Joe couldn't fault him. He was doing the same thing. This time of year, when the whole countryside had shaken off winter in exchange for a lush, thick coat of green growth, the view seemed as miraculous to them as it might have to an Eskimo.

"Other people's property, mostly," Euclid said.

"You worked on some nice houses."

Washburn responded simply by tilting his head toward the largely completed building beside them, sitting on its raw, scarred earth like a misplaced wedding cake.

"He ever show what we might call an unhealthy interest in those houses?" Joe asked.

Washburn again offered his version of a laugh—a small convulsion this time ending in a cough. "That's good," he said. "I like that. Yup, you could say he did."

"One more than another?"

"Sometimes." He paused to consider that before adding, "We also work on places that're being lived in; they aren't all under construction like this one."

"So, full of fancy stuff."

"Junk, more like it. I had to stop him from putting a little souvenir in his pocket more than once."

"Any place stick out in your memory?"

Washburn stroked his bristly chin a moment. "One on Tucker Peak, not long ago. Big place. Near the top."

Joe nodded. "Okay."

"'Nother outside Grafton, course. That would make sense. He liked that one. The old Ranney place."

Joe noticed that Les was writing that down out of Euclid's line of sight, as if doing so openly might jinx the oracle.

"There was one in Dummerston, too," Washburn continued, now on a roll. "On Miller Road. And that modern place in Newfane. I hated that one. Straw-bale construction. Total bitch to string—hay bales coated with stucco. No dead-air space. Terrible. He loved it, though. Like a kid in a candy store. I actually had him turn his pockets out there, just to make sure."

There was a long silence. The growl of the distant bulldozers undulated on the breeze.

Joe waited a long time before asking at last, "That it?"

Euclid slid off the back of the truck. "It's what I recall," he said, and walked off to return to work.

Lester finished writing and raised an eyebrow at his boss. Joe shrugged. "Guess we'll get the details from the foreman. Looks like we got Bobby's shopping list, though."

Mickey stiffened in his seat and jerked at the wheel, startled awake by the sudden roar of the rumble strip beneath his tires. Shit, he thought. Gotta keep awake. He blinked against the rain hitting the windshield, trying to concentrate on whatever showed up within the meager twin cones of light from the headlamps. Naturally, the car was a heap, barely fit for the road—a perfect reflection of his life. He was dead broke, surrounded by losers, and without prospects.

Except maybe for where he was headed.

He rolled down the window, hoping the swipe of passing rainwater against his face might help. It wasn't like he cared if the backseat got wet. It wasn't his car, and he didn't give a shit if Tony Leto had a fit later. Besides, if things worked out, he'd pay for the damages. Call it a fee for services rendered.

He'd give Tony that much—he hadn't known it at the time, but he had been useful after all. Mickey had plied him with booze, fogged his brain with dope, and flattered him with praise for most of the night, and had finally hit pay dirt. Or at least as close as he could get with a low-functioning toad like Tony.

The goal had been to figure out what James had done with the jewelry he'd made such a big deal about—something Mickey hadn't realized Tony was aware of until a slip of the tongue revealed that James had lost his driver's license due to a DUI and now routinely used Tony as his chauffeur.

How dumbass simple was that, Mickey had thought at the time. He'd been trying to figure out how to get the drop on James so he'd reveal how he was going to screw his partners out of their share of the take. And all the while, Tony the chauffeur had been holding the keys to the kingdom. Or at least the car.

Still, Tony had not gone down fast or easily, as Mickey's throbbing head was now reminding him. The son of a bitch had been like a sponge, taking everything in and letting nothing out. Meanwhile, Mickey had palmed the pills he'd been pretending to pop, and poured out booze when Tony's attention was elsewhere. Still, he'd had to take a lot on board, if only a third of Tony's load, and by the time he'd gotten what he was after, he half-wondered if he'd reap the benefits or die of an overdose.

Nevertheless, the worst was officially over. He might have been feeling like hell, but at least he was alive to know it. And Tony hadn't just spilled the beans; he'd even supplied the means for a field trip, if only by finally passing out so completely that Mickey knew the car was his for twenty-four hours at least.

Enough time, he hoped, to seal the deal.

Or something.

Because that part remained a little vague. What he'd gotten from Leto was that he and James would routinely drive to Northampton, in western Massachusetts, to deliver any and all jewelry to James's special buyer.

What was missing was everything else. Tony remembered one address, but only one among several, because every time they'd gone, he'd been told to stay in the car. He'd never met anyone, never witnessed any meetings, and never been told any details by James on the way back. And for all he'd known, that address was an empty shell.

He'd just been the driver.

But he had seen James go into that one building with the stolen goods and come out with an envelope full of cash.

That's what Mickey had needed to hear—enough for him to conduct a little business on his own, or at least try. After all, as he'd told himself before, where would either one of those dopes have been if it hadn't been for his special talent? He'd been the key there; he didn't need people like James or Tony. He needed to meet the fence, and shrink the supply-and-demand circle.

And get his ticket to the future.

The rumble strip made him jump once more.

Assuming he didn't kill himself beforehand.

Northampton lay below the intersection of Route 2 and I-91 as the latter dropped out of Vermont. He could've taken the Mass Pike instead of Route 2, but he wasn't sure of Tony's car, and he didn't want to spring for the toll. Which was just the kind of thinking he wanted to be free of from now on out.

He took Exit 20 onto King Street, the town's commercial strip of tacky outlets, gas stations, car dealerships, and junk-food restaurants, and worked his way toward downtown in the dawn's graying light, unsure of his bearings. He had heard a lot about Northampton—the fancy college, the music, the acidheads, the lesbians—but he'd never had a reason to go there before. It was a rich town, by his measure, but a poor place for his particular talents. He needed urban anonymity and clutter to function, and a large area in which to vanish. Northampton offered none of that.

He reached the junction of King and Main and swung right onto Main before the light changed. He immediately found himself in the center of downtown—normally a broad, sometimes daunting confluence of cars and pedestrians in near-random, freewheeling motion, now blessedly and eerily empty—where he came to an abrupt stop in the middle of the street.

He craned forward to take in the surrounding view—the curve of the road lined with a hodgepodge of architectural samplings, literally crowned at the far end by a multistory, castlelike city hall, looking fresh out of a Lego box.

"Holy shit," he muttered before self-consciously easing back into gear. No point being picked up for loitering by probably the only cop on duty.

He was surprised by what he was seeing, though. For all of the battered, destitute downtowns that he'd visited around New England, with every third store shuttered and the rest looking worse for wear, this one—even deserted at sunrise—seemed loaded for bear. There were dozens of businesses pushed together and stuffed with offerings, and they were out of this world—or at least out of Mickey's— running the gamut from Tibetan eateries to an eyebrow-weaving emporium.

This was one weird town.

He pulled over and consulted the map he'd printed off of Tony's computer before leaving Boston, twisting it around to make sense of it. He got oriented, rubbed his eyes to clear his blurred vision, and headed off, formulating what to do next.

The map brought him to an upscale warehouse of sorts, or what had once been a business equipped with bay doors. It had since been converted and was now an upscale hybrid, both commercial and residential, unmarked but very well cared for, and presumably owned by a single entity—whether discreet business or family, he couldn't tell.

He parked in the otherwise-empty lot, feeling exposed and self-conscious, and killed the engine.

Now what?

It wasn't what he'd been expecting. He'd anticipated an action plan—arriving someplace with an open door or some people to question or push around. A suggestion of what he should do next. Now he was feeling as disoriented as he had been in the middle of downtown.

He checked his watch. It was close to five in the morning. He could leave and drive around for a while, or find a Dunkin' Donuts to kill a couple of hours. Maybe this place would come alive.

He studied the building more carefully, trying to probe its function. But aside from exuding a sense of money, it told him nothing. Tony had said the place was "weird." Mickey hadn't understood what he'd meant.

A door opened at the far end, beyond the second bay, revealing a tall, good-looking woman dressed in jeans and a man's shirt. Her blond hair reflected the slowly brightening daylight.

She began walking straight toward him.

He considered starting the car and driving off while he had the chance, or maybe claiming that he was lost or feeling ill or looking for some name he'd make up.

Instead, he just sat there, watching her draw near.

She was slender, almost underfed, but she walked with purpose, her chin set and her expression intent. Even from a distance, she exuded a nervous, pent-up energy.

He rolled his window down as she approached, deciding to beat her to the punch. "Yes?"

"What are you doing here?" she demanded.

He opened his mouth to respond as he'd planned, then suddenly stopped and, perhaps encouraged by the impression she'd made on him, said instead, "James sent me."

She stared at him, quickly scanned the rusty car, looked around to check for anyone else, and said, "That figures." She turned on her heel and ordered him to follow her.

Mickey couldn't believe it. He fumbled with the door handle to get out and almost fell on the pavement, his legs wobbly and his head swimming.

"Come on," he muttered, staggering to catch up. The woman didn't look back.

She entered the structure the same way she'd appeared, not holding the door open. Still trying to clear his mind, he stepped into a small, bland lobby, as free of signage as the building's exterior. She was already partway through another door.

The next room was tile-floored, with a conference table in the middle, surrounded by chairs, and a sideboard along one wall sporting what appeared to be awards of some sort. Mickey couldn't figure out for what.

The woman turned on her heel and faced him, her expression grim. "Where's James?"

"Boston. This isn't really about him. I just said that to—"

"What *is* it about?" she cut him off.

He tried again. "That's what I'm saying. I work with him, but he doesn't know I'm here."

Her eyes hardened. "How did you know to come here, then?"

"Tony," he blurted out. "Tony Leto. His driver."

"Who else knows about this place?"

He looked at her in surprise. "What? Oh, I get it. Nobody. Tony didn't want to tell me, but I got a business proposition that'll—"

"When did Tony give you this address?" she cut him off again.

"Earlier tonight. Look, lady, you don't have to worry. Nobody knows I'm here, and Tony was so trashed, I doubt he'll remember anything about it, assuming he even survives what he took on board. He got pretty messed up."

She didn't smile so much as curl her upper lip. "I bet."

She stepped back half a foot, barely leaning against the sideboard now. "Lift up your shirt."

He laughed at the request. "You think I'm a cop?"

"Lift. Shouldn't be a problem if you're not."

Shaking his head, he grabbed his T-shirt and pulled it up to his chest. "If only the real cops could see me now," he said, smiling.

"Higher. All the way."

He did as requested, until the shirt blocked his view of her. He half-wondered if someday he might ask her to do the same thing in return. She wasn't bad on the eyes, even if she wasn't getting any younger.

He heard a slight noise, as if she'd shifted her weight, followed by "Okay, you can lower your hands."

As he exposed his face to her, for that split second, he saw her holding the heaviest of the awards as if it were a baseball bat, all curled up tight and ready to strike.

And then she let loose, smacking him across the temple.

He was dead before his legs buckled.

CHAPTER NINE

"Everybody still awake out there?" Joe asked on the radio.

One by one, his team responded in hushed tones, sounding like children caught reading under the covers. Except Willy, of course, who said, "Spare me."

Joe looked across at Marilyn Distelberg, who along with her husband, Bob, had allowed him to use their back office as a staging area. They ran the Newfane Country Store, famous for its huge old-timey sign advertising fudge and quilts to passing traffic—an icon often better recalled than the name of the store itself, and actually a disservice to its wealth of other offerings. Joe had felt like a trespasser in Santa's warehouse on the way in.

"He's had a long day," he explained.

The couple nodded. Joe had urged them to retire to their upstairs apartment, stressing the boring nature of most stakeouts, but they'd demurred, apparently finding his presence preferable to a good night's sleep. Marilyn had even conjured up some coffee and snacks.

He didn't blame them. He doubted that he would have slept,

either, knowing a cop was downstairs running a covert operation. He was also grateful—he was enjoying the company far more than if he'd been staring at the surrounding walls in silence, waiting for something that might not happen.

Newfane was the site of the straw-bale house that Euclid Washburn had found so annoying to wire. Through one of Willy's ubiquitous confidential sources, they had discovered that someone sounding suspiciously like Bobby Schultz might be targeting it tonight.

The VBI team wasn't alone. Joe had contacted the Windham County sheriff, whose office was on the far side of the store's parking lot, and asked if any of his deputies might like to join in. The response had been immediate and generous, making Joe cross his fingers in hopes that some of that enthusiasm would be met with a good result.

He gazed over at his hosts. "This must be a little bizarre, having us invade your lives like this."

Marilyn laughed—she was clearly the more talkative of the two. "Are you kidding? This is a total 'Dear Diary' moment. We'll amaze our kids with this one. They think we just sit around selling fudge all day and watching the dust settle on our glasses."

"We'll be cool for at least three minutes," Bob said softly.

"Nothing may happen," Joe cautioned, not for the first time. "I can't tell you how many of these I've been on that didn't pan out."

Marilyn waved her hand dismissively. "Doesn't matter. It's already been more fun than we've had all week. Our life here isn't as thrilling as people make it out to be."

Joe hesitated.

She smiled. "That was a joke."

"Right," he said, slightly embarrassed. The radio clicked beside him.

"Go ahead," he said into it.

"Got a pair of headlights. They got killed halfway up the hill, headin' this way," an unfamiliar voice reported.

"Looks like the van," Sammie Martens added from her vantage point.

Joe rose to his feet and addressed the Distelbergs. "Guess something's happening. I may be back, but if not, thanks again."

He left the office, walked the length of the darkened store, flanked by rows of cheese, toys, books, dry goods, and old-fashioned hard candy in antique jars, and slipped through the front door into the cool night air.

The straw-bale house stood on a hill on the edge of the village, out of sight but within walking distance of the store. Now that he'd been assured that the suspicious van had passed by, Joe felt comfortable walking up the middle of the steep road to the property, although ready to step in among the trees if warned.

Over the radio, which he had now equipped with an earpiece, he heard a running commentary on the van's progress—up the driveway, into the dooryard, coming to a full stop.

"I count three of them," Lester said.

"Roger that," Sam concurred.

"Including the driver," another voice added.

Willy, typically, was silent.

As Joe approached, he heard how the van's occupants had removed a ladder from the back and propped it against a side wall, and how one of the three hopeful thieves had then climbed it to jimmy a second-floor window.

A carbon copy of the Tucker Peak break-in.

The goal had been to let Schultz and his crew execute their plan and pinch them on the way out. But Joe was starting to worry about the familiarity of all this.

"Sam," he radioed. "It's Joe."

"Go ahead."

"Did any of you see anything that looked like a gas can? I don't want this place burned down like the first one."

"We're good," Willy said, without explanation.

"Okay," Joe replied, but he was instantly troubled. He only knew where Willy was supposed to be, based on their preop outline of the evening's activities. He had no idea where the man had actually ended up.

Willy's reassurance that all was well only heightened his concern.

Willy, for his part, was thoroughly enjoying himself. He loved the adrenaline that came when stalking human prey, even through the innards of a home he'd never visited.

Because that's where he was, of course: inside, with the burglars—not that they were aware of it. Unbeknownst to the rest of the team, Willy had managed to slip inside ahead of the van's occupants.

It hadn't been that difficult. The decision had been made earlier to kill the very alarm that the thieves thought they were defeating, thereby ruling out any mishap that might send them running prematurely—ergo the hiding out in the woods and in the Newfane Country Store. Beating them to the punch by waiting inside had not been part of the plan.

But as Willy drifted invisibly in their wake, watching them filling bags with pricey loot, he found his justification when he spied one of the men pull out a lighter and crouch down at the base of a window curtain.

Making sure the other two were already nearing the door, ensuring that he and the arsonist were the only two left behind, he silently stepped up behind the man, slipped his massive hand around his neck in a choke hold, and whispered. "Gently, asshole. Don't even breathe."

The thief did struggle, of course, if barely, since breathing was no longer an option, but Willy controlled him with ease, certainly long enough for his companions to step outside and be caught in a glaring, disorienting cocoon of lights and shouted orders.

Willy released his grip on his slowly drooping victim.

"Okay. All done. Time to step outside."

"You might want to look at this."

Joe rubbed his eyes and focused on the pictures Sam was holding out. "What are they?"

"I got 'em from the Burlington PD just before we headed out to Newfane. I figured they'd hold till later, but that was before we nabbed Schultz."

Frowning, Joe sat on the edge of his desk and started leafing through the collection. They'd repaired to the municipal building in Brattle-boro, complete with van and burglars, who were occupying cells in the basement. Joe had been about to interview Bobby Schultz.

"They busted an operator up there and found a lot of the missing items from the Tucker Peak job," Sam explained.

Joe moved the pictures closer to his desk lamp to better see their details. "I can see that. Burlington? Jeez. That's not what I would've expected."

"The fence had a room stacked to the ceiling. They're still processing how many cases are involved. The detective up there picked up on these because of the list we circulated."

"*You* circulated," Joe stressed, glancing up and smiling. "Nice work."

"They didn't find everything," she continued. "But it's a big chunk of it. The billionaire ought to be pleased, assuming he even knew what was missing."

Joe reached over to retrieve the master sheet of stolen items relating to the Hampton job and murmured, "Interesting."

"What?" she asked.

"No jewelry. It's all missing."

She took the photos back and flipped through them. "That's weird."

He slid off the desk and stretched. He hadn't slept in almost twenty-four hours by now. He circled around, settled into his seat, and reached for the phone. "Burlington PD?"

"Yeah," she said, glancing at her notes. "Kemp Wagenbach."

Joe began dialing. "Well, let's hope he's on duty."

He wasn't, but when Joe explained who he was and his purpose for calling, he was surprised to be told that he'd be patched through to Detective Wagenbach immediately.

He raised his eyebrows at Sam, who was listening on the speaker phone. "Service with a smile," he commented.

An artificially alert male voice soon answered, betraying a man who'd just been awakened. "Morning—Wagenbach."

"Sorry to be calling so early, Detective," Joe began. "This is Joe Gunther, of the VBI."

The voice sharpened. "I know who you are, sir. You addressed my graduating class at the Academy. This is a real honor."

Joe laughed self-consciously. "Thanks. I hope I didn't sound like a total dope. I usually try to avoid those things."

"You were great, sir. A real inspiration."

Joe moved on, now thoroughly embarrassed. "The reason I'm calling is that we just grabbed a burglar in the Brattleboro area who may be responsible for some of the stolen goods you just found as part of your . . ." He paused here to glance at Sammie helplessly. She quickly came to his rescue. "The Brooks McCandlish case. The superfence," she told Wagenbach.

"Special Agent Samantha Martens is on with me," Joe explained.

"Hi," Wagenbach said before adding, "Yeah, that was some stash, huh? What would you like to know?"

"Well, we noticed something interesting," Joe continued, "and I wondered if it had any significance. The jewelry from our Tucker Peak burglary is missing from the load you photographed at Mc-Candlish's, as if it had been split off from the rest. Can you shine any light on that?"

"Only vaguely," Wagenbach admitted, adding, "although it's funny that you noticed it, 'cause yours wasn't the only haul that was handled that way. I got McCandlish to open up a little, with the SA offering him a deal, and he said that more and more bad guys are using somebody in Northampton, Mass., just for jewels and gold and silverware. McCandlish said he didn't care, since he didn't like dealing with it anyhow, but when I pushed him for a name, he said he had no clue— that whoever it was kept way under the radar but that he paid top prices, like maybe twenty-five on the dollar. McCandlish said word had spread wide enough that people were stealing things they normally never touched when it was too hard to move and not worth the heat."

Joe nodded at the phone. "Interesting. And McCandlish was that big a player? I'd never heard of him."

"Oh yeah. Like a regional broker. The fence's fence, in some cases, not that he wouldn't deal direct. One of our CIs called him Mr. Wal-Mart. What we're getting out of him is that he mostly traded to Canada, which really surprised us. Kind of reverse smuggling. Lot of money for stolen goods up there, turns out. I guess their economy's better than ours."

Joe raised his eyebrows at Sam in an unspoken question. She shook her head, indicating that she had no additional questions.

"Speaking of Canada," Wagenbach said, "I guess we shouldn't be too surprised about a Massachusetts connection—or anything else, for that matter. Not in today's wired world. And we did find some jewels and shit like that in McCandlish's pile. It's not like everything was going to the mystery man in Northampton."

"All right, Detective," Joe told him. "Thanks for your help. Again, sorry to have disturbed you at home."

"No problem, sir. A real pleasure."

Joe put the receiver down and sat staring at his desktop for a few seconds, thinking. Then as he rose, he said to Sam, "Let's ask old Bobby what he's been up to lately."

Interrogations can be curious affairs—silent, confrontational, chatty, chesslike, and occasionally a combination of those and more. Generally, the interrogator works to maintain control and gain insight, while the subject either struggles to figure out where the conversation is headed or keeps silent.

In all cases, results rarely match expectations—for either party. Joe generally found what worked best was to first overwhelm his opponent with talk, to the point where, by the end, the poor bastard would confess just to get a little quiet. It wasn't a flawless technique, it demanded a certain knowledge of the person's background and history, and it had to match Joe's first impression that he stood at least a fair chance of success.

With Bobby Schultz, however, he was dealing with a man who needed no encouragement at all. As Joe entered the small room that the VBI borrowed from the police department for such purposes, a crestfallen novice criminal looked up at him with red-rimmed eyes and blurted, "I fucked up. I don't want to go to jail."

Joe raised his eyebrows. Okay, he thought, recalling Euclid Washburn's description of a childlike kleptomaniac. Abandoning plan A, he crossed the room, pulled out the only other chair, and sat down, preparing to do more listening than talking.

"You've been read your rights, Mr. Schultz?"

"Yes."

"And you understood them completely?"

"Yes."

"And you'd still like to talk to me?"

"I don't want to go to jail."

"I'm sure you don't. Too bad I'm not the one who decides that."

Schultz looked at him for a moment, before Joe added, "I might be able to help, though."

"You can?"

"I might. Depending on how this conversation goes, I'll talk to the prosecutor."

"And he decides?"

Joe smiled, wondering how he'd ended up with the only person in the state who'd apparently never seen a TV show.

"She plays a huge role there, yup."

Schultz slouched back, looking exhausted. "Okay. Then I did it."

Joe nodded. "I know. I was one of the people who caught you."

"You were there?" he asked, surprised.

"Yeah. My name's Joe Gunther. I work for the VBI."

"The VBI?"

"The police," Joe said. He sighed inwardly, frustrated at constantly having to explain for whom he worked.

He lowered his voice slightly. "So, Bobby, you want to help yourself out here?"

"Yeah. That's what I'm sayin'."

"Good. Then how 'bout you take me through this step by step, back to when you were working for the alarm company and started to think about what you wanted to do with the rest of your life."

Bobby Schultz proved as good as his word, although by the end of an hour and a half, it would have been hard to argue that he'd helped himself at all. In fact, he'd talked himself into a decent jail sentence by giving Joe almost everything he wanted. On the other hand, such was the way with more confessions than was commonly known.

Joe glanced over the notes he'd kept during the interrogation. "You said you sold what you took from Tucker Peak to Brooks McCandlish, in Burlington," he read. "What about the jewelry? It looks like it went somewhere else."

"It did," Bobby admitted. "McCandlish will take it if he has to, but his prices suck. I was told a guy in Mass. was a lot better, and he was."

"Who?"

Bobby shrugged. "Beats me. It was like one of those CIA movies. You call a cell number that only works once—at least that's what I was told—and then you meet somebody in a room where you can't tell who they are—"

"What d'you mean?" Joe interrupted.

"Dark room, bright lights behind the guy talkin', so it blinds you. Like I said, real Hollywood."

"Where was this?"

"Like a warehouse or somethin'. Nuthin' else in it. You could tell it was just for the deal, like the cell phone number. And I didn't drive there, so I don't know where it is. I went to some spot where they blindfolded me and took me in their car. It was kind of cool, after you got over being scared." Bobby smiled at Joe. By this time, his demeanor had become almost friendly, either because his confession had worked like a tonic or—as Joe thought more likely—only because he was a little simpleminded.

"You didn't see them?"

"Nope. They were real careful about that."

"Who gave you the phone number?"

"Nobody. It was on a Web site."

Joe skipped a beat, watching him. "A Web site," he repeated, not as a question.

The other man's eyes widened. "I'm not shittin' you. McCandlish was laughin' when he told me about it, 'cause he thought it was weird, too, but he told me to call the number on the Web site, so I did, and the voice on the other end told me what to do, after askin' so many questions I was startin' to think it wasn't worth it."

"What was the Web site?"

Bobby pulled a long face. "I knew you'd ask me that. I don't remember. I only wrote it down on a scrap of paper to remember for just then, 'cause I knew I could call McCandlish anytime for it." His face brightened then with a thought. "Ask *him*. He'll tell you."

"You go to a Web site," Joe restated, "you find a phone number, and the person who answers directs you to a meeting place. Just like that."

"Yeah," Bobby said brightly, adding after a pause, "Well, maybe not exactly, but pretty close."

Joe frowned. "Bob . . ." he began.

"Okay. Okay. I know. The phone number's not just sittin' there. Ya gotta get into the site by answerin' a bunch of questions. And it takes a couple of days; whoever it is has to check you out."

"Like a criminal dating service?" Joe asked incredulously.

Bobby laughed. "Yeah. That's good. I hadn't thought of that, but that's perfect." He slapped his knee in appreciation. "No cops invited. That's great."

A small pause in the conversation allowed Joe to change topics slightly. "Tell me about the burning thing, Bob. Why torch the places?"

Schultz looked slightly embarrassed. "Probably shouldn't have done that, huh?"

Joe tilted his head suggestively. "Maybe you thought you did it for good reason."

The ex-electrician nodded. "It did feel kind of right. At the time."

"Why's that?"

Bobby looked at him sincerely. "Those places, those people. It's like being on another planet, you know?"

"How so?"

"Well, you know. They're like palaces, and the people're like royalty. They love all the junk, and they hire you to protect it, and it all costs a fortune—like, way more than anythin' you've ever seen before. But they don't treat you right. I mean, we're just workin' there, doin' our jobs, but I had a couple of them back away from me when I came near, like I was covered with cow shit or somethin'. It made me mad."

"So the burning ties into that?"

"Yeah," he said meditatively, as if fresh from a philosophical revelation. "Kinda leavin' a message they could really understand."

It still surprised Joe, even after so many interviews, how a seemingly brainless act of violence or destruction could be occasionally tied to a core belief, instead of just a thoughtless outburst.

"How 'bout the town you went to?" he asked, returning to his original inquiry. "I know you don't know the address where you ended up, but what about before you got blindfolded?"

"Northampton" was the answer. "That's where I started out."

Jimmy picked up the phone. "McAuliffe."

"Jimmy, it's Chuck."

"Hey."

"I got that info you asked for, on Leto and the others."

McAuliffe reached for the file labeled "Hawthorn" on the corner of his desk and flipped it open. He picked up a pen. "Shoot."

"The James with no last name is James White. He and Leto are like Tweedle-Dee and Tweedle-Dummer, with Leto being the dummer. White fancies himself a mastermind, which is why he's spent only half his life in jail. Your informant was right about the Leto store being the clubhouse. The people I talked with said they meet in the basement while mom guards the door."

"'They' being who?" Jimmy asked, writing quickly. "Just the two of them?"

"Not always, but you're half right. I attached a list of names at the end of the report I e-mailed you—maybe four of which stand out, at least to my squad room."

"Any you like for the Beacon Hill job?"

"Mickey Roma," Chuck said without hesitation. "He's the smartest of the bunch, not so much a follower as the rest. Like I said, White likes 'em under his thumb."

"Why Roma?"

"He's got some skill sets. You know how these guys work, Jimmy—it's what you can do for them. I doubt Mickey Roma hung out with White for more than a job or two. It's all in my report. I just wanted to give you the heads-up on the highlights, and I'm running late for my doughnut break."

"Okay, okay, but Chuck," McAuliffe said, continuing to press him, "you saying White and company did do Beacon Hill?"

"Nope. I got nuthin' saying they did, nuthin' saying they didn't."

"What about White having a buyer, west of here someplace, just for the jewelry? Anything there?"

"Oh, yeah," Chuck said. "There's some chatter there—how he was hyped up about a new outlet a couple of years ago that fattened his margin. Course, you have to take this with a grain of salt—maybe a pound of it."

"Any particular town mentioned?"

Chuck laughed. "That was the weird part—unlikeliest place you'd think of to sell stolen goods—the capital of the high-on-the-hog, pouffie, back-to-nature, artsy crowd. Maybe that's why it's perfect."

McAuliffe tried to pin him down again, tiring of the run-on prattle. "Where, Chuck?"

"I don't actually believe it, to be honest. But the rumor is, Northampton. But that's it," he hastened to add. "No names, no addresses, nuthin'. Just Northampton."

Jimmy shook his head. "Thanks, Chuck. I owe you."

.   .   .

Patrol officer Anne Pape was slowly rolling through the no-man's-land separating Holyoke, Chicopee, and North Springfield, Massachusetts, passing an abandoned stretch of old warehouses and manufacturing plants of vague lineage. It was a good place for illicit activities, from drugs to sex to stolen car handoffs. At various times, there'd been illegals found locked in a panel truck, a meeting of two gangs swapping drugs for military-grade weapons, and even a guy customs grabbed who had an SUV filled with exotic birds. The whole area was a gritty, beaten-down, miniature Rust Belt version of the Wild West, as far as she was concerned.

And a good place to poke around, sometimes.

The larger urban setting was not without its risks, too, of course, and she wasn't thinking of the violence. Pape had begun her career in a quieter, rural jurisdiction, and had applied for a big-city opening to gain experience and upward mobility. But it carried a price. The sexism, the backstabbing, the politics, the jockeying for favor and attention—all were alive and well, despite any front-office protests to the contrary, and none of which had anything to do with the work she'd been hired for. That had its own set of pressures. Every day, she felt like she was entering a two-front combat area.

As a result, this present concrete wasteland was both a blessing and a threat, simultaneously supplying a break from the job and the potential danger of a bullet going straight through her windshield.

Having turned off her headlights earlier, she slowed to a stop and killed her parking lights at the sight of a slight movement far ahead. She silently stepped out of the cruiser, leaving the door open, and scanned the entire area. Only then did she reach into the vehicle, unhook the mic to tell dispatch that she was "out of the car and on portable" at this location, and release her shotgun from its mount against the ceiling's headliner. If she was going to check this out cowboy-style, she didn't want to go without the biggest firepower she had.

She moved away from the car, paused at the wall of the nearest warehouse to fit her portable radio with an earbud, made sure that she had a shell chambered, and proceeded toward where she could see what looked like a single human form hard at work doing something repetitive.

As she got nearer, her senses sharpened, along with her paranoia, and she repeatedly stopped to check her surroundings, increasingly doubting her choice of tactics. The sweat trickled freely beneath her body armor and across her forehead, and she kept blinking to keep it from obscuring her vision.

Ahead, she could make out a man crouching alongside a dark and silent automobile, engaged in the steady rhythm of working a car jack. As she left the wall on tiptoes to circle around and approach him from behind, Anne noticed that he'd already removed one wheel, replacing it with a couple of broken cinder blocks. The wheel was resting on the debris-strewn pavement, awaiting its fellows. She also saw, parked ahead of the dark sedan, a worn-out pickup truck with a thin plume of smoke pulsing from its tailpipe.

Satisfied that the two of them were alone, Anne readied her shotgun and shouted at the man, *"Police. Do not move."*

The man froze.

"Get down on your knees, release the tire iron, and place your hands behind your head."

She again checked around her, her voice having bounced off the surrounding walls, sounding tinny and frail. It was going well, but she felt like she might explode from the adrenaline.

"Cross one foot over the other and interlink your fingers."

For the first time, she heard a half-mumbled complaint, barely audible, as the man clumsily complied. "What the fuck?"

"*Shut up*," she ordered, and keyed her mic to update dispatch.

She carefully drew nearer, shotgun still pointed, and reached out for the man's hands.

"Do not move," she repeated as she seized hold of them with one hand, crushing them tightly so that he couldn't break free.

"Ow, lady," he complained. "That hurts."

She squeezed harder. "What did I say?"

"Just get this shit over, okay?" he whined, obviously a veteran of the process.

Feeling better by the moment, Anne placed the shotgun on the ground beside her, smoothly drew a pair of cuffs from her belt, and slapped them onto the man's wrists with a motion that she'd practiced a hundred times before.

All without a hitch.

"What's your name?" she asked, standing over him.

"Niles Freeman. Can I get up now?"

"No," she told him. "Swivel onto your ass and put your back against the tire."

Retrieving the shotgun, she shouldered it again and simultaneously hit the switch on the flashlight attached beneath its barrel. Looking along the gun's sights, she peered into the car's windows at a slight angle to avoid being blinded by her own reflection.

Behind the wheel, slumped over onto the passenger seat, as if taking a nap, was the body of a second man.

Pape stepped back as though pushed. *"Holy shit."*

She aimed the shotgun at the thief, catching the white of his startled eyes in the flashlight's bright glare.

"What the hell is that?" she demanded.

"What? What?" he shouted back. "What the fuck you talkin' about?"

"The body. There's a body in there."

He twisted around to stare stupidly at the car, as if it were transparent.

Anne, who had already begun recovering from her initial shock, asked in a more normal voice, "You didn't look inside?"

"I hadn't gotten to that part yet. I tried the doors and figured I'd break in later. I don't got a flashlight."

Glancing around, Anne got back on the radio, added the car's license plate to her general information, and requested detectives, a crime-scene team, and a supervisor.

"You get a hit on that plate?" she asked dispatch on her cell phone moments later. For discretions' sake, police officers increasingly used phones for even fundamental data.

"Car comes back to an Anthony Leto, out of Boston," came the response. "But the interesting thing," the dispatcher added, "is that someone reported it stolen by a Mickey Roma two nights ago. That who you got?"

The energy rush began draining from her as she stood with her phone in one hand and her shotgun like a deadweight in the other. Anne Pape turned to face the car and shook her head.

"Damned if I know."

CHAPTER TEN

Joe sat by his office window, watching the sky pale with the rising sun. It was a little after five in the morning, and the window was half-open, so he could enjoy the coming day—birds waking up, the early-spring air carrying the scent of new foliage.

He'd been at his desk for two hours already, having abandoned his bed and its memories in frustration. When he met Lyn, their relationship had been sweet and comforting, and certainly passionate. But it had also been free of the spikes and dips and obsessions of young love. He'd equated the feeling of finding her with the stability a boat might receive from a reliable mooring post.

Now he could only wish for such calm. Instead, he was suffering like a teenager flattened by loss, combined with an older man's sense of impermanence and doom.

Blessedly, however, and completely without cause—despite the hour and doleful ruminations—his brain made an unconnected, perhaps self-salvaging leap. He reached for the phone and dialed the Northampton Police Department.

"This is Joe Gunther, of the VBI in Vermont," he told the dispatcher who answered. "I'm taking a wild guess here, but is your chief sitting at his desk like I am right now?"

The man on the line let out an appreciative snort. "You two must go back. Yeah, he is. Let me put you through."

"Siegel."

Joe smiled at the gruff, low-toned response.

"You give up on sleep, too?"

There was a long, thoughtful pause, followed by "Joe?"

"You're good, Dan. We haven't talked in months."

Dan Siegel let out a deep chuckle. "Yeah, but we've been talking for forty years, easy. If we're not the two oldest bulls in the field, I'd like to see who is. How're you doin', pal? I heard you'd been kicked in the balls."

Not a Hallmark card type, Joe thought, still recognizing his sincerity. "Yeah, I've been better."

"Sorry to hear it. What can I do you for this time?"

It was the proverbial guy thing, in part—the once-over, light and quick. But Joe knew that it spoke of the man. Dan Siegel had ended up as chief of police of one of Massachusetts's more unusual towns by having a mixture of paradoxical qualities—hard-nosed and diplomatic, accommodating and by the book, sentimental and cynical. Being unpredictable had proven an asset in a supposedly broad-minded community ironically prone to pin you with a label, especially if you were presumed to be a conservative cop. Truth to tell, Joe had no clue as to his colleague's political leanings.

"We're working a B and E up here," Joe explained. "Just broke it up. We started tracking the stolen items and discovered that both down in my part of the state and up in Burlington, some of the jewelry was being split off and sold to a fence in Northampton. Whoever it is, he's paying well enough that not only are people seeking him out but they're even stealing things just because of his prices."

"Huh," Siegel said.

"What?"

"Funny coincidence. I was just reading the dailies about a body dump they discovered in Holyoke last night—some lowlife from Boston named Mickey Roma. He was found dead in a supposedly stolen car."

"Murdered?" Joe assumed some overlap would be coming.

"Unless you can commit suicide by beating yourself over the head. They're still processing the scene, and the autopsy's not done yet, but there's already a tie-in to what you're talking about."

"How so?"

"When they ran the names, there was a flag on Roma from a Boston burglary cop named James McAuliffe, who was inquiring about any stolen jewelry connections between Boston, Roma and his playmates, and Northampton."

"Did it ring any bells with you?" Joe asked.

He visualized Siegel shrugging as he said, "Jewelry's a big item down here—all the groovy, ex-hippie, millionaire crowd. We have a twice-a-year juried art show that's over-the-top and a few others just to meet the demand. But I never heard of any jewelry fence as such till now. This town sells the stuff; it doesn't steal it much."

"You talk with this Boston cop yet?"

"Joe. Look at the clock. Everybody except you and me has a life."

Joe persisted. "This is interesting, though. I wouldn't mind chasing it around a little. Could be the murder ties in somehow. Maybe there's a link between Vermont, you, and Boston."

"Okay," Siegel said, drawing the word out. "What're you proposing?"

"A sit-down, to begin with. What was the Boston cop's name again?"

"James McAuliffe."

"It wouldn't hurt to compare notes, find out what's overlapping, if anything. You might be sitting on something with teeth, Daniel."

Siegel was receptive. "That was running through my mind. I do video conferencing all the time. You have a setup for that where you are?"

Joe hesitated. The quick answer was no, although he had access to it through the police department downstairs, where younger people were available to guide him through the process. On the other hand, he could still feel the tugging of what had driven him out of bed in the middle of the night.

"If it's not a bother, I might drive down to sit with you at the meeting," he said.

Once more, Siegel applied the same insight as when he'd answered the phone. "You need to get out of the office for a while?"

"More like out of my own head," Joe conceded. "Let me know when you've set up a time with McAuliffe, and I'll be there."

"We live to serve, bud."

The line went dead.

Northampton had a tricky history. Home to Smith College, and stamped with its present countercultural reputation, it tended to forget that it once featured an anti-Irish double hanging in 1806, attended by a cheering throng, or that it gave birth to the Great Awakening in the early eighteenth century, through the efforts of fire-and-brimstone homeboy Jonathan Edwards. To be fair, a hundred years later, it became home to a utopian association promoting that all people should be "equal without distinction of sex, color or condition, sect or religion"—perhaps beginning a general outlook that had remained remarkably consistent ever since, more or less enthusiastically, depending on the times.

Brattleboro and Northampton had a closer kinship than was easily explained through proximity or similar ancestry. The residents of one had felt close to the other for decades, as if they recognized a common bloodline, or perhaps responded to a mutually compatible different drummer. But there were telling differences, as well, scale being the most prominent, and thus economic muscle power. Northampton had a college, whereas Brattleboro merely behaved as if it did. Northampton was three times its sister's size, located within the greater Springfield area, whose population exceeded that of all of Vermont's. And there was something else—a country mouse/city mouse disparity in sophistication and cultural self-confidence, which only served to highlight Brattleboro's longing to be more like its larger rival.

Nevertheless, in both places, the police had to step diplomatically and cautiously, and be forever on the lookout to prove that their citizens were better off with them than without. Here, Dan Siegel had Joe's sympathy. While Joe had spent decades working for the Brattleboro PD before switching to the broader-missioned VBI, he readily acknowledged that Northampton, with ten times the attitude, offered a far larger challenge to its cops than he had ever faced.

As he pulled off the interstate, traveled the King Street Miracle Mile version of Brattleboro's Putney Road, and finally turned right onto Main and into the heart of downtown, Joe was reminded of all this through the sheer press of people crowding the sidewalks and passing before the hood of his car. While "normal" people—to use a cop's vernacular—were amply represented, going about their business in coats and ties or casual Friday business attire, they were overwhelmingly outnumbered by the young, the unusual, and the downright strange. Big Bird could have strolled the street with nary a reaction beyond a passing thumbs-up or a supportive smile. There was an incubator quality about the place, suggesting that here, especially, people were allowed, reasonably and sometimes humorously, to push at the edges of convention.

Joe gradually executed another right turn and entered a street barren of exotica. Center Street was a standard assortment of concrete and redbrick industrial-era buildings, accompanied here and there by some unsuccessful attempts at 1970s urban renewal, including the police station, a single-story eyesore so lacking in grace that it only brought to mind the barracks of some banana republic militia. But it did have available parking, often a rarity in Northampton, and Joe left his vehicle in the lot, amid an assortment of marked and unmarked cruisers.

He was heading toward the front entrance to pay proper homage to the usual police station bells and whistles of dispatchers, buzzer-controlled doors, and the need for identification, when a glass side door yawned open, revealing Dan Siegel, who was leaning against the push bar.

"Come on in, Joe. Good drive?"

"All of forty-five minutes of barely turning the steering wheel," Joe reported, shaking hands and looking up. Dan Siegel was a giant, both in height and across the shoulders, which Joe had always envied in someone having to deal with politicians. It had to be an asset.

Siegel was already leading the way into the battered, claustrophobic, poorly lighted building. "We're back here. I called McAuliffe earlier and he said he'd be ready to come online whenever we were."

They passed a few doors, Siegel greeting people in uniform and not, while Joe merely exchanged glances. They eventually settled into a room that had a wall-mounted monitor of impressive dimensions. Say what you might about this department's outer skin, it contained some very nice equipment. The upcoming replacement building was only the most obvious example of how Siegel had worked for years to upgrade and improve what was a deceptively overtaxed police agency. The 120 calls per day and the twelve hundred arrests made during an average year were executed by a very young force of sixty-five sworn officers, operating in a town hosting almost fifty thousand people year-round. Northampton's resident population was only thirty thousand, but it swelled to the higher number because of its allure. It could be a double-edged sword in any argument that such numbers enhanced the local economy. Siegel ruefully admitted that almost half of those arrests featured out-of-towners, who also became entangled in over 80 percent of the car crashes. This was one of the downsides of being a popular place to visit.

Dan offered his colleague a cup of coffee and went about adjusting the teleconference linkup. In moments, the split screen before them awakened and they were treated not just to the view of a slightly rumpled man in need of a shave but also to that of a young uniformed woman with an almost disturbingly intense gaze.

"I figured I'd throw in the gal who found that dead guy outside Springfield," Siegel muttered as an aside.

All four quickly exchanged greetings, as much to make sure the equipment was functioning as out of politeness, but the moment allowed Joe to make the acquaintance, however virtually, of Officer Anne Pape.

Dan started things off. "Since I seem to be the focus of everybody's attention but have nothing yet to offer, why don't I ask what everyone's got. I'd definitely like to know what freight train is heading my way. Anne? And oh," he added, interrupting himself, "let's can all the Officer this and Special Agent that, okay? First names only should save us about fifteen minutes by the end of the day."

Both Joe and Jimmy McAuliffe either smiled or laughed gently. Anne Pape merely nodded, her eyes still glued to the camera. Joe wondered if she was heading places high and mighty, or straight toward a job-related stroke.

Dan resumed: "Anne? I'm guessing that you've gotten at least some preliminary intel back from the medical examiner, if nobody else."

"I have, Chief," she answered. "Death was from blunt-force trauma to the right parietal aspect of the head—a single blow. The toxicology report will be several weeks in coming."

"Right," Dan said encouragingly. "Any idea how he got that thump on the head?"

"Our crime-scene technicians haven't finished their report," she explained, "but it's looking like he was killed outside the car and placed behind the wheel."

"Do they think he was killed there or transported?" McAuliffe asked.

"Hard to say for sure, but since the steering wheel was wiped clean of any and all prints, I'm betting Roma was delivered from someplace else, probably to disguise where he died."

Dan nodded and addressed the Boston detective. "Jimmy, can you fill us in on how Mr. Roma got hold of the car? I heard he stole it."

"Yes and no," Jimmy told them. "The registered owner is Tony Leto, who's associated with a mid-level B and E bunch down here. They use his mother's store on Dorchester Ave. as a hangout. Leto's a card shy of a full deck, and he's probably the low man on the totem pole, but he does have a car, which Roma apparently wanted. According to what Leto's just told us, he and Roma started drinking the other night and got royally crocked before Roma 'Mickey Finned' him and took the car. Course, that's his version."

"Did Leto report the theft?" Pape asked.

"Not him—his mom—and I'm not sure what else he's not telling us, either. We have suspicions that this gang—if you can call them that— recently ripped off a place on Beacon Hill and put the owner in a coma. That places it higher on our priorities than your average smash-and-grab, but we haven't been able to move beyond that. I'll be sending you the report of what we've got so far, but it ain't much. Still—and this is where you come in, Dan—we have learned that these guys and others are working with a buyer in Northampton who specializes in jewels, gold, and silverware."

"Meaning that Roma was murdered in Northampton," Anne stated.

Dan and Jimmy both smiled. Joe just watched her face. She didn't react.

"Whoa," Dan said. "That's one theory, but we got a ways to go yet." He turned to his companion and said, "Joe, that's why you came down here—'cause you heard the same rumor. Tell us what you know and why you think my fair town is home to the King of Jewels."

"My story's like Jimmy's," Joe told them. "We've been having a rash of burglaries across the state, like everyone else, but the Burlington PD recently busted a clearinghouse fence of sorts on their patch, where we learned what Jimmy just said—that word's out to bring your jewelry and precious metals to Northampton if you want top dollar."

"And that's it?" Jimmy asked. "No names, no locations, no go-betweens? How the hell do these mopes know who to call?"

"It's a Web site, believe it or not," Joe explained, "And ballsy, too. I checked it out after a little research. Calls itself LotsforLoot.com. It's members only, of course—you have to answer a bunch of crooks-are-us questions at the portal to get in—so needless to say, I couldn't go beyond that, but my source told me that once you're in, there's a cell phone number that changes regularly. You call that, make arrangements, and then—in his case at least—you come down to Northampton, get blindfolded and transported somewhere, and do the trade at some ever-shifting site. Whoever's behind this has more fire walls than the Pentagon—layer on layer on layer—along with a totally 'up yours' attitude."

"What about tracing the Web site back to its creator?" Anne asked.

"We have our computer folks in Burlington trying that right now," Joe told her, "but it's not looking good."

There was a pause as they considered what they'd learned from their various perspectives. It was something to consider, since each had a specific self-interest, from Anne's homicide and Jimmy's aggravated assault to Dan's simple foreboding. Joe hovered somewhere in the middle.

Nevertheless, it was he who had the widest latitude in his job description, even being from out of state.

"Sounds like task-force material to me," Joe said, breaking the silence. "If we're right, and everything we're looking at is interrelated, we could do worse than try to find out why all the arrows are pointing at Northampton. That's assuming you have no objection, Dan."

"Not me," the chief said quickly. "I'm not going to turn down extra help. I'll formalize the arrangements as soon as you're ready."

"Guess I'm on board," Jimmy agreed, if without much enthusiasm, perhaps already sensing how little support he'd be getting from his brass.

Once more, Anne Pape only nodded curtly.

Jimmy McAuliffe had barely returned to his desk when his phone rang.

"Detective?" It was the receptionist downstairs. "There's a lady here wanting to talk to you. Mina Carson?"

He groaned. "Be right there."

Five minutes later, he escorted Mina into the same small, neglected meeting room they'd used before, waving at a chair as they entered. "Have a seat, Miss Carson."

She remained standing. "What've you found out, Detective? I thought you were going to call me."

"When I had something to say, yup."

"You've found nothing?" she asked incredulously.

In fact, Jimmy had been underwhelmed by the suggestion of a task force, and only hopeful that because there was now a homicide involved, his superiors would hand the case to someone else. He wasn't sure what it was about this one that he didn't like—whether it was because its victims were privileged, or the pins were harder to knock down than in a straight up smash-and-grab, or simply that he had too much on his desk to manage. But he hated that he might have to add to his load and interact with three other police agencies, including one from another state. He wasn't a lazy man, and had as good a solve rate as any of his colleagues, but he'd been feeling a little overwhelmed lately—a mental state not improved by this entitled, intense young woman who seemed to think hers were the only problems on the face of the earth.

"We've made some inroads," he allowed. "It hasn't been easy. I warned you at the start it might be slow going."

"I heard all that," she responded testily. "I'm the one who got you started down some of those inroads. I agreed to keep out of it if you kept me up-to-date. So, keep me up-to-date."

Jimmy heard the implied threat—that if he didn't give her something, she'd start meddling again. He quickly considered his options and made a choice.

"This is very preliminary," he began. "And it's over-the-top when it comes to the rules, so without being rude, I gotta ask you to keep your mouth shut, okay? You didn't hear anything I'm about to tell you."

"Fine. I understand." But her voice had changed from petulant to curious.

"We got some good information that your grandmother's items may have ended up in the Northampton area—that there's a fence out there running a two- or three-state business, at least."

"Who is he?" she asked.

"I can't tell you that. This is an ongoing investigation, irregardless of how you feel about me or how I'm doing. The point of what I'm telling you is that this is getting big enough that my bosses might take it away from me and kick it upstairs—maybe to a task force. We even connected it to an illegal Internet operation, so for all I know, the feds'll get involved next."

"You're kidding." Mina's enthusiasm was growing, much to Jimmy's satisfaction.

"Again," he stressed, "you gotta keep this under your hat, okay? We just found out that one of the people involved in this ring has been killed, probably by one of his own, so this is getting bigger all the time. We are not shoving this under the rug."

"Have you been to Northampton?" she asked.

Jimmy almost laughed. "No. I spoke to the chief there just a few minutes ago. They've got a top-notch police department over there, so I'll be coordinating with them. That's how it works. It's a good system and it's how we beat the bad guys all the time. But"—and he leaned toward her for emphasis—"it takes time. Can you live with that?"

She made a face but nodded. "Thank you. I'm sorry for being such a pest."

He smiled and opened the door to show her out. "Not a problem. I know how it must feel. How's your grandmother doing?"

"The same," she replied, heading toward the front entrance, "but thanks for asking. You'll keep me up-to-date?"

He waved at her. "Absolutely—soon as I get anything."

As she stepped outside, he prided himself on his strategy. By invoking murder, the feds, and faraway Northampton, he figured he had her positioned like the happy viewer of a TV cop show. Or, if not happy, at least placated.

Mina, for her part, hit the sidewalk outside, checked her watch, and calculated if she had time to look in on Billie before going home, packing a few things, and heading west to Northampton.

CHAPTER ELEVEN

"Heard you were planning a party in Northampton."

Joe looked up from his computer and raised his eyebrows at Willy, who'd just entered the office.

"A party?"

Even for Willy, he was not looking happy. "A task force," he said. He stayed in the doorway instead of heading for his corner desk.

"Yeah. Seemed reasonable, given what we got out of Bobby Schultz and that raid in Burlington. If somebody in Northampton is advertising for our stolen jewelry, we might as well go get him. It could lead back upstream and help us put a lid on this burglary epidemic that's been driving everybody crazy."

But he could tell that he'd already lost Willy's attention. He was now looking almost fidgety, which was rare. Impatient, all the time; but fidgety, no. Joe checked his watch.

"Shouldn't you be home with the family?" he asked, knowing that officially, at least, Willy had no assignment that should have been keeping him from Sammie and Emma.

It was a question guaranteed to elicit a harsh response—starting with a demand for Joe to mind his own business. Instead, Willy merely shrugged and said, "I guess."

Joe hit SAVE on his computer and leaned back, frowning. "You want in on the task force? Hang out in hippie-dippy land, as I think you once called it?"

Willy's scowl deepened, but he remained silent and kept staring at some middle distance on the floor.

"What's going on?" Joe asked softly and with a sinking feeling, guessing the general subject of his friend's discomfort, if not its specific nature.

"Nuthin. Just getting antsy."

Joe kept probing, feeling he had little to lose. "You and Sam getting on each other's nerves?"

Willy smiled humorlessly. "Like that's news?"

"You never had a kid before."

"I love Emma." His voice was hard.

Joe got up, circled his desk, and motioned to Lester's nearby office chair. "Sit."

As Willy numbly complied, Joe grabbed a guest chair and sat opposite him.

"I have never heard that word from your mouth, Willy—not for Sam, not for anybody. I *know* you love that girl. That wasn't the question."

He stopped there. Willy didn't bear up well against excess talk. He generally either controlled a conversation or left it.

"I knew I'd fuck this up," he murmured, averting his eyes.

Joe paused before saying, "I don't need gory details, but I gotta have more than that."

Willy began to fidget again, no doubt planning his escape.

Joe broke one of the cardinal rules and laid a hand on Willy's forearm.

Kunkle tensed and finally stared at him.

"Willy," Joe told him, "you came here to talk about this. Maybe not consciously, but you made a choice. In the bad old days, you would've climbed straight into a bottle. Today, you came here. So finish it. Talk."

Willy's face was set, as if he were being physically tortured. Joe stayed silent.

A minute later, Willy managed to say, "I can just tell."

"From Sam or from inside you?" Joe asked quickly.

"Me."

"So you haven't done anything? You're just sure you will?"

"I can feel it."

"Why? Did something happen?"

"It's little stuff."

"Like what?"

His hand was kneading his knee. "It's like it's building inside."

Joe thought about Willy's home before Sam had moved in—compulsively tidy and virtually bare. That sense of order had the feel of a fortress wall, built to control the chaos roiling within the man. Sam was not a messy person, but she certainly was more relaxed in her habits and housekeeping, especially now that they had a child.

"You feeling like the house isn't yours anymore?"

Willy sighed without comment.

"What else? Is Emma putting you in the shade a little—all her all the time?"

The scowl deepened. "She's a baby, for Christ's sake. She needs that shit."

"You could do with some of it, too, if by 'shit' you mean a little attention. You know this is pretty common, right? To feel displaced by a new baby?"

"Not a moron," he growled.

"Sam know any of this?" Joe asked.

"She's been askin'."

"Because you've been acting like a jerk, probably."

One of Willy's better traits was that he could take what he so routinely handed out. "Probably," he conceded.

"Want me to talk with her?"

That could have gone either way, a changeover that Joe was coming to identify as old Willy versus new. Still, it was a pleasant surprise to hear him say, "Couldn't hurt."

Sadly, however, that also told him that things had gotten pretty strained between them.

"When's the last time you were home?" Joe asked him.

"Couple of days."

Joe smiled slightly. "After everyone was asleep?"

Willy couldn't stand it anymore. He rose and crossed to the door. "Fuck you."

Joe merely shook his head and muttered, "You're welcome" at the empty doorway. But he was glad they'd talked, and after he'd had a chat with Sammie, he anticipated that he'd have Willy as a sidekick on his return trip to Northampton.

There were two ways of interpreting that, the first being that it would only encourage the family tensions that Willy had already begun. But Joe, despite his own present state of mind, remained an optimist by nature, and hoped for the second possibility—that given Sam and Willy's unorthodox history as a couple, perhaps a little time off, combined with some supportive conversation, might serve as the needed escape valve.

These were intense people who truly did love each other, but each had a complicated background and a combative style. Joe knew this—he'd been watching them up close for years. Couples therapy wouldn't stand a chance—that was a no-brainer in Willy's case alone.

But a small break, in which the heart could grow fonder? Joe couldn't see the harm.

Wú Méi's voice was soft in the darkness. "You are awake?"

"Yes," Lǐ Anming said immediately. She'd been staring at the patched ceiling for hours, studying the changing shapes painted there by the sporadically passing traffic. The windows were blocked by plywood, but in this room, at least, there was a narrow gap near the top. Not that the presence of a little light was disturbing. A good night's sleep wasn't something she'd enjoyed in years, or anticipated having in the foreseeable future.

"How long have you been traveling?"

"Four years. You?"

"Three. Have you heard from home?"

It was so common a question as to be trite by now. Few if any of them ever heard *from* home. This system involved hearing *about* their families from their handlers, or "snakes," as they were called, but they were never allowed actual contact. That was how the snakes kept them in place: If you step out of line, those back home will suffer. People like Lǐ Anming pledged up to thirty thousand dollars for their passage—to be paid in sweat equity. But what surfaced too late was that such equity would never suffice.

"No," Lǐ Anming told her.

The conversation stalled there, replaced by the restless nocturnal tossing and breathing of their bunk mates.

"What will you do after . . . this?"

Again, the question was familiar, echoing whatever hopefulness had spurred them on to their travels in the first place.

"Be an artist," Lǐ Anming dutifully replaced.

Wú Méi laughed softly. "Me, too."

Lǐ Anming considered that, recalling what she'd glimpsed from the van earlier, before asking, "Is it better here?"

"It is," her friend whispered back. "Ed is not too bad. The work is good. They leave you alone."

Lǐ Anming nodded to herself, appraising the news like the veteran she'd become. She did like what little she'd seen of their location—for the first time in her travels, in fact. The factory was dismal and frightening, like so many other condemned hideaways where she'd worked, but the town itself had affected her immediately and viscerally, producing something akin to real hope.

Joe began to introduce everyone around the table: "This is Dan Siegel, Northampton's chief, and Officer Anne Pape, on special assignment from the Holyoke PD."

"What sort of special assignment?" Willy asked with his usual grace. "Dealing with woodchucks?"

There was a little laughter to remove the sting, but Pape actually brightened and pointed at Kunkle. "Truer than you know. They took me off patrol to handle this 'cause they don't want to waste anyone in CIB on a body dumping, much less you guys." She looked around before adding, "With all due respect."

"Officer Pape discovered Mickey Roma's body," Joe explained to those present, not just to Willy, knowing too well how cops often didn't check their paperwork prior to a meeting. "Which for anyone who hasn't read the report is the young man from Boston we think was involved in a burglary gang and who may have traveled to Northampton to sell the jewelry from his take."

He continued pointing out the others in the room. "This motley crew of three represents the southeastern squad of the Vermont Bureau of Investigation, along with yours truly: Lester Spinney, Samantha Martens, and last but certainly not least, in his own mind, if nowhere else, Willy Kunkle. We also have, in spirit at least, Detective Jimmy McAuliffe, who's working the Boston aspect of this but whose bosses wouldn't let him make the trip here."

"Here" in this case was the basement of the municipal building in Brattleboro, which they'd almost arbitrarily chosen for their very first task-force meeting. They were again borrowing the police department's training room, the VBI quarters being too tight to accommodate even this small a group.

"In a nutshell," Joe continued, "what we've got so far is an arson/burglary in Tucker Peak, a body in Holyoke, a cold burglary in Boston, a hot one in Newfane, Vermont—complete with crew caught red-handed—and linkages from all of them running toward Northampton. The common denominator everywhere seems to be precious metals and jewelry, and the unacknowledged monster under the bed is that whatever organization or individual that's in Northampton has been operating for years by now."

He began pacing before the empty whiteboard behind him, as was his habit in such settings. "It's the tendency in broad-based investigations like this to poke and prod everything on the table to see what's got the most potential for development."

He paused to indicate Siegel. "Which is where Dan and I began thinking that between us, he and we Vermonters may be holding the best hand."

He glanced at Pape. "Anne, a few days ago, we followed up on a lead, staked out a home north of here, and nailed a guy named Bobby Schultz, who told us how he was planning to fence his hot jewels to a buyer in Northampton. This is via the LotsforLoot.com Web site you've already been briefed on. What Dan and I were thinking—as is our local state's attorney, since Bobby's been very cooperative—is that we should put together a little sting to see if whoever's behind the Web site might not open up to Bobby while we're watching over his shoulder."

"A stalking horse ploy," Spinney said quietly.

Several in the room stared at him.

His eyebrows rose. "Hunting trick from the old days. Man with the gun uses his horse as a screen while approaching the prey, who can't count and has no clue that horses don't have six legs. Hunter gets close enough, drops his rifle across the saddle, and bang."

"Thank you, Professor Spinney," said Willy, applauding.

Joe smiled and said to them all, "Precisely—a stalking horse ploy."

"The SA's on board with this?" Sammie asked.

"Yes. She considers Schultz worth a deal, especially if we can use him to shut down a major statewide organization for stolen goods. She is a politician, after all."

"Assuming your mysterious fence is as smart as you think, won't he know that Schultz is behind bars?" Anne Pape asked.

Willy laughed and answered her sarcastically. "This is Vermont, Officer Pape. We *cite* people for nonviolent felonies. We don't throw 'em in jail. I didn't bother checking, but Bobby could just as easily be out on his own right now as behind bars for lack of bail—unless the arson charge did the trick. Still, a good question."

"Bobby's behind bars," Joe said quickly. "But Willy's right about how easy it would be to get him out. Either we can lower the bail or fake getting it paid, or something, but Bobby'll then be free to claim that, pending whatever happens to him legally, he's back outside and robbing houses in his spare time. At that point, we'll run an article in the paper about some place being ripped off, and have Bobby mention it when he makes contact through the Web site."

"Does he show up to run the actual deal with the fence face-to-face?" Willy asked. "Or does one of us stand in for him?"

No one answered immediately.

"Doesn't he know what Schultz looks like?" Pape asked.

"We could test that out," Sammie said. "We could run searches, dig around, see if there're any photos of him."

"That won't work," Willy said dismissively. "A single phone call to his old boss would get you a verbal description."

Joe noticed that Sam looked hurt by the response—something that normally wouldn't have been true. Sam was made of tough stuff, and fully capable of constructively butting heads with Willy. Her sensitivity told Joe that maybe Willy's inner doubts weren't as private as he'd hoped they'd been.

"That is something to worry about," Lester said to further the discussion. "Somebody's already been killed as part of this, assuming we're right about Mickey. Do we really want to risk Bobby's life to make this happen?"

"You sort of look like him," Willy said, eyeing his boss. "A little makeup, a mustache, and a wig would do the rest."

Joe was surprised enough not to answer.

"He's right," Lester echoed.

Joe pushed his lips out thoughtfully and looked at Dan Siegel. "You'd have to watch my back like I was your mother."

Dan smiled. "How do you know I even like my mother?"

Mina Carson closed her hotel door, put down her suitcase, and crossed over to the window. The town's landmark hotel, the Northampton, was over eighty years old, had more than a hundred rooms, and exuded the old-time grace, luxury, and sense of privilege that had once stamped nearby Smith College at its snootiest prime.

But Mina wasn't here for nostalgic glamour. As she watched the cars and people avoiding one another in droves downtown, her demeanor was calculating. In fact, this choice of lodging ran in direct conflict with her purpose for being here. She wanted to find out not where aging debutantes went to relive their carefree years, but where thieves and felons came to do business. The hotel was convenient, she figured; close to everything in midtown. But if it came time to move, depending on what she learned, she'd trade this opulence for a flophouse in a moment.

Her resolve was solid, she had the money, the time, and the determination to see through whatever was coming next. She also had little to lose.

As things had turned out, she hadn't left Boston as she'd originally planned. She'd had to stay around to bury her beloved Billie.

CHAPTER TWELVE

Joe approached Sammie in the parking lot as she was unlocking her car after the task-force meeting. She looked over her shoulder at him and smiled. "I can see you in a wig and mustache. Make you look like Wayne Newton."

"Cute," he said, holding the door for her. "You on board with this idea?"

She leaned against the car, enjoying the warm breeze, which barely ruffled her hair. "I'm not nuts about your going undercover with people who may or may not have already killed somebody, but I'm assuming everything'll be set up to make it safe."

They both knew of her own report card in that department, where the question of security had often been cursory at best. Sammie was nothing if not occasionally given to risks. Some argued that the most recent proof of that was her involvement with Kunkle.

"How's Emma doing?" Joe asked.

Her expression softened. "Terrific. Every day I see something new happen. She's so full of beans, looking around, taking everything in. It's amazing to watch."

"And Willy?"

Her eyes settled on his. Her response was more balanced, almost careful, sounding very much like the cop she was. "Great. You hearing otherwise?"

"No, no," he comforted her. "We all go back so far. I was just wondering about him. He seems a little off."

They went back decades, in fact—which allowed them to skip what might have been the usual formalities of denial and saving face.

"I've been worrying about the same thing," she admitted. "I don't want the cause of it to be us." She frowned and added, "But of course he won't talk about it, the son of a bitch, and I don't dare push him, 'cause that'll sure as hell make him run. It's so frustrating."

"How's he acting?"

"Like he's coming out of his skin. He wanders around at night a lot, rarely eats with us anymore—basically, he's acting like he does when he's on a major case. A hundred and twenty percent distracted."

"You have any ideas what it is?"

She shook her head sadly. "He always said he wasn't cut out for this."

"You and Emma?"

She looked up at him. "Not because of us—sure as hell not because of Emma. He's crazy about her. But he sees himself as a shit magnet. That he's fated to bring on disaster wherever he goes. Like it's a law of nature he can't fix."

Joe ran the risk of being completely honest. "You think he's using that as an excuse to get out of the relationship?"

Her expression was truly anguished. "That's the crazy part. I don't. I think he's happier with us than he's ever been. He dotes on Emma, he's sweet and considerate with me, at least in private. . . ."

"He didn't seem that way back there." Joe indicated the municipal building with his thumb.

"I know," she agreed. "That struck me, too, but part of that's just Willy being Willy, you know? The public image thing combined with old habits. He takes pride in being a dipstick."

"Could be that's part of his problem," Joe mused. "You two are threatening the armor he's relied on for most of his life. If he softens up at home, then he becomes vulnerable when he's outside."

"But that's nuts!" she exclaimed. "His family's not the rest of the world. He can be as big an asshole as he likes out here." She waved her arm around.

"That sounds reasonable to us," Joe agreed. "But we're not talking about the most psychologically sophisticated man on the face of the earth—just one of the most complicated."

Sam smiled ruefully. "Yeah, good point."

"How 'bout I kidnap him for this little operation in Northampton?" Joe suggested. "Give him room to reassess? I'd recommend a shrink or a family counselor with anyone else, but not this boy."

In response, she stretched up to kiss him on the cheek. "Thanks, Joe. I know I'll always have my hands full with him, but he's worth the effort. He's a good guy, and a loyal one. He's just got too many voices in his head."

"I know," Joe said, pleased at having pulled off his sleight of hand. Sammie wasn't lacking in complexity herself, after all, and could have thrown a monkey wrench into his plan. But Joe was happy to try to keep them together. As dysfunctional as they could each be on occasion, they were in many ways the kids he'd never had, and he'd been among the very few to see the good in their unlikely pairing from the start, when the rest of the world had seen only a mating of fire and gas.

He reached out and squeezed her shoulder. "Leave it to me, then, at least for the time being. I'll see what I can figure out while we're playing buddy-buddy below the border. You just enjoy Emma."

Patrol Officer Nancy Millett eased out of her favorite fishing hole alongside Mount Tom Road, south of Interstate 91's Exit 18, and slowly began driving back toward town. This was good drag-racing territory late at night—straight, flat, and minimally populated—a place where some of the locals occasionally opened up to express their beer courage at the wheel.

But not tonight. What little traffic there'd been had been boringly sedate, and Millett had been reduced to listening to the other few cruisers tagging cars elsewhere in Northampton. The PD had divided the town into four basic patrol areas, weighted toward the north and northwest, where most people lived, but she'd drawn the outlying area to the south and east. Usually, that meant concentrating on a residential spaghetti bowl of short, twisting streets straddling Routes 5 and 10, but it also took in some rural stretches, including the one she'd just left, and the flats beyond the airport—an emptiness of farm fields and forest bordering the Connecticut River. Dark and vast, this expanse could be a magnet for hoboes and dopers, and sometimes others interested in a few minutes of illicit privacy.

It wasn't a policing hot spot, but it warranted a visit now and then, and its appeal for a young cop like Millett could be enhanced by a little subterfuge—like taking advantage of the bright moonlight to drive without headlights.

And so she proceeded along Pleasant, hung a sharp right, and passed under the interstate a second time, through a narrow cut in the berm that both supported the roadway and doubled as a diversion dam to stem the occasionally rambunctious Connecticut River from flooding downtown.

Somewhere along this last stretch, the pavement yielded to smooth dirt, and it was there that Millett rolled down all her windows, reduced her radio to a murmur, and killed her lights.

Instantly, she felt transformed—less encapsulated by her vehicle and more at one with her surroundings, which extended off to both sides like the dull surface of a gigantic tabletop, now painted a steely, featureless gray by the enormous moon.

She drove at a fast walking speed, as much to milk the moment as to spare herself too much jolting from the odd dip in the road's surface. The monochromatic light reduced depth of field to a minimum; while Millett could see ahead clearly enough, actually moving forward was like navigating a holographic black-and-white photograph.

Until she saw two spots of bright red suddenly flash far in the distance.

She increased her speed a hair, her boredom instantly gone. There were a few legitimate explanations why another car would be out here at this time of night, but they were far outnumbered by the less than legal alternatives.

As she drew closer to what became a very slow-moving van, Millett rummaged around in her duty bag to extract a small but powerful pair of binoculars, which she kept handy for just such opportunities. Driving with one hand, she brought the glasses to her eyes and struggled to focus on the van's rear license plate. Then, committing what she'd seen to memory, she replaced the binoculars and lit up her onboard computer to run the plate, all while still bumping along down the road.

The registration traced back to a Gregory Nimmocks, of Springfield, Mass., whose record revealed a slew of past violations. Unfortunately for Millett, there was nothing current. For a cop to "light up" a motorist, there had to be at least an articulable suspicion of something being amiss.

Millett therefore narrowed the gap between them, hoping to see something that would legitimize her pulling him over.

She didn't expect what she was suddenly delivered. From the roof of the van, there spewed a small burst of bright orange sparks, like some effervescent bioluminescence from a whale's blowhole.

"What the hell?" she said out loud, hitting her strobes, lights, and spotlight, simultaneously.

The van, despite its creeping speed, skidded to a stop, sending up a plume of dust from the road and an additional burst of sparks from its roof, along with a scream of pain that Millett clearly heard through her window.

She quickly called in her location, asked for backup, and exited her cruiser, moving out of her own light and into the darkness of the field, her gun drawn. She'd leapt from curious to heart-hammering focus in one second flat.

"*You in the van,*" she yelled. "*This is the police. Turn on your dome light, roll down your window, and hang both your hands out where I can see them.*"

The driver did as he'd been told, and from the license photo that Nancy had just seen on her computer screen, she recognized Gregory Nimmocks.

"Mr. Nimmocks," she then called out from the night. "Who else is in the vehicle?"

She could see Nimmocks trying to see beyond the glare surrounding the van to locate the source of her voice. "I got one guy in the back," he told her, looking around futilcly.

Peering into the distance, Nancy saw two pairs of headlights bouncing quickly toward them, each vehicle crowned by a flashing strobe bar. A muffled voice from the van's interior called out, "Get me a fucking ambulance. I been hurt bad. I need help."

Nancy waited until her backup had positioned themselves to cover Nimmocks before she moved to the rear of the van with a colleague, where they stood to either side of the back doors. One of them grabbed the handle and yanked it open, while both covered whoever was inside with their weapons.

What they found was a second man, curled up on the floorboards, rocking back and forth and cradling a wounded right arm. Beside him was a square pedestal bolted in place and supporting what looked like a toy version of a steel foundry oven, complete with narrow smokestack running up through the roof of the van. Visible through the open door of the furnace was a small cauldron filled with glowing red metal, the smoke from which made the van's interior look like something straight out of a 1950s Vincent Price horror movie.

"What the fuck is that?" Millett asked aloud.

"It was a smelter," Dan Siegel told Joe and Willy in his office four days later. "These crazy bastards were stealing gold and silver from people's houses and jewelry stores and then melting it down in the back of the van. They figured it was a foolproof way to avoid being caught, as if being mobile would make them invisible."

"What were they going to do with it?" Joe asked.

"Sell it, duh," Willy said softly.

Siegel raised his eyebrows, but Joe acted as if not a word had been spoken, which—given his exposure to Willy's one-liners—was understandable.

"What he said," Siegel agreed with a slightly confused smile, adding, "Although we couldn't get the name of a buyer before the two of them lawyered up. They did say it was someone local, which fits in with why you're here." He tilted his head slightly. "Speaking of which, I take it you came up with something?"

Joe smiled. "Yeah. You're now looking at the new and improved Bobby Schultz. It may be a long shot, but we put the real Bobby on the Internet after we floated a story in the paper about a house that had been burgled in Bratt. He typed in LotsforLoot.com and entered in his bona fides and was told to show up at someplace called Prospect House, near here, tomorrow night."

Siegel stared at them for a moment before repeating, "Prospect House."

"That one got you the Kewpie doll," Willy remarked to Joe, watching Siegel.

"Supposed to be located in Skinner State Park?" Joe said.

"Oh, I know what it is," their host commented. "I've even been there a few times. Nice hike; nice view. Most people call it the Summit House now, but it used to be a hotel back in the day, before the Civil War, in fact. I think you been snookered, though."

"They tore it down?" Willy suggested.

Siegel smiled thinly. "They might yet. It is closed. The last owner willed it to the state in the forties. The state, in turn, opens it for special occasions only, although less and less often as funds get tighter and tighter. Mostly, it just sits there, rotting and waiting for someone to put in a bid and save it from demolition. You can't go into it. It's sealed off."

"Nice job, boss," Willy said with a smirk.

Siegel shifted his gaze to Joe's subordinate and commented pleasantly, "You're quite the asshole, aren't you?"

Willy smiled. "Happy you don't own me?"

Siegel's eyes lingered on Willy long enough to make clear that he wouldn't have survived the initial job interview, and then he turned to Joe. "What do you think?"

Joe had been considering that. "There is a building, right? One of our team found it on Google Maps or Google World, or some bloody thing."

"Oh yeah. It's there all right. Even looks pretty good, although it needs paint. I don't know that I'd jump up and down on the porch that runs around it, though."

"Then it's conceivable that the deal's legit—an out-of-the-way meeting place, hard for cops to bug or stake out."

Siegel made a face. "Conceivable in a movie, maybe. There's only one road in or out, straight up the mountain. The building's almost a thousand feet off the valley floor. And," he couldn't resist adding, "I don't see a paraglider making a dramatic escape after the deal is done— not for a few bucks' worth of silverware."

That last comment did bring things back into perspective. Even Willy said, "Good point. James Bond it ain't."

"What're our choices, though? It's what we got," Joe argued.

Dan nodded. "Okay. What details were you given?"

"Just that," Joe told him. "Tomorrow night—time and details to come via phone. Schultz had to leave a number to call." Joe held up a cell and waggled it back and forth.

"It's not consistent," Willy said out of the blue.

"What isn't?"

"The setup. Bobby was blindfolded last time. Why would they change a good plan, asking him to come up to the front door?"

" 'Cause they know him now?" Joe suggested.

Surprisingly, Willy didn't write that off. "Maybe."

"We could head up today and at least check it out—get a lay of the land," Joe suggested.

Willy, the veteran of covert ops, shook his head. "Not you and me, we couldn't. Assume you're right about them trusting Bobby. They'd still be smart to stake the place out ahead of time. They see us scouting it out, they'll know we're cops. And I bet they will be there, 'cause otherwise, they wouldn't have given out the location, they would've been vaguer, like they were with Bobby the first time. Could be a test, trying to draw us out. We have to stay under wraps, or at least you do, Bobby, baby," he said, smiling at Joe. "I could do it alone, if you want."

Joe was already shaking his head. "I got a better idea. How 'bout we use Les and Sammie? They're just a phone call away."

"That would get around using any of my people, who might be recognized," Siegel volunteered. "And I can outfit 'em with covert cameras and sound. They can look like tourists taking in the sights."

Joe nodded. "That's it, then."

Willy sat in the far corner of his motel room, near the bathroom, where he'd positioned the guest chair normally situated by the window. The lights were out, the curtains were open, and it was late. He could hear Northampton transitioning into its urban midnight mode, which he knew from experience was when the emergency calls became most interesting.

Under normal circumstances, he and Joe would have been sharing a room, but even there, his boss had cut him the slack few others knew to give. Like the local chief—Siegel. No doubt there that he wanted Willy gone. Stamped all over his face. Old school.

Joe was old, too, of course—no getting around that. But old school? Not hardly. He was traditional—so bad at the electronic stuff that Willy was amazed he carried a cell phone. But he kept an open mind.

Or maybe it was just that he kept Willy employed.

Who knew why.

Willy took his gaze off the almost metallic glitter of the dark, sharp-edged scenery outside—all streetlights and neon and reflections from shiny, hard surfaces. It was raining a little, which added to the brittle feel. He surveyed the room and took in the two neat beds, the bare counter supporting only the blank-faced TV, the empty table by the window. The place was almost as untouched as when ready for oc-cupancy. Willy had been there for days, and yet all signs of his pres-ence could have been removed in two minutes.

He liked it that way.

Spare.

What was it about that? He knew it was making him restless with his new family. He'd once been able to associate being invisible with safety, as if the devils that haunted him would be diminished if there was little of him to see. And that included his environment. He'd once comforted himself with the thought that if a fire destroyed his house, he wouldn't miss a thing. Not that he'd have much to miss, the house was so empty.

Just like this motel room.

It was all metaphor, of course. He knew that—surface symbolism for deeper issues. He'd heard it before.

Well, no longer. Now his life was full of people and possessions and responsibilities. Sammie was a pragmatist, and trained by the military. She knew how to live lean and travel light. But the quantity of crap that a newborn demanded, even for a trip across town, was beyond belief. Willy had functioned for weeks behind enemy lines with only a small pack and a rifle—a very long time ago.

He didn't begrudge Emma her need for a car seat, a stroller, a sunshade, her diaper bag, extra clothes, and formula. He could see it clearly, when he was rational: the love of a new mother, the harmony of a new family, the peace it could bring him—and the flashes of happiness when he allowed himself to acknowledge them.

But the old craziness was beginning to climb up inside, like a jealous, thwarted lover.

And he wasn't sure how to handle it.

CHAPTER THIRTEEN

"I can't believe you almost brought Emma," Lester said, adjusting the pack he'd slung over his shoulder.

Sammie laughed. They were both dressed in shorts and sneakers. She had her hair wrapped in a red bandanna, looked vaguely like a college student, and was carrying a camera. She waved her hand in the air. "Look around, Les. This place is beautiful, and what a view. She would've loved it."

"We're on a recon mission," Les, the father of two teenagers, pointed out. "How do you know what might happen up there?" He indicated the white wooden building looming above them, looking like a toy house precariously abandoned on top of a pile of rocks.

"I know, I know," Sam agreed, her mood undiminished. "She's not here, right? I was just thinking out loud. But you have to agree. It's a beautiful day and a hell of a view."

He could, and did. Through the surrounding trees, the ancient glacier-carved trough of the Connecticut River Valley stretched out below them, with Northampton clustered on the far bank of the river, peaceful and picturesque.

They continued up the last few serpentine curves, left the trees behind, and, fifteen minutes later, came upon the peeling, battered, tightly shuttered old hotel.

Sammie paused like the tourist she was playing and took a picture. "Can you imagine putting this thing way up here in the 1850s? That must've been a trick."

Lester stopped beside her and draped his arm across her shoulder, kissing her cheek for anyone who might be watching, although they appeared to be alone. "It is pretty neat, I gotta say."

The building did seem to defy its setting. It so dominated the mountain's peak, no one could even walk around it, except by either crawling under the wraparound deck or defying the barriers across the bottom of the access stairs. And even then, they would have run the risk of falling through the deck's rotting boards. The confusion of support members made the entire structure look like an ungainly wooden locust that had picked the worst of all places to land.

Sammie moved to a nearby outcropping to admire the view, now completely unencumbered by trees. She snapped a few more shots while speaking softly into the mic by her collar. The device connected her to Joe Gunther, far downhill in a command vehicle.

"No sign of anyone. The building looks buttoned up tight. Access to the porch is nailed off and placarded."

"Feel free to scramble around," Joe's voice told her in an earbud under her bandanna. "The video is coming in beautifully."

The camera lens he was referring to was fastened like a small decorative pin to the front of her blouse.

"Hey, Les," she called out to her colleague, who was checking out the building's other side. "Since there's nobody to squeal on us, you wanna break a few rules?"

He turned and pointed happily to the closed-off stairs leading up. "You mean that? Absolutely."

Feeling like actors on a stage, before an audience they couldn't see, they helped each other over the barricade and cautiously made their way up to the deck, exchanging loud comments about their fears of being caught. Sam made sure to point her covert lens carefully and slowly at every aspect of the building she thought worthy of being recorded.

They also swapped the camera back and forth for more detailed poses against the front door and whatever boarded-up windows they thought might serve Joe as access points later, in his disguise as Bobby Schultz.

Lester even tried prying one of the side doors open, saying loudly, "I wonder what it looks like inside."

"We'll get caught," Sam protested, joining in.

But access was tight, and they eventually gave up, knowing they shouldn't overplay their hand. Placing their feet carefully, they retreated to the rocky terrain below, laughing nervously as they went.

An hour later, they slipped into the van where Joe, Willy, and Dan awaited them. Attached to one wall of the vehicle's interior was a narrow shelf, above which was an array of audio and video recording equipment and several flat screens, one of which featured a rerun of their outing.

Sammie nodded at the screen. "All come through okay?"

Joe nodded. "You see anything you didn't comment on?"

They both shook their heads, and Lester elaborated. "Place looks untouched. When I muckled onto the plywood blocking the door, it was nailed tight. I couldn't see anything that showed any recent activity. It's weird, in a way, since you'd expect a place like that to be a magnet for late-night vandals."

"It has been," Siegel told them. "But it's tighter'n Fort Knox now. Also, word's out that it's hard to break into and that they've upped the patrols. That's why I'm having a hard time believing you aren't being dicked around with this thing."

Joe could only shrug. "Well, we have to give it a shot."

Joe used Bobby Schultz's van to approach the barrier blocking the Skinner Park road after hours, where, abandoning their earlier plan for what he thought better suited Schultz's personality, he eased the nose of the vehicle against where the lock met the metal post and snapped it open by sheer force, causing the gate to spring wide. He then drove through, got out, reclosed the gate, looping the shattered chain to hold it in place, and continued up the miles-long drive to the mountain's top.

Bobby Schultz hadn't struck him as a hiker.

It was an unusual experience repeating this trip alone and at midnight, instead of by proxy via closed-circuit TV. The trees lining the narrow, empty road were black and claustrophobic, their heads lost in the cloud-covered night sky. The knowledge that he was so removed from the beaten path only served to make him feel the many eyes he imagined were watching his slow progress. The van's dim yellow headlights merely emphasized how little he could see.

At last, he felt the trees pulling away, and a compensatory space opened up around him, accompanied by the appearance of the dark and ethereal structure, shimmering ahead like an extinguished alien ship.

He put the van into park, killed its engine, and got out, holding a large satchel filled with the swag they'd thought might be typical for such a meeting.

He felt awkward wearing a wig, and he kept fighting the urge to constantly check on his mustache.

"I'm out of the van," he said softly, using the same equipment Sammie had the day before.

There was no response, as agreed. Joe had made it clear that he'd be distracted enough without any voices in his ear. He knew they were close by. That was the compromise they'd chosen in exchange for the site's remoteness—Joe could go solo, but backup would be near, regardless of any risk that they might be seen.

Flashlight in hand, he walked up the last incline between the parking area and the hotel, and was surprised to find a stepladder opened before the barrier at the foot of the deck. Carefully, he used it to gain access to the creaking wooden stairs. As he climbed, testing each tread for its strength, he was aware of the vastness around him. As far as he could see beyond the rough wooden railing by his hand, there was only blackness, punctuated by the twinkling of tiny urban lights very far away. Northampton looked like a blurred smudge on a gigantic X-ray negative, throwing its glow against the low clouds just above Joe's head.

He paused at the top, uncertain about how to proceed. In the terse phone call he'd exchanged with the fence, after logging on to the LotsforLoot.com Web site, he'd only been instructed to come here, not what to do once he'd arrived.

Out of curiosity, he crossed to the door before him, which was covered with plywood, and gave it the same kind of tug that Lester had earlier.

The door swung back silently on newly oiled hinges.

"Whoa," Joe murmured, stepping quickly free of the sudden opening and cautiously peering around with his flashlight.

He called out, "Anyone there?"

There was no response, which by now didn't surprise him. Half of this whole arrangement was obviously oriented around security, the other half being pure theatrics.

He stepped into a large room, possibly once a lobby or parlor, and played his light across a scattering of dusty furniture, some broken, but most looking ready for the next busload of phantom tourists. There were pictures on the walls, books on the shelves, candles set up on a functional but attractive sideboard. A thin rug absorbed his footfalls. He half-expected to see Miss Havisham sitting before the ruins of her wedding cake. After checking the front room carefully, he moved down a central hallway.

About halfway along, he paused, sensing more than seeing something ahead. He killed the flashlight and instantly saw a faint glow spilling into the hall from a side room.

"Okay," he commented quietly. "Showtime."

He turned his light back on and continued, noticing along the way that most of the doors to either side were ajar, revealing a series of simple bedrooms overlooking the dark night through surprisingly small windows. He imagined that both the age of the structure and the occasionally violent weather dictated an absence of picture windows anywhere, including in the parlor he'd just left.

He stopped on the threshold of the room that had attracted him, stared at what faced him from the center of a table placed where a bed would have been normally.

It was a flat-screen monitor, showing this very room, along with the chair that had been placed opposite it.

As soon as Joe appeared and took it all in, a disembodied voice spoke, so disguised and flattened by a modulator that he couldn't distinguish the speaker's gender.

"Sit down in the chair facing the screen."

Joe crossed the room, sat in the chair, and placed his bag on the floor beside him. His wig was prickling the top of his scalp.

"State your name."

"Bob Schultz. Where the hell are you?"

Joe tried to see the rest of the room by the monitor's glow, and he thought he could make out a large box on the floor in the background, which he took to be a power source for the screen. He knew there was no electricity to the building anymore.

"That's not important. Did you bring what you talked about on the phone?"

"Yeah."

"Hold it up."

"You got X-ray eyes? It's in a bag." Joe retrieved it and dangled it before him, seeing himself as if on TV. He thought he looked silly.

"There's a smaller table tucked under the one with the monitor. Pull it toward you and spill the contents onto it."

Not having known what to expect, Joe was relieved to comply, if disappointed to still be alone. This particular scenario had not occurred to him.

Nor was what happened next. Without a sound or movement, the room silently exploded into bright light, brought there by two tripod-mounted lamps that he hadn't noticed standing guard in opposite corners of the room.

He stared around, half out of his seat. "What the—"

He looked at the TV, expecting to see the wizard responsible. Instead, he just saw himself again, now as sharply revealed as if he were standing in a lineup. The thought made him uncomfortable. It was still possible that the orchestrators of this were but one room over, ready to move in.

"What is this bullshit?" he asked, slowly settling back down.

"Just what you were looking for, Bobby. Nothing more or less."

"I was looking for a buyer for this shit."

"You better hope it's not that."

Joe frowned as he thought Bobby might. "Don't give me that. Let's cut the crap and deal, already."

"That's what we're doing," the voice said calmly. He was still trying to decipher some identifying feature—be it a lisp, a stutter, or an accent. Nothing stood out. "Spread it out so the camera can get a good look at it. Use the monitor to gauge the best angle."

Joe moved the loot around, wondering how they would handle the next step. The voice asked him to hold up a couple of items so that the camera mounted at the top of the screen could more clearly see the details. It was equipped with a macro lens, allowing it access to karat markings and jeweler's stampings when Joe was instructed to display them.

After they were done, the voice demanded, "What's your price, Bobby?"

"Ten thousand."

"Seriously."

"Eight."

"You're wasting time."

"What'll you give for it? It's good stuff, and I took the risk of getting it."

"I'm tearing up. Two."

Joe made a show of disgust, flailing his arms. "That is a rip-off. I was told you paid top dollar."

"We pay for the goods, not your wet dreams."

"That is not fair. Four at least."

"Pack it up and have a nice day, Bobby. Don't come back."

"What the fuck? We're supposed to deal here. That's how it's done. You're just screwing with me. Three. Otherwise, I will take off."

"Two thousand five hundred. That's it."

"Two thousand seven hundred and fifty."

"No. Two five, or we're done."

Joe blew out a puff of air, dejected. "You asshole."

"Deal?"

He paused for a moment before conceding. "Yeah."

"Leave everything there, go to room six at the end of the hall, and take your money from the middle of the bed."

Joe scowled at the screen, as if taunting himself. "What the fuck? Where *are* you?"

"You want the money or not?"

"Course I want the money."

"Then go to room six. If you go anywhere else, you will die; if you spend more than four minutes in this building from this moment on, you will die."

"You're full of shit."

"You're wasting time again."

Joe stared at the monitor belligerently. "I'll take my stuff *and* the money. You can fuck yourself."

"If you do, you will die. Do you really think you're alone up here?" The screen and the lights went out at the same instant, freezing Joe in total darkness.

He didn't say anything. In the sudden silence, he distinctly heard the sound of something or someone moving elsewhere in the building. It was so subtle, it could have been a figment of his imagination.

Except for the perfect timing of it.

"Asshole," he said one last time, and left the room, wondering if the sound hadn't come from another hidden speaker somewhere.

He went down to room six, located a brown paper bag in the center of a bed with no mattress, and looked inside. There was a wad of dollar bills, amounting to—he had no doubt—the precise agreed-upon sum.

He also didn't doubt that there were other bags of money in other rooms, containing differing amounts.

What he didn't know was whether it was worth his life to check that theory out.

Which, of course, was the whole point.

"Nice and tidy," he murmured admiringly, and left the building.

CHAPTER FOURTEEN

"Are you kidding me?" Willy burst out. "You believe that? That they rigged the whole building? Like a *Mission Impossible* movie?"

Dan Siegel spoke quietly in Joe's stead. "They rigged the door and the closed-circuit video. They also found a way to get in there afterward and clean the place out. Why not plant a booby trap or two? If Joe's right, there was a lot of cash spread around."

Therein, Joe knew, was perhaps Willy's biggest complaint—that when they'd returned the following morning, again low profile, just in case they were being watched, they'd found the building as if it had never been touched. Under the guise of a state maintenance crew, complete with official-looking truck, they'd even had to pry out the nails holding the door shut.

"So we got nothing," Willy concluded.

"Not even from the money," Siegel conceded, settling back comfortably in his office chair. "No prints that jumped out; no serial numbers of note. It's just your run-of-the-mill currency. Same with the paper bag—plain as mud."

"Definitely your cut-above-average crooks," Joe mused.

"Swell," Willy grumbled. "Let's make sure to alert the media."

Joe rose from his seat and walked over to Siegel's window to look out onto the street. "On the other hand, we did come out of it with more than a bag of cash."

"Meaning what?"

He didn't turn around as he spoke. "Meaning that we also gained some insight about how they operate."

He faced them to tick off a few items on his fingertips. "They've got money and brains enough to pull this off, and they know how to work it all by remote control. And they're full enough of themselves not to wander too far from what appears be a Northampton base of operations. They also seem to be specialists in what they fence, since they make it crystal clear to leave your stolen weapons, toasters, and TV sets at home when you deal with them."

"Which gives us what in the end?" asked Dan.

Joe raised both eyebrows at his host's question. "The opportunity to explore what they're up to. What do *you* do with stolen jewelry, gemstones, gold, and silver?"

"Retire," Willy answered.

Siegel laughed abruptly before saying, "You pass it down the line, maybe overseas, maybe melted down—like those yahoos we caught in the van—maybe to a central depository. Maybe even to a bunch of specialist receivers."

Joe nodded. "Okay, having said all that, does it ring any bells for you either in the context of Northampton's daily crime profile or generally?"

The police chief lifted his chin and studied the ceiling for a moment before finally shaking his head. "We get B and Es like everyone, car thefts, purse snatches, whatever. We don't get much organized crime. I do have a guy I use now and then for the odd jewelry theft," he added. "He's sort of the grand old man of the artsy-fartsy crafts movement that came out of the sixties. Doesn't get around like he used to—sticks close to town now, whereas he used to travel all over the world back in the day—but he's still sharp, and he knows everybody. We could start by talking with him, since we already know that this town's jewelry central, at least for our purposes."

"It's not all artsy-fartsy, though," Willy pointed out. "From what I've seen in the photos, a lot of the items being flushed through this pipeline are antiques, or at least they date back to the late nineteenth century."

Siegel stared at him, and Joe realized that the chief had no idea of Kunkle's unexpectedly artistic side, both as a producer of pen and ink drawings and as an occasional art collector. A very small sampling of both could be found in his house.

"Right," Siegel said, catching himself gaping. "Well, I got someone for that, too. Smith College has a no-slouch art museum, and we've used their curator as a source." He paused to rethink his strategy. "In fact, let's switch them around. Go to plan B. We'll interview the curator first, to get the basics on what Northampton has to offer. She's on the board of a couple of outfits that decide whose art gets accepted for display in the local shows. Then you can hit the guy I was just talking about; he's more the insider for the commercial ins and outs." He stood up, as if the plan had been fully discussed and decided upon. "Plus, we might get lucky—one of 'em might be dealing hot goods out of their trunk."

. . .

The $35 million Smith College Museum of Art had been rebuilt on the footprint of its predecessor, which, in addition to being too small, leaky, and having poor ventilation, had begun suffering from the dubious architectural failings of so many buildings created in the early 1970s.

The replacement appeared to suffer from none of those problems. Representing perhaps a third of the overall fine arts center—the rest of it housed the art library and the art department's offices—the museum was small but soothingly lighted, made airy by a central atrium under skylights, and filled with pleasingly eccentric details, one startling highlight of which was the decoration of public bathrooms on the bottom floor. The tiling—including the toilets, urinals, and sinks—had been lavishly and playfully painted with bright blue plants and fish and oversized water droplets, to the satisfaction and surprise of any art lover in need of relief.

Curiously to Joe, that lightheartedness in no way matched the personality of the consultant Dan Siegel introduced them to after taking them on a whirlwind tour of the place. Dr. Louise Marshall was very short, very round, and very nervous, constantly picking things up and replacing them without a glance, and peering around whoever was addressing her as if she either aspired to meet the person next in line or was simply seeking a means of escape.

As they were undergoing the ritual of settling into the seats scattered around her large first-floor office, Joe seriously reconsidered the value of this visit.

"Lou," Siegel began after the introductions were over. "These guys are hoping you can fill 'em in on the local art scene. Not so much who's who, but how and why Northampton's a hub for custom jewelry design and higher-end"—he affected a snobby accent—"objets d'art, like some of the samples you have around here."

A broad smile creased her almost perfectly spherical face, transforming her demeanor with a girlish interest. "Art skullduggery in Northampton? How exciting."

"I didn't say that, Lou," he cautioned as Willy sighed impatiently, his eyes already wandering around the room. "We're just asking about Northampton in the context of a case we're working on. I thought of you because you have a ritzy bunch of patrons, you cater to a different population from the one we see up and down Main, and you sit on all the local art boards."

"Northampton, the nuthouse for the artistic and the idle rich?" she proposed ruefully.

That made Willy laugh.

Sitting at her desk, Marshall picked up a pen and then put it back down immediately. "Okay. One-word answer? Money. That and dumb luck and Smith College alumnae and the lack of appeal of neighboring Springfield and Holyoke. Not to mention how far we are from Boston and how close we are to the Berkshires and Tanglewood—but not too close—plus a dozen other influences. *That's* why we're an art magnet."

Joe was beginning to warm to this eccentric woman. "Money may explain why art comes here to roost," he said. "But what about the low-life fellow travelers trying to ride its coattails by stealing, counterfeiting, exploiting, conning old ladies, and trying to sell you fake masterpieces to hang on your walls?"

The curator removed her glasses, put them back on, and smiled again. "I like the question. If this were the Museum of Fine Arts, I'd expect it, but who would think of taking little old *us* to the cleaners? What a lovely idea."

" 'Lovely'?" Willy echoed quietly.

She heard him. "Well, certainly flattering, and, I would add, smart. Not only is Boston filled with all that, but the FBI has a huge office right downtown." She waved at Siegel. "Not to disparage, Daniel, but you guys aren't the FBI. You wouldn't know an art fraud if it crushed your toes."

Siegel returned the smile. "And yet, here we are."

She clapped her hands happily, which Joe thought would send Willy out of the room.

"Excellent point," she said before addressing Joe. "And I do think this region is ripe for what you're suggesting. It is an arts center, but it has been almost completely overlooked by the malevolent forces that plague most of its ilk. That might make an interesting topic for a paper, in fact." She paused to pull over a pad, onto which she scribbled a note, although, given her flightiness, Joe suspected that it might as easily have been a grocery item as the thought she'd just expressed.

"But you're unaware of any actual illicit activities in the local art trade?" Siegel asked.

She raised her eyebrows. "Ah, but that's the point, possibly, no? Ignorance is not evidence. Someone may have had the same thought I just had about exploiting the boonies, and acted on it accordingly, all to no one's knowledge. Is it indiscreet to ask the nature of these questions?"

The three men exchanged glances.

"Yes is an acceptable response," she suggested.

"We're actually not sure," Joe conceded. "We've had indications there might be something cooking along those lines, but we're sort of using you to get the lay of the land first, before we start flipping over rocks."

She was already nodding. "There is a biannual art and craft show called Paradise City, which is also one of the nicknames of this whole town, in fact. It takes place out on the fairgrounds, near the airport, and it's a juried show, meaning that every exhibitor must submit his or her wares for approval. They also have to pay a hefty fee. Both conditions imply—if they don't guarantee—that whatever goes on display will be of high quality and probably quite pricey.

"There's also something that caters to more middle-class folks. It's called the Twist Fair. That's twice a year and more resembles a bazaar in feeling. Not as hoity-toity.

"Both of those and a bunch of other offerings and events help to elevate the area's pedigree, as do heaps of arts and crafts stores, an unusual number of local artists, and, to be honest"—she raised both small hands, as if revealing the rabbit springing from a hat—"the presence of a brand-new, high-caliber, well-attended art museum and gallery."

She abruptly slid off her chair, got to her feet, crossed the room as if on a mission, adjusted something on the windowsill invisible to everyone else in the room, and sat back down, speaking all the while.

"Add to that a pretty well-heeled, well-educated upper crust, and you have the makings of an environment that might be quite attractive to a stolen-art ring, or a counterfeiting gang, or whatever it is you're after."

She picked up a tidy sheaf of papers, tapped their ends on her tabletop to even up what already looked immaculate, and replaced it carefully before her, suggesting simultaneously, "If I were you, I'd speak with David Cone."

"He's next on the list," Siegel assured her, telling his colleagues in an aside, "The one I was telling you about."

"Why him?" Willy asked.

"Well," she answered, "among the factors I listed that have made this town an arts magnet, David Cone is the headliner. He came here in the sixties, along with a few others who shared his vision, and hit it big-time."

"As what?"

Marshall paused thoughtfully. "The Hawaiians say of the first missionaries that they came to the islands to do good, and did well. I would say of David that he did both. He helped enrich this town and made a fortune doing it."

"That doesn't tell me much," Willy said brusquely.

She didn't take offense. "True, but it sets the stage. He arrived as an artist—a street jeweler—eventually opened a store, bought a few properties, began shipping his work to a wider market, bought a lot more properties, and became one of the wealthiest businessmen we have. At one point, it was rumored that David Cone owned a piece of almost everything commercial around here you could think of."

She shoved away from her desk, opened a lower drawer, and extracted a plastic jug of mixed nuts only slightly smaller than herself, which she placed on the edge facing her guests.

"Nuts?" she offered cheerily.

They ignored the offer, as she did herself.

"He wasn't the only one," she continued. "That entire time period was when Northampton went from being a *Father Knows Best* backwater of hardware stores and men's haberdashers catering to Smithie dads to what we know and love today. And much of it was because of practical idealists like David, people who saw they could create a community that reflected their own values. The Boston Brahmins who built Holyoke never lived there or cared about it, and it's a mess right now. The pioneers of the new Northampton wanted their children to grow up, go to school, and stay here. They invested in a place to live, not a factory town. Big difference."

She took them in with a single glance and sat back, slightly embarrassed. "Wow, that wound me up. Mr . . . Kunkle? That's right, isn't it?"

"Yeah," he said.

"You do know how to get me going."

Oh, please, Joe thought.

Willy smiled.

"All that being said," Joe commented, "do you think whoever might be operating illegally here is a newcomer, or one of the old guard gone rogue?"

Siegel snorted his dismissal of the question's open-ended nature, but Marshall understood what he was after.

"I would look at that," she said. "Anyone can come here and set up shop, but it helps to know the movers and shakers. This is a small town, in many ways. An outsider might step on toes that an insider would know to avoid, if you get my meaning."

Joe nodded his thanks. "I do."

She squinched up one corner of her mouth ruefully. "I don't feel I've been of much help to you."

"I wouldn't say that," Siegel said. "Gents?"

Willy surprised them by speaking up first. "You've been terrific, Dr. Marshall. Good background, good insights. Just what we needed. Now all we have to do is go out and arrest David Cone."

Laughter followed as they all stood to make their good-byes. As he closed the door to her office on the way out, Joe addressed Willy softly. "For real?"

Willy stared at him deadpan and replied, "Fucking nutcase. Totally useless."

. . .

They didn't bother with a car. Downtown Northampton's curved, slop-
ing, blocks-long Main Street encouraged walking, window-shopping,
and gawking at passersby, and was more redolent of a European setting
than of the average New England mill town.

As they hit the heart of the place, this was in part what led Dan
Siegel to announce like a tourist guide, "Voilà, the house that Cone
built."

Willy and Joe forced themselves to look away from a young woman
totally painted in silver, who was standing on the sidewalk, pretending to be a statue. In front of them stood a stately brick-clad building
vaguely reminiscent of something Thomas Jefferson would have fa-
vored. Its sign boldly stated DAVID CONE HEIRLOOMS.

"Subtle," Willy said.

"Doesn't need to be," their guide explained. "Lou mentioned
David for good reason. This town has a bunch of heavy hitters—the
regional hospital, the college, even a government contractor that
makes periscopes. It used to have a state mental home that housed
twenty-five hundred patients on a fifty-acre campus and employed almost a thousand people. Cone Heirlooms is on a par with all those."

"Why?" Joe asked.

Siegel held open the building's front door and ushered them in.
"Ask the man himself. That's why we're here."

"Malls, direct orders, and the Internet, in that order," they were told fifteen minutes later on the building's top floor by a large, broad-shouldered
man with a ring of white hair circling a tanned bald pate. David Cone,
expansive, well dressed, sporting a gold watch, a bracelet, several rings,
and a gold chain worthy of the seventies, greeted them in his office

and fussed over offering them a choice of bottled water, iced tea, or bottled beer from a well-stocked designer bar.

Siegel had begun the conversation by repeating Joe's question of moments earlier.

"I started out like any of the kids you see down there on a Saturday night," Cone said, gesturing out the window toward a sweeping view of downtown. "Grinding out original pieces, one by one, mostly to score with pretty girls. But it took me about twenty minutes to realize that, beside getting laid, none of them knew what they were doing—not as businessmen. So I turned the whole process upside down, looked at the market first, then at how to mass-produce what could pass as original art. Only then did I analyze the art itself, figuring out how to crank out the most for the cheapest cost, while making it look modern and arty and handmade. Jewelry stores and kiosks in malls were my first outlets, and then I branched out from there. Hardly brain surgery," he concluded. "I just saw what no one else was looking at."

"You trained as an artist?" Joe asked.

"Not like you'd think," their host admitted, still bustling about with ice and glasses. "I never liked the crap my mother wore when I was growing up. I know no normal kid notices his mom's jewelry, but I was a little weird that way. So, with her permission, I began fooling with some of it—giving it style. I wish I could say that I was a revolutionary or a radical hippie or that I went to India and saw the light and came home with a bagful of ideas and smelling of hashish. But I just got bored with the fifties—Eisenhower and martinis and the suburbs and the Red Menace."

He finished addressing their needs and settled into a leather armchair off to the side of a yacht-size desk. He was charming and well-spoken, and despite his self-deprecating patter, Joe imagined that he had all the mores and manners of a well-bred shark, albeit tutored in the latest business etiquette. Joe had no doubts that he'd boned up as much on the politics of power seating and how to order off the menu at trendy eateries as he had on the jewelry market. In that way, he was probably just an ironically hip—if much more successful—version of the parent he'd been disparaging.

And a bit at odds, Joe thought as well, with the town that he'd made his own. David Cone reminded him of a tycoon from Greenwich, Connecticut, who'd forgotten to get off the train at his station.

"I did go to art school—never graduated," he was saying, "and I checked out the New York scene afterward, trying to find my direction in life, but I didn't like the pretentiousness of all those people who claimed that failure made them better artists. I'm no Picasso or Michelangelo; I wanted to make nice things that people wanted to wear; plus, I liked hanging out with the business types in New York more than with the artists. So I jumped ship. I heard this was a nice quiet place with cheap real estate where you could set up a business and support a family. Back then, you could buy half a city block for seventy-five thousand dollars. There wasn't much happening, but there was a growing energy in the air, and you could just feel the town yearning to change into something more interesting—much to the unhappiness of the old Hamp crowd, I might add, who resent it to this day."

"Hamp," Siegel explained, "is what the local old-timers call the town, as opposed to NoHo, which is one of the groovy new labels. The whole new-versus-old debate is bullshit, of course, but it catches the flavor of the thing."

"What about now?" Willy asked. "You couldn't buy diddly for seventy-five grand."

Cone nodded in agreement. "How true. It's come full circle. Now we're the cutting edge of spiffiness—the go-to center for the supercool. Who knew, right?" He laughed. "I just hope we never lose that strain of pure crazy that makes us unique."

"This kind of brings up why we're here," said Joe, trying to segue. "It was suggested by a couple of people that because of your early arrival here and the success you've made of your business, you might be able to help us out with a little problem."

Cone smiled broadly. "I'll give it my best shot. I should warn you that I'm also semiretired. I'm hoping the next generation will carry things forward. I come in every day, and try to keep abreast, but I'm learning to take it easy a little in my old age."

"Of course," Joe said obligingly. "Still, it's probably more of a history lesson we're after than anything hot off the presses—at least to start with."

"Okay. Fire away."

Joe smiled. "Before I do, I want to stress that we'd like to keep this conversation private."

Cone was already cutting him off with a raised hand. "That goes without saying. Dan can tell you that I'm in a business that still operates mostly on tradition. We've got computers and cell phones and all that, but believe me, when it comes to sealing a contract, more times than not, it's still who you know, a handshake deal, or a verbal agreement. That's just to say that what's said here stays here."

Joe nodded his thanks. "I appreciate that, David."

But before he could go on, Dan interjected a comment. "Dave, we just busted a couple of guys who were riding around in the middle of the Meadows with a smelter in the back of their van. They were melting down stolen gold and silver for sale as raw material."

Cone's eyes were widening throughout. "In the back of a van? How could they breathe?"

"They had a small chimney," Joe explained. He'd picked up on Dan's strategy of engaging Cone by mentioning an actual crime, instead of using the broad picture approach. "In fact, that's what got them caught. The cruiser behind them saw the sparks."

"The point being, Dave," Siegel continued, "they were hoping to sell their raw material locally."

"Really?" Cone sounded genuinely curious.

"Yeah, but we can't connect the dots. I've been chief in this town a long time," Dan said, "but I have no clue how that might work, much less who might be involved."

Cone knit his eyebrows. "You mean who'd want the raw material? It's gold, right? You know the going price for gold right now? It's over-the-top. It's a seller's market. The answer is, anybody."

"What about other uses for it?" Joe asked. "It wasn't just precious metal they had. There were stones and jewelry, too. One of the leads we've been following—which has nothing to do with the guys in the van—suggests a recycling of other people's art pieces into new ones, things like earrings and bracelets and rings and whatnot."

Cone was looking doubtful. "Okay. I see what you're saying. I'm not sure I get the point, though. I mean, why bother? Just steal it, break it apart, melt what's too hard or too recognizable to move, alter the stones a hair, and sell it."

"Who to, though?" Joe asked. "I wouldn't know what to do with a ruby or a lump of gold, but I could see how operators like yourself might like access to cheap raw materials. It would have to improve your bottom line."

David Cone laughed. "My bottom line? Goodness, Joe, I run a sixty-million-dollar business. That's what I meant when I said I owed it all to malls and the Internet. David Cone designs sell across the globe. You can buy them in China. I have a factory over there. I start screwing around with two losers in a van trying to kill themselves on smelter fumes, and I'm dead. The feds would have my ass, and my competition would eat it up."

His face brightened suddenly as he said, "You know, you ought to look into those fly-by-night outfits that move from motel to motel, pretending to assess your family treasures. You've seen the ads?"

Siegel and Joe nodded.

"That would more likely be the market you're describing. People take stolen goods to those events all the time, 'cause they're so far under the radar. It's actually kind of ironic, when you think about it, since it's crooks cheating crooks. The only sad thing is when regular people actually *are* selling grandma's jewelry, hoping to pay for her funeral or something. Those poor bastards are just getting screwed."

He became more animated. "I went to one of those once, just to see for myself. I couldn't believe it. I mean, I know it's a dog-eat-dog world, but this was pathetic. There was a couple I helped out when the guy at the table told them what they were offering was gold plate. Totally outrageous. It was a good piece. Not a beauty, but it was real gold. And he was feeding them a line, saying, 'I don't want you to go away with nothing, so I'll make you a deal anyhow; just don't tell my boss.' They were about to go through with it."

Willy's voice landed heavily into the middle of the conversation. "Can we move on? This has jack to do with why we're here."

Cone stopped dead in his tracks.

Joe made no apologies. "David, we need a handle on what might be going on here. What about the idea that some operator is paying top dollar for old valuables? What might he be doing with what he's buying?"

The older man became thoughtful. "The silver? I have no idea. The price right now wouldn't justify buying it as a raw material. Gold or platinum? That could be, if your end goal was casting grain."

"Which is what?" Siegel asked.

"I buy . . ." Cone began, then corrected himself. "I should say, we buy gold in the form of wire, sheet, or casting grain—which is a kind of pellet material. The first two are pure and perfect and of very high quality—or should be. Casting grain can be made from recycled metal, because it's suitable for items that need to contain more alloys to make them stronger—things that'll be subjected to a lot of wear and tear, like a bracelet or your cheaper wedding bands. You could go to a place like L.A. or New York or Boston and find unscrupulous bulk buyers who couldn't care less what goes into the casting grain. It's all mixed together anyhow in the end, so who would care? That's where I was heading when I brought up the traveling motel operators." Here he looked balefully at Willy. "They'd be perfect for that kind of conduit. They could and do pay bottom dollar, convert what they buy, and then sell it as casting grain on the one hand and loose stones on the other.

"There is another option, which is where I thought you might be going before the smelter came up, and that's estate jewelry, which is the older stuff you see in a lot of the big-city antique stores—pins, bracelets, earrings, rings, necklaces . . . on and on. Some of those pieces can fetch fifty thousand dollars apiece. That's appealing to some shady operators because of the money on one hand and the lack of paperwork on the other. Ideally, you're supposed to have a receipt or a photograph or a credible appraisal to make an heirloom like that legit. But don't kid a kidder, right? An unscrupulous dealer who's given a really nice piece? If he can turn it around fast enough and with a minimum of fuss and advertising, who's to know that it was stolen to start with?"

He nodded agreeably at Dan. "And with all due respect, the police are way behind the eight ball here. No one's trained to look for this. It's white-collar or victimless crime, or whatever you want to call it, but it's sure not drugs and murder. There's no funding to pay you folks to chase it down."

There was a sound at the door, and a tall middle-aged woman— well dressed and carefully made up—entered and took them in with the air of a politely affronted home owner discovering uninvited guests raiding her fridge.

"David?" she said, crossing over and resting a hand on his shoulder.

He beamed at the three men. "This is Donna, my companion and associate," he told them, adding, "These men are from the police. They're just asking for some background information."

She smiled thinly. "Donna Lee Hawkins. How interesting. Well, you've certainly come to the right place. David is the sage."

She strolled over to an armchair near his and settled down, crossing her legs elegantly and saying, "Please don't mind me. I find everything he says fascinating."

Cone laughed. "Donna's far too modest. She actually helps run things around here. I think you'll find her knowledge as valuable as mine, and probably more up-to-date."

The cops eyed one another but left it alone, recognizing that the interview would most likely end if they objected to the interloper.

"Are we still considering this conversation confidential?" Willy asked, eyeing Donna with distaste.

Cone waved that away airily. "Of course, of course. Goes without saying."

Hawkins turned her full gaze on Willy, the look in her eyes wishing him to vanish into a puff of smoke.

"You were talking about casting grain," Siegel resumed cautiously, transparently sharing Willy's doubts. "But we're finding a lot more than just gold. What would you do with the rest? Throw it out?"

"No, no," Cone protested, addressing his companion. "Sweetheart, they think they've stumbled across a jewelry gang, and they're wondering how people like that might dispose of the loot."

"How neat," she said, sounding distinctly unenthralled.

"Anyhow," Cone explained, "like I said, they would sell off the gems, same as the metal. Buyers for antiques that don't qualify as estate pieces or can't be melted down might be artists, small jewelry stores, auctions, eBay, even flea markets. You name it."

"There's virtually no regulation or enforcement," Hawkins said unexpectedly, repeating Cone's earlier theme. "You can pretty much do as you like."

"Except for some newer diamonds," he commented. "Diamonds can have laser inscriptions on them, like tattoos. Makes them trickier to pass off."

"Even there, though, it's easy," she argued. "Three minutes with a grinder and the inscription goes away and the diamond changes appearance. Doesn't take much."

"How do you know all this?" Willy asked her flatly.

She gave him that hostess smile again. "It's the company I keep."

Cone laughed with too much enthusiasm. "Watch out, Donna. You'll have us thrown in the slammer."

Joe decided that he no longer wanted to keep this going, even though he had more questions to ask. He stood up as he said, "I wouldn't worry about that, David. You've been a huge help, and we really appreciate it."

His two colleagues followed suit, Willy looking as if he wanted to slap a pair of cuffs on Hawkins there and then.

They made their formal farewells, shaking hands all around and thanking Cone for the beverages and his time.

In the elevator, Joe turned to Dan. "Ever see her before?"

"Seen only. At a restaurant or a social thing or two. Thought she was just a bimbo. He's had about five wives. Hard to keep track."

"I bet keeping track is exactly what she does," Willy commented darkly.

"That's okay," Joe said to the lighted numbers slowly counting down above the double doors. "We'll be chatting with Mr. Cone again soon, and I wouldn't mind taking a peek at Ms. Donna Lee Hawkins's background in the meantime."

CHAPTER FIFTEEN

Mina stepped through the doorway of the small shop, her arrival announced by an ancient, almost comforting tinny bell weakly pinging above her head. She looked up to admire the nostalgic brass artifact—a relic in a world of electronic buzzers and closed-circuit surveillance.

"May I help you?" a cultivated voice said from the back of the gloomy shop. A white-haired man appeared from behind a counter beyond the clutter of dusty glass display cases and antique furniture.

"I was just admiring your doorbell," she said.

"I thought about upgrading it. My insurance company even recommended it," the man said, approaching slowly. "But I suppose it's obvious that I prefer the old ways. Besides, that thing's been serving me well for quite a while."

He stuck his hand out. "Walter Finney. Welcome to Finney's Antiques."

"Mina." She hesitated before adding, "Shepard," wondering where that name had come from. She was instantly irritated with herself for not having preplanned this better. Despite not being engaged in anything criminal, she was instinctively aware that she was somehow breaking the rules.

"How can I help you, Miss Shepard?" Finney asked. "Or are you just interested in looking around? If the latter," he added with a broad smile, "I promise to leave you alone. Nothing worse than a storekeeper hovering at your shoulder, driving you to distraction."

Mina laughed. "No, actually, I appreciate the help. I heard through the grapevine that you buy antiques as well as sell them?"

His eyebrows rose. "Oh, yes. Always happy to see an interesting piece." He took half a step back and glanced down at the cloth bag she was carrying. "Do you have something with you now?"

"I do," she admitted, and removed a small, ornate clock from the bag, a gift from Billie, but something she'd never truly liked.

She handed it over. "What do you think of that?"

He admired it by the light from the front window. "Very pretty. A Waltham, nicely preserved. Do you know if it's ever been worked on? Or is it all original?"

She gave him a blank stare before replying. "I don't know. I *think* it's original."

Walter nodded vigorously. "Good. Let's have a closer look, then."

He led the way to the back and circled around the counter that separated the sales area from what appeared to be an office beyond. On his side of the counter was a narrow workbench, and he sat down there, slipped on a visor with a magnifier lens attached to it, and switched on a lamp.

"All right—let's get better acquainted," he said gently to the clock as Mina placed her elbows on the countertop and studied him.

"Do you do a lot of this kind of work?" she asked as he carefully applied a tiny screwdriver to the clock's backing. "Assess antiques for their value?"

"Well," he replied, not bothering to look up, "it's not like being a stockbroker in the eighties, but every week someone comes in with an item or two. It's interesting and often challenging, and it keeps my hand in. I used to work in Chicago, a hundred years ago, so it's hardly that kind of pace, but I enjoy it better here."

"So there's enough action to keep you in business?"

He chuckled. "Ah, that's an interesting question, carefully worded. I have to admit that if I hadn't done so well in my previous life, I probably couldn't afford this one. There are a lot of nice pieces that reach me, mostly from older local families, but I have to be careful that what I take in has at least a vague hope of appealing to someone else."

He glanced up, winked, and said, "It's a hit-or-miss business, to be sure," then returned to scrutinizing the clock.

Mina nodded to his bowed head. "The value of some of it must be pretty impressive."

"I do get to see some beauties," he said cheerfully. "Although, I find mostly the opposite to be true—where the owners overinflate the value of their treasures. Sadly, I'm usually the bearer of bad news there. It's not like the *Antiques Roadshow* on TV, I'm afraid. Not usually."

"But there can be a lot of money to be made," she insisted.

He repeated his quick glance up, but less genially and more observantly. "True," he said, removing the clock's back.

"And there's really no telling where some of this comes from, I imagine," she suggested. "It's not like rare stamps or famous paintings, where provenance has to be really solid." She paused before saying, "I mean, that clock could be from anywhere."

Walter Finney gently placed the item in question onto the bench, sat back, and pushed the magnifier lens up onto his forehead to better see her face-to-face. "Is it?" he asked.

"Does it matter?" she asked in turn.

"It does to me," he replied quietly, taking her in very carefully.

She leaned a little closer, pressing against the countertop, despite their being the only two people in the store. "Mr. Finney, the reason I'm asking is that my grandmother was killed in Boston and some of her things were stolen, and I have reason to believe that they were brought here to Northampton to be sold."

"Are the police pursuing this?" he asked.

"I hope they are, but they're pretty busy, and Northampton's a long way from Boston. I'm not saying anything bad about them, but . . ."

He was nodding. "I understand. I'm very sorry for your loss."

In the face of his kindness and concern, she could feel her tears welling up. "Thank you." She tried to focus on why she was there. "But you can see why I'm asking questions. I don't just want to sit around and wait for results that may never come in, and I don't want any opportunities to be overlooked. That's already happened once, and if it hadn't been for me, they would have missed it entirely."

Finney returned to studying the clock, speaking as he did so. He'd been fed his fair share of sob stories in the past, and while this one felt genuine, he had no way of knowing for sure. "I do feel for you, miss, but I'm afraid you may have come to the single worst place in Northampton for this kind of information. I'm a one-man shop and I pretty much mind my own business. I have no idea what criminal activity might be going on out there."

"But you do know if this is a good town for valuables to be bought and sold," she insisted.

"The money's here, certainly," he replied. "And it's a well-known artisan center, complete with galleries and craft shows and what have you. It's even the home base for a major supplier of jewelry and fashion accessories—David Cone Heirlooms. Its headquarters are right downtown. Not that he deals in much like this." He hefted the clock in his hand. "I do think, though," he felt duty-bound to add, "that if I were a thief, I wouldn't come here to get rid of my stolen property. I'd stick to some metropolitan center. More anonymity and better money."

"But that's just it," she told him. "The rumor is that if you want top dollar, come here."

He shook his head doubtfully. "Have you considered that perhaps you were misled?"

She pressed her lips together in response.

He sighed, nodded, and sat back again. "Did you want an opinion about your clock? Or was all this a ruse to start a conversation?"

"Mostly a ruse," she confessed. "Although, if you have an opinion, I'd be curious."

He smiled slightly and set to work reassembling the clock. "It is an original. The gears are in good shape. It needs lubricating, and the spring's seen better times, no pun intended. But overall, you should be able to get four hundred dollars for it, depending on the market at the time." He finished attaching the back and handed it to her. "That having been said, I would just hang on to it in memory of your aunt."

"Grandmother," she corrected him.

He nodded slightly, having made the mistake on purpose. "My error."

He removed the visor, killed the lamp, and came around the counter to escort her to the front door. "I am sorry I couldn't be of more use to you, Miss . . . I apologize. I've already forgotten your name."

"Shepard," she said, and turned to face him at the door. She shook his hand. "I want to thank you for your help. I didn't mean to play that trick on you; I just wasn't sure how to proceed."

"Next time," he counseled, "just ask." He reached out and touched her forearm as she turned to go, adding, "If I think or hear of anything that might be helpful, how do I get hold of you?"

"I'm staying in town," she said quickly, and then hesitated. "Why don't I just drop by in a few days."

"Of course," he agreed. "Best of luck."

He stood by the door, watching her walk away for a couple of minutes before he retreated to his workbench and picked up the phone.

He dialed the private number from memory.

"Dan Siegel," the voice on the other end announced.

"It's Walter."

"Walter," Dan said, obviously pleased. "You forget the next game's at your house?"

"No, no. I got that. I already called the health inspector to make sure it's condemned for that night alone." He chuckled to be friendly but then came straight to the point. "This is actually a business call, Dan. I just had a visitor at the store I thought you should hear about. It's got me a little worried. A young woman, calling herself Shepard and saying that she's staying in town, brought me a small piece for appraisal, but it was clear that Shepard was an alias and that she wanted information other than the worth of her little clock."

"What kind of information?" Dan asked seriously, his interest piqued.

"It was odd," Walter admitted. "She told me that her grandmother had been killed in Boston and her valuables stolen—by which I think she meant mostly antiques and collectibles—and that she had reason to believe they had been or were being sold off here in Northampton.

I told her I thought that was unlikely, but she seemed pretty set on it. She reminded me of Nancy Drew, but with an edge, if you get my meaning."

"I do, Walt. Was she a total whack job?"

"No, no. In truth, she was very sweet. But angry. She said the Boston police had dropped the ball once already and were likely to do so again. I definitely felt I was speaking with a vigilante toward the end, even if she was well-spoken and quite pretty."

"You're a dirty old man, Walter."

Finney smiled at the phone. "I'm a lover of fine art. And I do apologize if this seems silly."

"Don't worry about it," Dan reassured him. "We get calls like this all the time—heads-up from concerned citizens. They're all good. You never know, right? Better blow the whistle than beat yourself up after something bad happens."

"So you think there's nothing to it?"

Dan laughed comfortingly. "Probably. I mean, like you said, it's a bit of a reach, right? Still, we'll look into it, and I thank you for making the call. Give me a description of this beauty while you're at it, will you? Just so I can say I've done my job."

Finney complied, displaying the accuracy of a professional appraiser.

"Okay," Dan said afterward. "Got it, although if you think any of this'll cut you slack at the game this Friday, you've lost your mind. You know that, right?"

Walter laughed in turn, eased by his friend's relaxed manner. "I would expect nothing else, Dan. Thanks for listening."

Dan Siegel hung up his phone at the police department and looked across at his guest.

"We may have a small problem, Joe."

Gunther nodded with long-practiced nonchalance. "I was expecting nothing else," he said.

The two of them walked slowly, hand in hand, between College Lane and Paradise Pond on the Smith campus, approaching the botanical gardens and the ornate greenhouse at a leisurely pace, looking like the stylish, well-dressed couple they were, out for a stroll to enjoy the sunset at the end of a pleasant spring day. Below them, stretching away from the broad embankment to their right, the water sparkled fiercely in the reflected light, coursing noisily toward the picturesque low-head dam a few hundred yards downstream. This side of the Smith campus was as meticulously New England rural as some of its other parts were British pseudo-Gothic.

But the hand-holding was not as friendly as it appeared. She had a firm grip on him, and her voice, though low, was distinctly hard.

"How complicated is it to understand that there should never, ever, be any e-mails between us even hinting at all this? No texting, no notes, no phone calls—nothing except face-to-face talks in the open. Is that like quantum physics to you? Or are you just dying to get caught? You do know that we'll go to jail if that happens, right?"

"I just wrote that we needed to meet," he complained, sounding peevish.

"No," she insisted. "You wrote, 'Meet me ASAP. May be trouble brewing.' Did you think I wouldn't agree if you didn't get hysterical? Did you think that somehow we wouldn't see each other like we do about ten times a week?"

"Oh, come on," he said, trying but failing to pull his hand away.

"'Trouble brewing' could have referred to anything. If pressed, I could say it had something to do with my car, and that our trip to Boston might be messed up."

"Like we couldn't rent a car?" she demanded. "Or use mine? Is that really the problem?"

He didn't respond.

"No," she answered for him. "It's not, which is something they could check out."

"Then I'd come up with something else."

"Are you that out to lunch? You don't get to pick and choose excuses with the cops till they hear one they like."

She changed her voice and softened her grip, making her approach both gentler and more pleasant, if not quite believable. "Sweetheart, I know I come on a little strong. I'm not trying to bust your chops. It's just that we have it so good right now, I don't want us to get sloppy. We live in times where every computer is open to scrutiny, every phone can be tapped, every transaction can be had through a search warrant. I mean, have you ever looked around and seen how many cameras there are everywhere? In stores, banks, ATMs. Traffic lights have them; they're on the tops of buildings and on poles in the park. It's crazy. I will guarantee you that if one's not on us right now, it soon will be, probably from one of those buildings." She gestured toward the campus sprawled out across the street—in stark contrast to the peaceful fields and water beside them—a jumble of halls, labs, dorms, student centers, and service buildings.

"I know," he conceded mournfully.

She kept her eyes straight ahead as they walked, the pleasant setting invisible to her. She hadn't told him of her lethal encounter with the thief from Boston, and the effort she'd gone through dumping the body in Holyoke.

There was a lot she hadn't told him about how she'd gotten them to where they were.

"The systems we have running," she explained softly, "are as bulletproof as I can make them. The Web site, the blindfolding of clients, the audio-video links like what we rigged up at the Summit House—all those have been checked and double-checked. I don't bore you with that stuff because you're the talent, the artist, and I know how you hate it anyhow. But I can only do so much, and regular e-mails and the rest are where things get tougher for me. Besides, like I told you, people would get suspicious if it got out that all our techie gear was hyperprotected. It would look like we had something to hide. That's why I've made such a big deal that both our houses should always be kept so that the cops can come in anytime they want—complete with bug-sniffing equipment or whatever—and not find a thing."

"I know," he repeated. "Sorry I screwed up."

She leaned into him and gave him a quick and calculated kiss on the cheek. "You didn't really, honey. I'm just being oversensitive. I'm the one who should apologize."

Not that she did.

She pointed with her free hand. "Let's go down Green Street."

They checked for traffic before cutting over. Green Street marked one of the campus boundaries, with a preponderance of clearly stamped college buildings on one side and more run-of-the-mill town architecture on the other.

As they reached the sidewalk, she mimicked laughing softly and tossed her hair, visualizing how she might look on one of those ubiquitous cameras.

"So," she said conversationally. "Tell me what's bothering you."

"I don't like the police dropping by to ask questions. What if they know about us and are trying to stir things up? Maybe we should close down for a while."

She looked at him as if he'd just sprouted a second nose. "Do you really believe that?"

It was asked with such incredulity that he became angry. "They're not morons."

"They're not geniuses, either," she shot back. "What do you think? That they learn how to crack cases by watching TV? Good cop/bad cop? Little gray cells? The game is afoot? Most of them barely graduated from high school—lunkheads straight out of the military and dumber than dirt. You are so gullible sometimes. There's a good reason you see all those videos of cops beating the crap out of people. They're like barely trained apes, most of them."

He finally managed to snatch his hand free from hers, causing her to look around nervously, as if a member of her supposed hidden audience might step into view to complain. "If they're such idiots, then why do you go to such lengths to cover up what we're doing?" he asked.

She proved her coolheadedness by acknowledging his point after an irritated pursing of her lips. "Okay," she conceded. "So maybe I'm overstating it. Not liking them doesn't make them incompetent, although I don't know how swift these particular cops could be, coming from Vermont. Nothing happens up there. What I'm really saying is that the whole reason we keep our security so tight is because we planned for everybody and everything—locals, feds, even Vermonters. We knew that the people breaking into houses and supplying our raw material were dopers and half-wits; we knew the cops would wake up sooner or later and start sniffing around Northampton. It was that inevitability that we calculated when planning our security. We *talked* about that."

Appearances notwithstanding, he'd enjoyed riling her, which he often did to counterbalance her controlling nature—and to boost his own self-esteem. He therefore chose this moment to release a second concern to interrupt her increasingly self-congratulatory monologue. "I had another visitor today, too—a young woman. She was asking questions about the jewelry business, legit and otherwise."

That stalled her. She cut him a look, knowing full well that she'd been baited. He so reminded her of a spoiled child sometimes.

"Who was she?"

"She didn't say. Not specifically."

She stopped in the middle of the sidewalk, almost causing a collision with a student who'd been about to pass them. "Don't."

He raised his eyebrows as if preparing to protest, then gave her a broad smile. "Okay, okay. Don't get your panties in a twist. She was a kid is all." He looked around at the few coeds in proximity. "Like one of these. I mean, I didn't like the questions, but she told me she was writing a paper about the economics of crime and the black market and wondered if any of that affected my business."

She resumed walking, no longer interested in holding hands or acting for unseen cameras, despite being on a block that was more likely to have them than where they'd just been. "And you waited to tell me this on a stroll around town? You know, you better get your head in the game here, or *you're* gonna be the reason we go down."

"She was a kid," he protested.

She glared at him. "And you jam me up for reacting about the cops? You don't actually believe her story, do you? You wouldn't have brought it up if you did. You would've kept it to yourself so you could fantasize about fucking her when you're doing me."

"Oh, please," he said, his mouth open.

She wasn't buying it, maintaining her rapid pace toward downtown. "Spare me. We're like a mongoose and a cobra, you and me."

"I," he corrected her. He was pleased to catch her out. He knew how she hated such missteps, and how they highlighted the difference in their educational upbringings—he a preppy; she more seat of the pants, despite her degree in art history. She usually stumbled grammatically when she was angry, which was one reason he pushed her there so often.

"Whatever," she responded. "This girl really a Smithie?"

He stopped his taunting, his genuine concern overriding his more juvenile needs. "No. She was older, and pretty intense. I didn't buy the research story. That's why I couldn't figure her out."

"Where's she from?"

"She wouldn't tell me. She said from out of town. I asked where she was staying. She said nowhere in particular. It was all vague."

She'd begun to slow her pace, already recovering from their spat, and so he fell in beside her once more as they resumed their leisurely appearance.

"I'm sorry I jerked you around," he said for the record. "I was worried about her. She called herself Mina, by the way. No last name. She seemed more focused on her questions than on me, if that's a help—like I was just part of a research trip."

She was nodding throughout his explanation, but she stayed silent when he was done. She could be a good listener and always kept her own counsel. She also sensed that he'd told her all that was relevant, and would merely repeat it if she pressed him for more.

What was needed now was for him to feel validated, so that he stayed in the slot that she'd assigned him in her overall scheme to become rich, successful, and, ironically, free of the likes of him.

She reached out and stroked his back with a circular motion. "I'm sorry, too, sweetie. You were right to give me the heads-up about this Mina person. We've put so much into this operation, and it's worked so well for so long. . . . I'll figure out who she is."

He nodded, staring straight ahead, before eventually turning toward her and reaching out for her hand. "Thanks," he said. "I just hate to stick our necks out too far."

She muttered something unintelligible and soothing, all while thinking, You haven't got a clue.

CHAPTER SIXTEEN

The knocking that interrupted them wasn't against the door, which was open, but the jamb, and was timid in both force and pattern. Every head in the room turned to take in Anne Pape, who was standing there awkwardly in a jacket and a pair of slacks.

"Hi, Officer Pape," Joe greeted her. "You're looking very well turned out. They bump you up to detective?"

She reddened slightly and lingered in the doorway. With Joe were Willy and Dan Siegel. They were in a small windowless room that Dan had declared their task-force office until the case either developed beyond its confines or was solved.

"They thought I'd blend in better out of uniform."

Willy laughed, predictably, but not for the reason that Joe feared. "Right," Willy said scornfully. "What they thought is that this is a body dumping from outside, not their problem, and they didn't want to waste a detective on it. Am I right?"

Her embarrassment deepened, but she didn't duck the charge. "You are right, Special Agent Kunkle."

Joe, shaking his head, stood up and gently took hold of her arm, guiding her to an available chair. "Look, let's get this straight. You're on board, and I'm happy for the company. I don't care what your rank is, or your experience, or what your problems may be back home. We'll figure out what you've got to offer as we go. In the meantime, you're Anne, I'm Joe, he's Dan, and the idiot with the 'tude is Willy. Him, you'll just have to get used to. The only missing member of our party is Jimmy—"

"McAuliffe," said the Boston detective as he stepped into view. "Sorry I'm late."

Everyone stood to exchange handshakes, except Willy, who gave a half wave from his tilted-back seat.

"Good drive?" Dan asked as everyone settled down.

"Boring, mostly. I took the Mass Pike over and cut north on the interstate. Hope I don't have to do that too many times. Makes me restless."

Willy nodded sympathetically as Joe said, "I'm reading between the lines here, but you're saying you'll only be here now and then?"

"Well," Jimmy replied, "I'm here now. I don't know about then."

"Politics?" Anne asked, echoing her own situation.

He chuckled and pulled out a chair. "That and money. I'm not saying I'm not in. This thing's a homicide for us now, what with the old woman dying, and she was no street bum, so the pressure's on. But I'm a long way from Boston. My hanging around could go either way, depending on how lucky and/or high profile we get."

"And on how complicated your life gets," Joe added. "What did you say that granddaughter's name was?"

"Hawthorn's?" Jimmy asked, surprised. "Mina Carson. Why?"

"She's in town," Dan told him. "I got a call from a local antiques dealer, friend of mine; she came in asking questions about how and where to unload the kind of stuff that was stolen from her grandmother. I then asked around and found out he wasn't the only one. She's here playing private eye."

"That fucking woman's like a bad tooth," Jimmy muttered. "She promised she'd let me handle this."

"You have a picture of her?" Anne asked. "We could confirm it by showing it to the antiques dealer, just to make sure."

Jimmy looked at her wiltingly. "She's a pain in the ass, not a suspect. I don't have a picture."

Surprisingly, Willy came to Anne's rescue. "Still a good idea. The Internet probably has something. If not Facebook, then maybe a society snapshot. Didn't the granddaughter hang out with the old woman a lot?"

Jimmy glanced from Anne to Willy and shrugged. "Sure. That might work."

Anne turned toward one of the available computers in the room as Joe resumed, "In any case, she's a fly in the ointment, but not why we're here."

"True enough," Dan agreed. "In the middle of all this fussing around with jurisdiction and who's on first and what this woman's up to, we shouldn't lose sight of the fact that we're facing a double homicide."

"Yeah," Willy said lazily, "but whose, right? I mean, Jimmy's got one, for sure. Maybe he owns 'em both. We have no clue where Mickey Roma got beaned." He looked at Anne. "That's why your people are running away from it, isn't it?"

Anne apparently enjoyed Willy's style. She smiled slightly as she was typing and nodded without comment.

"Thanks a lot," Jimmy said. "I shoulda stayed home."

"No, no, no," Joe said. "I mean, yes, we don't know where he was killed, but it's a good guess it wasn't Boston. We go down that path, we might as well say he drove down to New York, got whacked, and was beamed back to Holyoke. There's got to be some common sense applied here, which suggests that we're on the right track where we are."

"All roads leading to Northampton?" Dan quipped.

"Right," Joe agreed. "Or at least suggesting that Northampton bears some serious scrutiny."

"I say we just arrest Cone's girlfriend and call it a day," Willy said.

Joe didn't totally disagree with that sentiment. "I didn't like her, either," he said, turning to Dan. "Did we ever run her through the system? We talked about it when we left his office."

Dan leaned forward and extracted a sheaf of papers from the table where they were sitting. "Donna Lee Hawkins. From her background and general involvements, it looks like she's more a fellow traveler than a doer. She's never served time, but she's obviously made some arrangements to avoid it." He flipped through a few pages, refreshing his memory. "We're talking Ponzi schemes, bank and insurance fraud, white-collar rip-offs. Nothing violent, and, like I said, nothing that was pinned on her—she was always the girlfriend at the time, and always accommodating with the prosecution afterward."

"Nice," Willy commented. "So now it's Cone? What the hell. He gave me the creeps, too. Ruthless bastard playing the aging country squire."

Joe merely glanced at Dan, who'd introduced them to Cone in the first place. Siegel shook his head. "I don't see it. He's full of himself, but that could be said of you." He indicated Willy, who responded with a thumbs-up. "He's been in this town for decades," he went on. "And no one can say he ever kept a low profile. His place has been burgled once or twice—not lately, though—and he's been sued by the odd unhappy customer or employee—again, not recently. That happens to people with money. On the flip side," he added, "like I said before, he's been helpful as a resource. I'm not suggesting that someone inside his organization isn't crooked, but I don't see David as that guy."

"I'm glad you mentioned it," Joe said. "We were actually getting some interesting information from him when Donna walked in and interrupted. But I didn't want her in the mix. Gut reaction."

"Hear, hear," Willy echoed.

"You think we could have another shot at him alone?" Joe asked.

"Sure," Dan replied, making a note of it.

"Not to be rude," Jimmy said suddenly, "but who the hell's David?"

"Sorry," Joe responded. "Biggest jeweler in town."

"One of the biggest independents in the country," Dan explained. "We're talking multiple millions a year."

Jimmy nodded with appreciation. "I get the interest in him now. Sounds like enough to kill over."

Dan was evidently feeling a little defensive. "Except that we have absolutely nothing linking him to any of this."

"So let's tear into him," Willy suggested airily. "A guy like that—no way he's clean, no matter how many butts he's kissed to hide it."

Siegel's face darkened at that remark, which is when Anne diplomatically asked Jimmy, "This her?" and pushed away from the computer so they could all see the screen.

Ignoring both Dan and Willy, Joe and his Boston counterpart rose to consult the image Anne had brought up.

"Yeah," Jimmy announced. "What a pain."

"You print that out?" Joe asked.

Dan took advantage of the question to get up and turned on a printer in the corner. "Should work," he said.

It did, and Joe and the others soon had copies of Mina's picture in their hands.

"I don't mind chasing her down if she's driving you crazy," Joe volunteered.

"Knock your socks off," Jimmy said, regaining his seat before asking, "So, what's the plan?"

"We tried a covert buy," Dan began.

"How 'bout a GPS chip?" Joe said abruptly, cutting off whatever Dan had been about to say next.

That created a pause, into which Willy dropped his opinion. "Cool. I like it."

"The covert buy didn't work," Joe explained, "because we hadn't anticipated that the buyers would conduct it remotely." He glanced at Jimmy and added, "We took some loot along, but when we showed up, I had to deal with a remote TV hookup—leave the goods, take the money that had already been left there. Clever on their part, dumb on ours, but who knew?"

"But we didn't blow our cover," Willy continued. "That leaves the door open for us to try it again. Hell, it's no different from your run-of-the-mill drug buy. We always do several of those before we move in. Standard practice. I think this is a natural—plant a bug in something like a locket or whatever and see where it takes us. Two can play at this electronic shit."

Dan was mulling it over. "Why not?" he said. "We don't have anything else on the front burner. Let's set it up."

. . .

Joe had been sitting in the lobby of the Hotel Northampton for barely an hour before he recognized the young woman entering from the King Street entrance. He'd aimed for the time when most businesses close and people choose between dining out or simply calling it a day. He had already invested most of the afternoon tracing Mina Carson's steps, interviewing an assortment of store owners and antique dealers, until he'd found a sharp-eyed clerk who'd recognized the telltale hotel key card in Mina's wallet when she'd made a small purchase.

Joe rose from his armchair and sidled up to her as she stood before the elevator doors.

"Miss Carson?" he asked quietly, displaying his badge without fanfare. "Could we have a brief chat?"

She stiffened and took half a step away from him. "Who are you?"

"Joe Gunther," he explained. "I work for a special investigations unit in Vermont. I'm chasing the same case you are."

His phrasing caught her attention. "You know about me?"

"I know of your loss. I was sad to hear about your grandmother—terrible thing."

She stared at him a moment, taking his measure, as he was doing in turn. Joe was struck by how this woman resembled Lyn Silva—in contrast to the photograph that Anne had pulled off the Internet. Younger, of course, and with hair differently colored and cut, but familiar in her athletic build and focused energy.

The resemblance was a shock, and it gave him an unexpected emotional jolt. He was all too familiar with personal loss—comrades in arms; many friends and colleagues; his wife, Ellen, years ago; Lyn. Each death had put him through the wringer in various ways, depending on his age, the circumstances, and how each person had touched his spirit.

But this last one had hit him the hardest with its random cruelty. Lyn had been no combatant or cop or victim of disease. There'd been no available rationalization to lessen her being snatched away. She'd been not just a true innocent but someone who'd made the effort to improve life—her own and everyone's around her—and against considerable odds.

She'd been a fighter, as the cliché might have it, if a loving and gentle one, and it was that feature Joe was seeing in the eyes of the woman before him.

"I would really appreciate comparing notes with you," he told her. "If you wouldn't mind."

"You know Detective McAuliffe, from Boston?" she asked, her expression suspicious.

"We've met. I can't say I know him. He's one of a group of us that's trying to sort this out."

She finally allowed for a quick nod of the head. "All right. Where do you want to do this?"

"Wherever you're comfortable."

She looked a little hapless for a moment, scanning the oddly retrofitted lobby for a quiet corner. The coincidental arrival of a small but boisterous group further complicated her decision.

"How 'bout I buy you some tea or a cup of coffee?" he offered, having noticed the small café/bar at the building's south end, around the corner from the elevators and down the corridor.

Unexpectedly, she accepted. He gestured for her to precede him to the Coolidge Park Café, a two-level establishment overlooking the town's central intersection, whose audible bustling was barely noticeable through the insulated glass. Outside, on the café's veranda, tables had been put out for guests to enjoy the warm weather, although no one was there at the moment. Joe noticed a couple of trees were clad in colorful knit sheaths—remnants of an overnight "Yarn Bombing," where area knitters had sneaked out under cover of darkness to decorate trees and make them appear like arboreal ballet dancers, sporting leg warmers and standing on their heads.

In the distance, as in a silent movie, a group of protesters, holding signs Joe didn't bother reading, walked up and down the sidewalk. He chose an inside table by one of the broad windows, quiet and beyond the muted talk emanating from the bar at the room's other end.

"So," she said quickly, as soon as she'd sat and crossed both legs and arms. "What do you want?"

He maintained the tone he'd set with his inclusive opening line. "As bad as this has been for you, it turns out that the people responsible have been running amok across two states at least, and your grandmother isn't the only one who's been killed. That's why the task force I mentioned. 'So,' as you put it," he said with a smile, "I thought it might be a good idea to trade a little information, since you're already here and hard at work."

She gave him that appraising silent gaze for a moment. "You're not going to give me shit for impeding a police investigation?"

"Would you like me to?"

At last, a half smile. "I think I heard it already."

"So I've been told."

A waiter appeared, and Joe ordered two coffees after consulting with Mina.

"What brought you to Northampton?" he asked once they were alone.

"Detective McAuliffe mentioned it," she said simply. "He swore me to secrecy, said that the case might go federal, and basically told me anything he could think of to get me off his back."

"Which didn't work."

"I'm not on his back," she said almost sweetly. "I seem to be on yours now."

"You haven't done anything to mess me up," Joe assured her.

"And yet there you sit."

He smiled in concession. "Well, we had heard you were in town, although that mostly made me wonder what you might've found out."

"Meaning you're going to deputize me and let me join the force?"

Their coffees arrived, along with the regulation minute of fussing with sugar and cream—or not.

One sip later, Joe cradled his jaw in his hand, his elbow on the arm of his chair, and watched her ignore her own cup before asking, "Your whole world's been kicked off-kilter, hasn't it?"

She looked at him, startled. "What?"

"Your grandmother."

She flushed, and tears sprang to her eyes, but her voice was angry when she said, "She was murdered, *Detective*." The last word was emphasized bitterly.

"Call me Joe," he countered gently, adding, "and I know she was, which, in part, is why I'm here in another state instead of where I belong. Miss Carson, if there's something I've learned, it's that humans can be unbelievably cruel to one another and that there's often no way to predict when or how that cruelty will lash out and hit us. You can duck it most of the time—avoiding bad sections of town, or not picking fights in bars. But your grandmother was at home, minding her own business, having done no harm to anyone over an entire lifetime. Isn't that right?"

She'd pulled a handkerchief from her pocket and was wiping her eyes. "Yes."

"That's mostly what keeps me doing this," he went on. "I'll follow the letter of the law if one punk swats another. That's my job. But in cases like your grandmother's, I'll put in the extra effort. She didn't deserve what happened to her—nor did you—so you both get the best I can give, for as long as it takes."

She let her hands drop to her lap and stared out the window at the bored-looking protesters. "Thank you," she murmured to them.

He tried again. "What have you discovered while you've been here?"

"Nothing," she said flatly, facing him again.

"You hit all the stores and dealers?"

"Most of them," she conceded. "That was probably pretty stupid. I didn't want to go to the cops. . . . Not that it mattered." She shifted her attention to him. "You found me anyhow, right? All of a day later."

She let out a sigh, and he barely heard her say, "It's just so frustrating. . . ."

"What's your angle been?" he asked, already knowing from his research.

She moved slightly beyond her reverie to fumble within the large bag she'd placed on the floor beside her, extracting a small, rectangular, intricately worked clock, which she handed him. "I'd give some of them that, pretend I wanted to hock it, and then chat them up about how and where one would fence stolen goods. With others, I'd tell the truth and explain about Billie. With a couple, where it didn't look like they traded in antiques—more business types, in the bigger places—I just pretended I was a student writing a research paper and asked them questions."

He studied the clock without expression as she added, "I know, totally lame, and all it did was make everybody suspicious. How many of them called you? I bet that nice old man did. Mr. Finney. I could see him angling for information by the end, trying to find out who I was and where I was staying. And I even told him the truth about Billie. Was he the one who called you?"

Joe sidestepped, instinctively wanting to avoid burning an informant. "I'm not the local here. I was just told that word had gotten back to the PD about your inquiries. Still, concerning your efforts, did you get anything to go on, even by implication?"

She shook her head.

He was struck by her silence and spoke next with a pointed emphasis. "Mina. You have not been abandoned. I know you felt that way in Boston, but even McAuliffe is here now, far from home, working hard. That's the way we get these things done in the end—by working as a team. You aren't a cop. We know that. But we also respect your loss and your commitment to finding Billie's killer. I will keep you in the loop. I promise that. But with one request. You know what that is, right?"

"That I tell you what I know?"

"Do you know something?"

She shook her head again, but this time, he thought, more in irritation than denial. "I'm not holding out on you," she insisted. "I already said I don't know anything."

His own fears told him otherwise. He suddenly yielded to a flash of unusual emotion, again remembering Lyn and how fate had abruptly taken her. He rose to hide his feelings and stood at the window, staring out as she had earlier.

"Be careful," he said, avoiding eye contact. "If you don't help us—and through us, every other potential victim out there—you'll not only find yourself in a minefield between the police and some ruthless, dangerous people but wondering later about some of the choices you're making right now."

He turned to look down at her. "I have lost too many friends for you not to hear me on this. You have *got* to keep us informed if you stay here, and I *urge* you to leave right now. Go home, mourn Billie, put your and her affairs in order, contact me daily if you want, but *please*, don't do anything on your own to find out who killed her. I do not want to investigate your death. Do you understand?"

Scowling, she'd risen in the middle of this and gathered her bag, telling him through her body language that he'd come on too strong.

"Are we done?" she asked.

"Will you be going home?"

She frowned. "I am doing nothing to break the law. If I choose to stay, I will."

With that, she walked back toward the elevator.

"Great," he said to himself.

CHAPTER SEVENTEEN

She walked, tense and angry, into his ornate penthouse office and looked around to make sure he was alone. She closed the door against the secretarial noises outside and approached his large desk, her body rigid. He'd decorated the office himself, which she hated—all wood and unread books and leather furniture and wannabe Hemingway hormones.

He looked up at her and smiled lazily. "Hey there. If it isn't my Bonnie Parker."

The reference stopped her cold, the vision of Mickey's body at her feet, his head bleeding, still fresh in her memory.

"What do you mean?"

Her voice betrayed her alarm. His smile remained, but his eyes widened as he pushed away from his desk.

"Relax, honey. You know, Bonnie and Clyde. Her name was Bonnie Parker."

She scowled furiously. "I know what the fuck her name was. Do you think I'm stupid?"

He held up both hands and struggled to rise. "Of course not. Relax. Have a seat." He tried to ease her into one of his guest chairs, but she pushed him away.

"What the hell is your problem?" he responded, retreating.

Still standing, she almost threw the mug shot of a man onto his lap. "Not *my* problem. Our problem. How many times have I told you to adhere to protocol and follow the security procedures I set up? But, *oh no.* The cops're too dumb, we're too smart, nobody cares." She pointed at the photograph he was still focusing on. "That's proof that we're not too smart—or *you* aren't—and that they're far from dumb." She whirled around. "They might as well be right outside that door, and not to ask a bunch of idiotic questions about the art business, either."

"I'm the one who said I was worried in the first place," he protested.

"About the wrong thing, moron," she countered, leaning over him. "Look at that."

He tossed the picture onto his desk. "I did. So what?"

"Do you recognize him?" she said slowly, as if addressing a child.

"No, I don't. Why should I?"

"Because you did the deal with him from Summit House. He was the guy who sold you the goods."

That stopped him cold. He stared at her, dumbfounded, and then reached out to study the photograph more carefully. "It's vaguely like him, but it's not. You're wrong."

She smiled triumphantly and straightened, at last stepping back to sit down. She brushed her carefully made-up forehead with the tips of two fingers and shook her head sadly. "I never should have let you conduct that transaction."

"I've done them before."

"Twice," she amended. "Both times with morons, and I shouldn't have let you do those. Sign of weakness, or love, or whatever."

He let his frustration finally show. "What the hell are you talking about?"

But she was enjoying her victory, even though it accompanied bad news. "Do you remember the man you dealt with?"

"Bobby Schultz," he said with confidence. "He checked out straight down the line, from the Web site application to the final interview before the meet."

"Did you use our sources to get a copy of his mug shot?"

He hesitated.

"Sweetie?" she asked leadingly, the endearment venomous.

She indicated the picture once more. "Well, that's it. Meet the real Bobby Schultz."

His lips parted slightly, and the blood drained from his cheeks.

"You wanna guess who you talked to?" she asked. "Or even what police agency he's from?"

He didn't correct her grammar.

"What're we going to do?" he almost whispered.

She studied her nails. "Gee. There's a question. What do you think, Clyde?"

Mina entered the showroom and looked around at the rows of glistening display cases stretching off in ordered ranks from the ornate entrance. The place was as quiet as a museum, and similarly lighted— dramatic and yet unobtrusive. Gentle, barely audible classical music murmured in the background.

The guard at the door greeted her quietly. "Good afternoon, ma'am. Welcome to David Cone Heirlooms."

She smiled and nodded. "Hi."

Once more, as had been the norm since beginning this quest, she had only a vague notion of what she was doing. The common de-nominator in her earlier research among the art galleries and antique stores in and around Northampton had been that David Cone Heir-looms was the King Kong of competitors—the biggest buyer, seller, manufacturer, and influence in the region, not only dealing in original and previously owned works but acting as a conduit for other people's products, as well. Over the years, according to her sources, Cone had never met an obstacle he wasn't willing to absorb. In the words of one of the more inventive and minor of his rivals—the owner of a store called the Flea Shoppe—Cone "would sell tires off his rear loading dock if he could rationalize it." She'd visited the corporate offices ear-lier, of course, in her bogus student researcher role, and interviewed some stuffed shirt, but this was her first sight of the flagship store.

Looking around at the variety offered in this mecca, she could see the Flea Shoppe man's point. There were affordable earrings, rings, necklaces, and bracelets; pricier custom-made versions of the same, from both "the David Cone Studio" and other designers, whose names she recognized from shopping in Boston; and even a large selection of antiques, which, before now, she hadn't realized were even sold by Cone. This last area was an example, according to her homework, of where the company had recently entered a new, if somewhat related, commercial field.

Scuttlebutt had it that David might be easing out of operations—in favor of a younger generation—and that the antiques business and the

Cone Studio line of more ornate and individualized items were examples of that. But no formal announcement had been made. David had cut his teeth mass-producing clean, elegant, almost Nordic-looking pieces, whose appeal had been that they could be worn with almost anything.

Now, things had become trickier, more online and consumer-friendly, and less reliant on traditional commercial channels. The implication was that David had gotten lucky here, too, passing on the reins just as greater savvy and a less traditional approach were called for.

David Cone Heirlooms, in short, had been generally credited over the years with being innovative, pro-active, tough-minded, and incredibly fortunate.

Much to the resentment of some of Mina's sources.

She walked alongside the display cases, absorbing their contents and reviewing what she'd learned, envisioning this man—whose image was liberally displayed throughout the store—starting out as the street artist that his biography claimed. It seemed less than credible to her that one person could have had such a perfect mixture of Midas touch and artistic ability. Most creative types she knew were terrible at business, although she did have to concede that this image fit a time-worn and sometimes self-serving cliché.

Her other niggling peeve was Cone's reputation as a great artist. He'd made his reputation selling to the middle class through the most commercial of outlets—hardly the customer base for true "high art," she thought with some understandable snobbery. And the signs on the walls and counters around her all bragged that the fancy custom stuff nowadays was coming from his studio—not necessarily from his own hands. As with so many organizations centered around an iconic figure, who was to know the true influence of that person? Was David Cone a legitimate Julia Child or a trademarked Betty Crocker?

Mina was still lost in this reverie when she found herself among the most expensive of the so-called studio offerings.

It was, she had to admit, a remarkable and innovative selection of old and new, traditional and exotic, and cleverly reflective of the cultural commingling that was becoming common the entire world over. She'd been trained in the arts, and was quick to recognize the erosion of some cultural resistance on one hand and the enduring influence of many traditional styles on the other. Asian, African, and Western art, once highly distinct and foreign to one another, had all begun to soften at the edges, leading to new hybrids that appealed to a wider audience.

What she saw for sale around her seemed to fit the Cone battle plan of catering to as many people as possible, including those who identified themselves as the discriminating elite.

She paused a moment, her hand resting on top of a showcase, as if considering a purchase. In fact, her thoughts had wandered from research to her own plight, stopping her in her tracks.

What the hell *was* she doing? Had that Vermont cop been right? He'd seemed so concerned, unlike Jimmy McAuliffe—as if he had a personal stake in her welfare. She'd actually felt bad, walking away from him, which had heightened her discomfort. Cops weren't supposed to make you worry about *their* feelings.

Still . . . He had made her think beyond her loss and rage, if only for a moment. What was she going to do without Billie? She'd had moments when she'd taken the old lady for granted, even finding her irritating. But now? Was her present obsession based on revenge, or on avoiding the unknown ahead?

She rubbed her eyes and focused on the items before her—a category the store had labeled "Old Meets New." It was a tired concept, to take a fragment of something old and gussy it up with a modern twist—like an old hat adorned with a modern peace symbol. But here, they'd done a tasteful job of it. Mina resumed walking down the aisle, taking a break from both her hunt and her self-doubts to simply enjoy the items on exhibit.

Then, perhaps inevitably, she came to an abrupt halt, overcome by emotion.

Leaning against the counter to steady herself, she stared, transfixed, at a pendant whose simplicity was offset by the addition of a tiny antique cameo. A cameo Mina had enjoyed playing with as a child, as it had once sat in the center of one of Billie's rings.

"Can I help you with anything?" a smoothly modulated female voice asked.

Mina's head snapped up to face a saleswoman, who was smiling politely.

"I noticed you were enjoying that piece," the woman said.

Horrified by it would be the better phrase, Mina thought. She forced a half smile. "Yes. The pendant."

"Very pretty." The clerk slid open the cabinet from her side and reached in to extract the piece. "And a very nice way to set off such beautiful craftsmanship. The simple setting catches the eye, and then the cameo pulls you in closer." She laid it out on a black padded cloth she'd made magically appear from somewhere Mina hadn't noticed.

Mina leaned over, her face barely five inches above it. She recognized every detail. As a kid, she'd held Billie's hand, kneeling beside her chair, and let her fingertips trace this exact white-and-pink profile of an aristocratic lady, framed in a tiny oval of leaves, one of which was minutely fractured.

"How much is it?" she asked, her head still bowed.

"Fifteen hundred dollars," the woman said. "Quite a bargain, given its delicacy and uniqueness."

Mina straightened, reacting only to an image of violence and death. Her earlier reservations, born of Joe Gunther's concern, were wiped from her mind.

Her voice was calm. "It is distinctive. Did you make it?"

The woman smiled. "I could never do anything so beautiful. But it is a product of the Cone Studio."

To gain leverage, Mina extracted her wallet and held it nonchalantly in her hand. "That's what I meant, of course. But tell me, is the Cone Studio an amalgamation of artists from all over, or is there actually a studio?"

"Oh, no," the saleslady said, her eyebrows raised as she quickly glanced at the wallet, "the studio's real."

"It's here? In Northampton?"

The smile froze slightly. "I can't say, exactly" was the studied reply. "It's nearby, but it's not open to the public, if that's what you're asking. That's too bad, isn't it? I would love to see them at work. Can you imagine the attention to detail?"

You have no idea, Mina almost said, asking instead, "But you're sure it's local? It's important to me that it's not from someplace like China or something."

The woman was already shaking her head. "No, no, no, no. That's one thing we're all told when we're hired—in honor of how David

Cone came to be . . . well, David Cone—all the studio's products are made locally, by local talent."

And from locally stolen property, Mina thought. She opened her wallet. "That's neat. So many big operations have gone overseas. I heard that Cone does have a Chinese factory."

The woman wore her most guileless expression. "That's absolutely true, but it's only for our mass-market line, so that we can stay competitive." She waved her arm out wide. "Everything in this section is made in the U S of A."

"But the studio must have other outlets than this store, surely?" Mina said. "To keep all those artists employed?"

"Oh, we do. The Internet, don't you know? That keeps us very busy."

Mina nodded and pulled out a credit card. "How's it work? They just deliver a truckload every week?"

The woman laughed. "Like L.L.Bean delivering boots? That's very funny. You're good. No, no. Our manager goes out there every so often and resupplies us as needed. You are right about the other side of the store, though, come to think of it—there's a loading dock out back where I see trucks sometimes—but I don't know much about that. There's also a warehouse where they handle most of the shipping. I've never been there, either, but I hear it's pretty busy."

The clerk delicately relieved Mina of her card. "Credit or debit?"

"We could put a tail on her," Joe mused aloud later in their cramped task-force office.

"Absolutely," Dan said in mock agreement. "I got a whole crew just sitting around the squad room. I'll put 'em right on it."

"Why a tail?" Willy asked his boss pointedly, sensing the kind of thinking that he liked the most.

"She's focused, committed, and totally free of the rules and regs that tie our hands," Joe answered.

"Like a missile we could track?" Willy suggested.

"Crudely put," Joe agreed.

"That is so wrong," Anne blurted out, and then looked around nervously.

Willy just laughed, but even Jimmy had to add, "I like the idea, but it does run against the notion of using civilians as bait. It's not like she's a suspect, or even a snitch."

Joe was nodding agreeably. "We wire civilians all the time with microphones and ask them to record incriminating conversations with bad guys. For the moment, we're stuck with her anyhow. Hell, we're already worried about her safety, but we can't arrest her, throw her out of town, or even assign her protection, since the threat's not been identified. So what's left? Why not tail her, for her sake and ours."

But Dan was not buying it. "Great idea if she'd proved she was as good as Batman at catching crooks. So far, all she's done is blunder around and make everybody suspicious. She's not serious, Joe. We want to spend resources, let's go after the best idea I've heard so far, which is to take another run at LotsforLoot with a GPS-bugged bauble. We've already got the paperwork lined up."

"I agree," Jimmy said. "We nail these guys, that's another way of making her safe. And it doesn't set her up in anyone's sights."

Joe sensed the overall mood and let it drop, although a glance at Willy made him think that Mina might have landed at least one guardian angel in any case.

"Okay," he said, addressing Dan's first objection. "I feel your pain in the manpower department. We'd better not forget that she's out there, though, whether we like it or not. Are we, in fact, all ready to go with the GPS?"

Dan opened a file he'd placed before him earlier and extracted a small envelope. Out of it slithered a gold bracelet with semiprecious stones. "Got this from Property. Not something I'd wear myself, but the techies planted a GPS under one of the stones, and they're promising it'll work." He looked at Anne, who, among all of them, had shown the best ability with computers. "You all set with contacting the Web site?"

She nodded toward a laptop on the counter lining the wall. "Your guys rigged that up so that there's no tracing it back to the PD. We should be good as long as Joe's got everything he needs to imitate Bobby Schultz again."

Joe slid his chair over beside her, groaning, "Hate that mustache. You ready?"

Far across Northampton, Lǐ Anming put the finishing touches on another creation, glancing guiltily in Ed's direction to make sure that he wasn't paying attention. It wouldn't have made any difference, of course. He was interested in groping her, not in what she was doing, which was beyond his comprehension anyhow.

She turned the piece over in her hands, both admiring her handiwork and the subterfuge she'd carried out—both of them elegant, subtle, and, she hoped, worthy of attention.

Her task was to separate the cameos, stones, mountings, insets, and the rest from one another, then to construct brand-new pieces that would stand on their own as originals. She had no idea what lay behind it all. Objectively, it was absurd to break up antique jewelry to create replacements of equal or lesser value. So it wasn't a great leap to imagine the likely source of the older work. After all, Lǐ Anming fully appreciated the nature of her own illegal employment here, along with its worth to others.

As a result, she'd hatched a plot several days earlier, as much for her own self-empowerment as out of any hope for salvation, whereby she would subtly bring attention to each new creation, not with her name, but with a telling detail from one of the older pieces. Thus, if she felt that an erstwhile antique's prominent features might serve to bring attention to its theft by being visible in her new version, then she would work to bring that about. It wasn't always possible—some pieces didn't lend themselves to the purpose. But it worked occasionally, and gave her great satisfaction, as now with the necklace she was holding.

She hadn't even told Wú Méi of her plan. Given how they lived and the pressures they were under, sexual and otherwise, she didn't trust anyone with a secret like this. Besides, her entire defense, if caught, was going to be ignorance. "I'm just a stupid Asian girl," she was prepared to protest, "following instructions."

The amazing thing was that so far, no one had confronted her. She placed the necklace with satisfaction into the cardboard box marked "Finished," then began considering her next challenge.

Joe killed his engine in the parking lot and stepped out into the cool early-evening air. He was in Greenfield, Massachusetts, at around suppertime, having been called by a representative of the governor of Vermont for a mysterious meeting with the boss herself. He'd been inclined to call Gail on her cell immediately, of course, to hassle her a little on the formality of it all, but then he had thought better of it.

They'd been operating on different planes for some time now, and while true and trusted friends, he was still old-fashioned enough in his manners not to make presumptions.

He crossed the street and approached the family restaurant he'd been directed to, already noticing the tall young man with the military haircut, who was wearing his suit and tie as if it were a uniform. Unlike so many governors, Vermont's tended to be accompanied by a single member of the security detail, assigned by the state police, and exemplifying once again the state's overall practical frugality. The governor didn't have a mansion, either, nor did state senators or representatives have private office space. Say what they might about Vermont's occasional offbeat style, people couldn't complain about its leadership being hard to reach.

Joe stopped before the young man, who smiled and nodded in recognition, extending his hand in greeting. "Special Agent Gunther. This is a true honor. I'm Trooper John Carter."

"I've heard good things about you, John," Joe told him honestly. It was often the case that the governor's detail was chosen from among the more promising of the state police rank and file. They served not only a security role, after all, but were subtle—if purely physical—representatives of their agency's best interests, especially when the boss happened to be a liberal Democrat.

Joe therefore couldn't resist adding, "I hope you've been considering the VBI. I think you'd like it there."

Carter smiled and raised his eyebrows in appreciation, but, true to the party line, he merely said, "The governor's waiting for you in a private room downstairs, sir. Take the staircase to the left, just inside the door, and enjoy your dinner."

Joe patted him on the shoulder, slipped him his business card, and passed by, hearing the young man's quiet laughter as he headed down-stairs.

The restaurant was a Greenfield tradition, if maybe living on oxygen lately, like many of its patrons. It served the same old-timey, rib-sticking, lard-laced food that it had served for generations—increasingly under threat from both the healthy-food crowd and those inclined to eat off their laps as they drove. In addition to the main dining room on the ground floor, where the place's founder had once toured the tables like a doting patriarch, greeting customers by name, there were more private rooms downstairs for quiet gatherings, which, Joe imagined, were becoming sadly few and far between.

Good for an out-of-state governor who was passing through town and in need of a meal and an impromptu quiet meeting, but not so great if that governor was a strict vegetarian. Joe therefore entered the small, dimly lighted room with some amused anticipation about what he might find on Gail's plate.

There were two people waiting for him—Gail and one of her trusted sidekicks, a young woman Joe had met just once, Alice Drim. Alice virtually leaped to her feet when he entered, crossing the room to shake his hand. Gail stayed seated, smiling broadly, and pointed to the seat by her side. Given the upbeat reception, Joe followed his instincts by shaking Alice's hand and kissing the chief executive on the cheek as he sat.

He also made a show of leaning toward Gail's plate and admiring the remnants of a small scattering of greenery at its center. She laughed, understanding the gesture. "I know, I know. It was a side salad with pretensions—the best they could do, given their menu and my short-comings as an omnivore."

Joe nodded in agreement. "You might've done better at a fast-food restaurant, these days."

She shook her head. "I realize that now, but I do love this place. It's a classic. I didn't even know it existed until we walked in. John suggested it when dinner was mentioned. We're on our way back from a meeting in Boston. I should've known he'd think I had the eating habits of his grandmother. They've bent over backward, though, so I couldn't be happier."

"We didn't know when you might get here, Mr. Gunther," Alice said. "Have you had dinner? I could order you something."

Joe waved his hand. "No, thanks. I'm all set."

Gail laughed. "Knowing him, he probably had a slice of Spam smeared with peanut butter about twelve hours ago. Am I right?"

Joe smiled ruefully. In fact, he had no memory about what or when he'd eaten last. It was true that he generally survived off of whatever snack was closest.

Nevertheless, it was Gail who followed up by asking, "Kidding aside, Joe, you're sure you wouldn't like something? A burger, maybe? You're the state's guest, after all."

He shook his head again. "I'm good. I am sorry I'm running a little late."

Gail dismissed that. "You kidding? We didn't reach out till about forty-five minutes ago. I was hoping we could meet in Brattleboro, until my spies told me you were in Northampton. That's when some quick-thinking person came up with this place."

He nodded at the familiarity of the process and raised his eyebrow at her. "Sammie, eh?"

She winked at him. "I never discuss my sources."

She glanced at her empty plate and looked up, as if struck by a sudden thought. "What's the weather like outside? Still nice?"

"Sure," he replied, surprised. He still had no inkling as to why he'd been summoned.

Gail pushed back her chair and stood up, addressing Alice. "Let John know we'll be taking a stroll down the main drag, just to take a breather and have a chat. Shouldn't be more than twenty minutes."

"He'll want to keep an eye on you," Alice warned.

"That's fine. I just want to pick Joe's brain about a couple of things."

Still mystified, Joe followed the two women upstairs, stood by while the arrangements were quickly made, and then fell in beside his old partner and companion for a turn down the street—complete with an armed guard a respectful ten paces behind them.

As they rounded the corner from Federal onto Main and headed west, Gail was the first to acknowledge the situation. "I guess it wouldn't be much weirder if a helicopter was hovering overhead."

Joe laughed. "It's not bad. I was just thinking a few minutes ago how Vermont keeps all this low-key, even with someone having taken a potshot at you before the election."

She was silent at the reference to Lyn's dying by her side on that occasion.

"Sorry," he added, embarrassed.

She slid her arm through his, looking straight ahead. "Don't be. I didn't know her, and yet I think of her every day—how she came to be there, and what she meant to you."

"I appreciate that," he told her.

They walked awhile in silence, each weighing a topic that would be shared by them forevermore.

He was the first to change the subject. "Brattleboro's not on the way between Boston and Montpelier."

She looked up at him. "What?"

"When you called from the road," he said. "You said you were headed back from Boston, and only reached out 'cause I was on the way—till you found out about the Northampton job."

She gave him an embarrassed look. "Busted."

"What's up?"

"I just wanted to see you."

He laughed. "Not so easy anymore, huh?"

She joined in briefly but without conviction. "No kidding. I'll tell Alice later, so John can hear, of course, that I needed to fly a Department of Public Safety issue by you, for your input; ergo the detour and the privacy."

He squeezed her hand, which was resting atop his forearm. "You always walk arm in arm with your consultants?"

This time, she laughed outright, leaving her hand in place. "Oh Lord. Everyone knows our history. I just don't want people to think we're getting back together."

He nodded and smiled supportively but said nothing, reminded by the comment of how they'd ended up apart, and of how occasionally—despite her political chops—she could still string together a phrase in just exactly the wrong way.

"I do think about that sometimes," he said conversationally. "How politicians can lead a private life."

"It's easier if they have a family," she said. "At least that's what I'm finding out. Being single makes you more available to the press, somehow. They're nosier than if I had a husband and kids at home. I've already started hearing that I'm a closet lesbian, and that poor people like Alice are either being sworn to secrecy or are part of my harem."

"Who's saying that?" Joe asked, startled.

She shrugged. "Nobody. Somebody. You know how it goes. It's a little like dealing with mosquitoes, in a way—if you're busy doing something, you don't tend to mind them. But let your mind wander for a moment, and they're all you can see."

He didn't answer, at once sympathetic with all that was on her mind and with all that she wanted to accomplish, while hearing how mundane she sounded. It reminded him of how easily people of her stature were not allowed to complain like regular human beings.

As if coming to the same realization, she stopped, broke away, and faced him. "Thanks, Joe."

"For what? I don't feel like I've done anything."

"You came. You're here. Like always."

He studied her face, seeing something unexpected—a vulnerability, combined with a plea to be heard.

He glanced back at Alice and John, who were standing next to each other like assigned dates at a social—awkward and restless. He was more conscious and protective than she about how exposed she'd appeared to him in that moment.

He took Gail's arm again and resumed walking. "Talk to me."

She hesitated and addressed their shoes when she spoke. "It's hard to say."

He thought back a moment. "That I came to see you when you asked?"

"It's more than that." She looked into his face. "It's true what I said about being governor, and how much I love it."

"But . . ." he suggested.

She smiled ruefully. "The excitement, the workload, the having to make decisions that matter—it's amazing stuff."

Her voice trailed off and she looked away again. He let her deal with her thoughts without interruption.

"This isn't going to sound right," she finally said, so softly that he barely heard her.

"Try me," he urged.

"I miss you." She squeezed his forearm for emphasis as she explained, "Not us. I don't mean that. I mean, I do mean that . . . sort of." She laughed and shook her head. "Shit."

He tried helping her. "I'm on my own. And I heard you were, too, nowadays."

"Well," she conceded, "that's true. But I'm not suggesting that."

She stopped and faced him a second time, her expression making him wonder how credible her cover story was going to sound to her companions later. "Joe," she said. "We're best friends. We've both gone through hell at one point or another. It happens to people with our mileage. But somehow, through it all, I—at least—have always felt this connection to you. I felt it when you were with Lyn, and not because of longing or jealousy or loneliness, or any of that crap. It's just a permanent thing. Here." She tapped her chest. "I feel more complete knowing you're out there."

He nodded in recognition. "I know. I feel it, too."

Now it was her turn to resume walking, evidently lightened by what he'd said. "That's why I called. Why I had John head home this way. I needed to tell you that."

"What do you want to do with it?" he asked practically, his own emotions mothballed enough at the moment to make him feel more like an analyst than the ex-lover he was.

That approach seemed to be what she was seeking. "Nothing," she said almost happily. "Right now, I just want that back. You lost Lyn and I won the election, and somehow in the midst of it, we both lost each other."

She stared at him wonderingly. "Is that too much melodrama? I know it's a little crazy, but I'm really not asking for anything here. I just want to know that you're still in my life. That you're okay."

She stopped one last time and reached up to hold his face in her hands. "You're my shoreline, Joe, or some other stupid poetry line. I mean, I understand that you're sad and heartbroken and all the rest of it, but I need to know that you can still feel your feet on the ground. Can you do that?"

He gave her a half smile. "I can. I'm good."

She kissed his cheek. "Then I can do what I'm doing, and I think a lot of others can keep doing what they're doing, too. You do that—it's your gift—for more people than you probably know."

She turned in the direction they'd come from, causing John and Alice to part ways to let them pass, and said to Joe in a louder voice as they began retracing their steps, "So, tell me how your case is going."

Which he did, as he might have done to any close friend whose discretion he trusted, while not going into too much detail—

Including the assignment they'd planned for him later that night.

CHAPTER EIGHTEEN

"What the hell is the deal?"

Joe got back behind the wheel, adjusted the earbud slightly, and spoke softly into the mic taped inside his shirt collar. "Don't know. Did you hear the instructions?"

"Corner of Amity Street and University Drive in Amherst, yeah," Dan responded, sounding frustrated. "Floodlights, blindfolds, computer hookups, and now this. Is there any ransom movie these people haven't seen?"

"Apparently not," Joe replied, pulling away from the curb and the pay phone that he'd just used.

This was the fourth stop he'd been told to make after being instructed, as Bobby Schultz, on the LotsforLoot site, to be at a certain street corner at a certain time late that night. He'd been told that just after the first of the pay phones had begun ringing.

It hadn't actually been the usual TV or movie scenario, however, with the hero panting from place to place at a dead run, his imperiled sweetheart's life at stake. Nothing so dramatic. The reverse had been true. A couple of times, Joe had waited up to fifteen minutes for the phone to ring. If not for the same concerns that were bothering Dan Siegel, in fact, he might have been on the verge of boredom by now.

But not quite.

"What do you think?" Dan asked.

"Not much," Joe replied, looking as if he were muttering to himself. "But I'm not crazy about it. If they're this hinky, I may have to lose the earpiece."

"You can't do that" was Dan's blunt response.

"They may have scanners to pick up the frequency."

"Two people are dead, Joe. You are under my command here. You keep the earpiece, or you abort."

"You're still on my tail, aren't you?" Joe countered. "It's not like I'm flying solo."

Dan was unrelenting. "I said what I said, Joe."

"Okay. You're the boss."

But the wild hair that Joe covertly shared with Willy Kunkle was on the ascendant. Whether it was his meeting with Mina, who'd so reminded him of Lyn, or the frustration of being manipulated by a nemesis as elusive now as when they'd all started out, he wasn't sure. He did know that his patience was wearing thin, and his anxiety about Mina's safety was increasing. He'd seen the same look in Lyn's eye as he had in Mina's, when Lyn had taken on the task of discovering what had caused the deaths of her brother and father, years earlier. That entire adventure had been a near thing, and even so, he'd lost her, if to something unrelated. He barely knew Mina Carson, but he was determined that no such fate should befall her. Enough was enough.

He reached the assigned corner in Amherst and saw the pay phone reflected in the light from the nearby streetlamp—all but ignored in these cell-crazy times. The street was virtually empty at this time of night—two students walking hand in hand down the block; a pair of headlights in the distance.

He parked illegally, got out of Bobby Schultz's borrowed van, and loitered by the phone.

It rang eight minutes later.

"Can we get this done?" he asked irritably.

"All in good time," the electronically altered voice responded calmly. "Head down One sixteen. When you get to Potwine, on your left, pull over and locate a rock on the southeast corner with a red X painted on it."

"You're shitting me."

"Did you get that? Do you know what the southeast corner is?"

"Fuck you."

"This is your deal to screw up, Mr. Schultz. Your choice."

"I got it. I got it."

The phone went dead.

Amazed by this latest spy thriller twist, Joe returned to the van and found 116 south, heading out of Amherst, away from the lights, and toward Hampshire College.

"You get that?" he asked, as if speaking to his empty passenger seat.

"Roger. Any idea what's under the rock?"

"Right now? A treasure map and a flintlock pistol."

It wasn't either. Ten minutes later, Joe discovered a disposable cell phone, under the advertised rock.

"Shoulda known," he murmured, and opened it up.

"What?" Dan asked.

"Drop phone," he said. "Back to sit and wait."

But the phone buzzed almost immediately.

"What?" Joe asked in turn.

"Cheer up. We're almost there. Keep the phone and follow directions."

Joe resumed driving, the phone wedged into the crook of his neck.

"South on One sixteen," said the voice.

Joe started gaining speed, trusting that Dan would understand that he couldn't talk now that he was on an open phone.

"You go by Hampshire College yet?"

"Just," Joe told his guide.

"Good. When you reach Bay Road, go straight across and keep on One sixteen."

He did so, seeing no traffic to either side.

"I just crossed Bay," he said, keeping Dan up-to-date, although both he and the car had also been equipped with tracers.

"About three thousand feet down, slow down."

"Is this almost over?" he asked, staying true to his role.

"You see a road sign for Military Road?" was the response.

He did, right above a stop sign.

"Military Road," he repeated for Dan. "Got it. You want me to take it?"

"Yes."

He rolled into what was less a road and more of an odd-shaped parking area alongside a low-lying equipment shed and a wooden sign labeled DEPARTMENT OF CONSERVATION AND RECREATION BUREAU OF FOREST FIRE CONTROL. There were a few empty trucks sitting quietly in the yard.

"Keep going," he was told.

"To the end?" he asked.

"You'll find a gate there. Pull over, out of the way, and take your goods and this phone with you. You'll be on foot from here on."

"I'm not into hiking in the middle of the night," Joe complained. "And the gate's closed anyhow."

"Not entirely. Squeeze through at the edge and walk up the driveway."

Joe parked, got out, and paused at the gate to look around. The moon revealed strands of barbed wire topping the chain link, and a nearby pylon crowned with an ancient-looking surveillance camera, peering down at him like an enormous old bird of prey.

"What is this place? It's got cameras, for Christ's sake."

"They don't work anymore. It's an abandoned military base."

"Says who? Am I gonna get my ass shot off?"

The voice sounded a little testy for the first time. "You want to go home empty-handed? Go home."

"All right, all right," Joe groused, fitting through the narrow gap in the gate that had been left open for him. "Now what?"

"Just walk."

He glanced over his shoulder as he left the gate area and proceeded up the length of a broad paved combination of a parking lot and a very wide driveway. The camera stayed where it was, presumably sightlessly riveted by the facility's entrance.

To his left was a long, looming hill, curved like a gigantic bread loaf, paralleling the road and covered with grass. Its crest buttressed into a tree-covered mountain above it, which, in turn, disappeared into the night. Joe could barely make out what looked like several ventilation shafts about midway up the curvature, poking out of the hill into the moonlight.

"Where're we going?" he asked, his growing disquiet not play-acting.

"About a hundred yards ahead, to your left."

Mounted into the hillside was a double glass door. Joe stopped and studied it. He was reminded of those tiny shed entrances that could be seen along the edges of some cemeteries. People thought they contained tools and equipment—which they sometimes did—but he knew that where he came from, at least, they also held bodies in storage over the winter, in preparation for the spring thaw.

The comparison was not comforting.

"It looks locked," he said into the phone.

"It's not. Just for you."

"I don't like it. It's a dead end."

"It's an old bunker, Bobby, built in the late fifties for the Strategic Air Command. It was a backup command post they used to control our missiles and bombers. It's part of a college library now."

"A library?" he asked stupidly, once again feeling all too much in character.

"The college bought it for the storage. Forty thousand square feet. Nice quiet place to conduct our business. You want more history, or you want to get this over with?"

Still, Joe demurred, helped by Dan's whisper in his other ear. "Don't do it, Joe. I know this place. The guy's being straight. It's built to withstand a nuclear attack. There's one way in, one way out. Stay put."

"How'd you get a key?" Joe asked the voice.

"How did we get into the Summit House?" was the reply. "Everyone can be bought, Bobby. You want to do business, or you want to get lost? Now's the time."

Joe considered his dilemma. He knew that Dan was right: reassess and/or abort. Officer safety was the cardinal rule in law enforcement, fictional theatrical excesses notwithstanding. No assignment was worth your life.

And his life wasn't even being threatened—the guy on the phone was the one who was paranoid.

But there was still Mina, wandering around like the proverbial loose cannon and very much at risk, if and when she finally made contact with these very same people.

Mina, who reminded Joe so much of Lyn.

He walked up to the glass door and gave it a tentative pull. As it swung open, there was nothing but darkness ahead of him, and no sign of life.

He stepped inside.

"Joe? Joe?" came Dan's voice, but amid a growing crackling, as if from interference.

"You in?" the voice asked in his other ear, sounding surprisingly loud and clear.

Joe felt like the cartoon character with a devil on one shoulder and an angel on the other.

"I'm in," he said.

"There's a flashlight in front of you, in the middle of the floor."

He saw the dull glimmer of something shiny and cylindrical ahead. After retrieving it, he turned it on and found himself in a cramped, ugly lobby lined with faded historical photos of the bunker under construction, its walls thicker than any of the nearby laborers were tall. Joe had heard about some of these structures, the mother ship of them being Cheyenne Mountain, out west, where the military tracked and controlled the country's airborne nuclear arsenal during the Cold

War. He had no idea that there was one just outside Amherst, Massachusetts.

"Keep going forward, through the far door, and take the stairs up."

At once determined and fascinated, Joe forged on, and found the
static from the earbud abruptly rendered mute by the concrete, lead-
lined shell surrounding him.

He was on his own.

That realization did give him pause. Whoever was on the other
end of the phone had to have been aware of the building's abilities to
block radio transmissions—the fact that the cell was still working proved
it. They'd rigged things so that only their device would work.

They wanted him isolated.

So, what was different from the first encounter in Summit House?
This gang had been cautious there, too, and kept a scrupulous arm's
length, even running the risk of his going through all the guest bedrooms and collecting more than his allotment of cash. Of course, Joe
had assumed that some enforcement provision had been put in place
for precisely that kind of misbehavior—which implied that a similarly
lethal backup plan had been worked out for this scenario.

He kept climbing the concrete stairs, the sound of his footsteps
smacking off the hard walls like methodically thrown objects.

He wasn't happy. His instincts were in sympathy with Dan's, but
still he continued, stubborn in his need to gain some headway.

Upstairs, because of the lack of windows in this three-story building, lights had been turned on, allowing him to pocket the flashlight.
The effect remained unsettling, though, making him feel like a small
rodent inside the Hoover Dam. The ceilings towered overhead; the
hallways he was told to navigate were resonant, cold, and left him

feeling exposed. He was instructed to step through a door, and when he entered the biggest room he thought he'd ever seen, it was an impression he'd almost been anticipating.

The cavern he entered had maybe forty-foot high walls, which were proportionally balanced by an equally gigantic floorspace. On the wall behind him, halfway up, was a glassed-in balcony—really an observation booth, as at a high-end sports arena. In faded letters across its glass access door, the words SENIOR BATTLE STAFF ONLY were painted.

Joe felt ready for the ceiling to come off and reveal a huge, God-like, pink-faced scientist wearing glasses and a goatee.

Thankfully, all that happened was the familiar robotic voice saying, "Move to the table in the middle of the room."

He did so, stepping around several piles of crates. On the table was what looked like the same setup he'd seen on top of the mountain, complete with computer screen and small camera.

There was a click on the phone as it went dead.

"Sit down, Bobby," the computer said.

As he had at the Summit House, Joe placed his bag of offerings within view of the camera lens and saw himself on the screen as he sat.

"Who are you, Bobby?"

Joe sympathized with all the people he'd made uncomfortable during interrogations over the years, because he immediately felt his heart rate increase and his palms moisten at the question.

"What do you mean? I'm Bobby Schultz."

"And I'm Elmer Fudd. You have a lot of heavily armed friends, Bobby. How can you afford them?"

"What?"

"Beats me. I'd say they're cops, from their outfits, and they're pouring into this building like ants as we speak. Not very subtle. What were you hoping to accomplish? To suffer the same embarrassment you did last time? Congratulations. I think you succeeded."

The screen went dead.

Joe pressed his lips together and let out a puff of air, already hearing through the closed door the sounds of people getting closer. He waited patiently for Dan, the task-force members, and the local enlisted SWAT officers to join him—all parts of the backup Dan had insisted upon earlier.

No point adding his own death by friendly fire to this mess.

Dan, Joe, and Willy were all back at the Northampton police station, hours later, drinking coffee, when one of Dan's technicians from downstairs stuck his head into the windowless, stale-smelling room.

"Anything?" Dan asked without enthusiasm.

"Nope," the technician reported. "We ran the monitor, the camera, the transmitter, and even the wiring through every check we could think of. There's nothing to go on. No prints, no serial numbers, no area records of similar equipment being stolen. You name it, we tried it. All that stuff might as well have been dropped from the sky. Whoever you're dealing with knows how to cover their tracks."

"Thanks. Appreciate the effort."

"Sure thing, Chief."

Jimmy McAuliffe and Anne Pape were no longer among them, both having opted to go home. And from the look on Jimmy's face when he left, Joe hadn't been confident that they'd see him again on this case. Anne was more gung ho, but he'd already been surprised that her superiors hadn't pulled her in. There had still been nothing found linking Mickey Roma to Holyoke, other than the initial premise that he'd been dumped there to cover the killer's tracks.

"At least you didn't lose the GPS to these guys," Willy commented. "They're expensive."

Joe looked at him, eyebrows raised. "That's upbeat."

Willy smiled sarcastically and glanced at their host. "Hey, gotta throw the dog a bone."

Dan frowned. "Thanks. Any bright ideas about what to do now? I'll have checks run on everybody in the library system who's got a key to that place, but I doubt we'll get anything out of it. These folks are clever enough to have filched a key and copied it without its owner knowing."

Joe had been thinking about what else to do in the wake of their latest disappointment. "I'd like to finish that conversation we started with your pal David Cone."

"You think he's in on this?"

"I think he'd have good reason to be. He's in the business, he likes making money, he's clearly ruthless and ambitious, and he's got the best cover I know for dealing in hot jewelry and precious metals. I can't think of a reason not to put him under a microscope."

"And I didn't like his girlfriend," Willy said.

Joe jerked his thumb at his colleague. "You need any more reason than that?"

CHAPTER NINETEEN

He sat on the sofa beside her, his hands clasped in his lap, staring intently at the recording they'd made of the police entering the bunker turned library annex, captured through the building's old closed-circuit surveillance system, which they'd adapted for this purpose.

"Look at them," he said, his voice tight. "They're like Ninjas. Look at the guns."

"They're cops," she said scornfully. "Of course they have guns. What did you expect?"

He was shaking his head. "This is getting out of control."

"That's exactly what it isn't getting," she said sharply, twisting in her seat. She pointed at the recording. "They've got nothing right now—twice in a row—despite your screwups."

He faced her, his mouth half-open. "My screwups? What've I done wrong? I may've let the cop pull a fast one the first time, but otherwise, I'm the one who told you about them sniffing around, about the girl asking questions."

She rose abruptly and began pacing. She was struggling for self-control—traditionally not a strong point.

"You are not disciplined," she said calmly, addressing the floor at her feet. "You weren't brought up that way. It's not your fault. You're an artist, and you were indulged. Again, nothing you could do anything about."

She turned to face him, inspired by a line of thought. "Do you remember when we got together? Your frustration? Your sense that you'd never really achieved anything?"

His gaze slid away. He didn't answer.

"You had ambition," she said. "No real goals, but lots of ambition. That's what clicked between us. Do you remember that?"

He gave her a crooked smile. "I remember the sex," he said.

She quelled her anger and replaced it with a laugh. "And the first real money we made? That was right up there with the sex, wasn't it." She stated it as a fact. In truth, in her own memory, that was highly accurate—the best orgasm she'd ever had with this man had been on the night of their first major financial score.

But he was back to his original theme. "Haven't we made enough? We're doing well—better than we thought we would. You said we were way ahead of schedule."

She approached him and sat on the edge of the coffee table. "Honey, it's only a schedule. We're no way close to what we can do, and we're not in any trouble, either." She took up his hands in hers. "Didn't we talk about the risks from the start? Wasn't that part of the appeal? To build our own empire? To know what we could do, in real terms? Despite convention? Despite the law? Tell me honestly—don't you walk taller than you used to, before we began?"

Again, he didn't answer, but she could tell he was mulling it over. A teenager in arrested development, she thought, but a necessary ally. The schedule was one thing; her own grand plan was another.

But right now, she needed him back on track. She loosened her hand from his and slid it between his legs, smiling as she leaned in to kiss him. "And speaking of sex," she said, "it's been a while, hasn't it? Too much work, too little play? No wonder you're unhappy."

With her other hand, she deftly unbuttoned her blouse, slowly feeling him respond. There you go, she thought to herself as he reached up to fondle her breast. Just a little yank on the leash now and then. A small-enough price to pay.

Mina adjusted her position slightly, shoving at the bunched-up jacket behind her with her elbow to improve its cushioning effect. She'd had to park her car at an angle to Cone's rear loading dock—combining discretion with a good surveillance spot—but the trade-off had been to be wedged behind the wheel. Fine for the first half hour but a little hard on the body after triple that time.

Willy had no such complaints. Unknown to Mina or anyone else, he lay on his stomach near the edge of a flat shed roof, one story above her car, comfortable in the knowledge that he could stay put for over a day without complaint. For a man as driven and challenged as he, the discomforts of complete and utter stillness—where the mere act of breathing was a regretted, if necessary, compromise—came as a contradictory pleasure. It put him in as close as he ever got to a Zen-like state—overcoming his restless spirit with virtual invisibility.

It was the same with his home, as squared away as he was not; and his work, as obsessively thorough as he felt incomplete. It was also why he sketched, which only Joe knew about—and now Sammie, of course. It allowed him to lose himself in concentration.

He wasn't sketching now, though. He was in full view of anyone looking in his direction from a nearby window. Except that all they'd see was what looked like a ragged piece of tarp, discarded and forgotten, lying heaped, stained, and wrinkled on the roof. "Hiding in plain sight" was the common saying—certainly hiding where they least expected to find you.

He thought about Sammie now, as he had been for days, and little Emma. They were both in that house, he assumed, it being after working hours, with the light slowly fading. Sam would have relieved the sitter, and replaced the daily bottled breast milk with the real McCoy, no doubt to Emma's contentment. They'd be sitting in the rocker in the front room, Sam gazing out over the front lawn and the quiet horseshoe-shaped street beyond it.

True to Willy's psyche, however, the image filled him with tension, the two people within it altering the perfect, lifeless balance of the house, introducing influences at once spontaneous and uncontrollable. He loved them both—of that, he had no doubts. A man committed to shadows and deflection, and with personality so abrasive as to repel, he knew he would give his life for either person.

But his dual love for them and a compulsion for structured solitude were driving him to the edge of despair—a realization that only heightened his already-considerable self-loathing.

An approaching engine distracted Mina from her discomfort and made her slump farther down into her seat. An unlabeled van drove by, cut a three-corner turn in the lot, and stopped with its rear doors facing the loading dock.

This was of interest to both covert observers. UPS had already come by, along with a couple of clearly identified trucks bearing supplies, but this vehicle was different. It was older, nondescript, even worn and rusted to the point where no company would have chosen to be associated with it. To Willy, it was a clone of himself right now—something hiding in the open. To Mina, while it looked out of place, it also filled her with expectation, its uniqueness teasing her with the chance that she had maybe caught a scent in her hunt.

The driver, dressed casually in jeans and a T-shirt, swung out of the vehicle, walked around to the back, and threw open the rear doors. Leaning inside, he removed several cardboard boxes, one at a time, and placed them onto the dock behind him, handling them gently. After he was done, he slammed the doors, climbed onto the dock, and repeated the process, carrying each box inside. Both Mina and Willy noticed that the boxes were also unmarked and merely tucked shut, rather than taped, suggesting a local origin.

Five minutes later, the driver reappeared, jumped off the dock, slid behind the wheel, and aimed for the parking area's exit. As Mina started her car to follow, Willy slipped from under his tarp, vanished into a nearby open window, and ran through the building and down a flight of stairs to where he'd left his own vehicle. He reached it just as Mina pulled into traffic.

The small convoy worked its way through Northampton's thick early-evening traffic, forever compounded by people darting, starling-like, across the current, mostly oblivious to lights, crosswalks, or common sense. At the uphill section near Smith College, however, where Main briefly became Elm, things began opening up.

From then on, the three vehicles blended in with the flow. Northampton's downtown became scenic Florence, then Look Park, and finally

Leeds and the part of Northampton Township that was more woods and fields than residential blocks.

By then, Willy, from practiced habit, had killed his lights so as not to draw Mina's attention to her rearview mirror, the traffic having thinned enough to have made the three of them the only ones on the road. The faint residue of the dying day helped to keep him from hitting the ditch.

Once the van left what was now only marked "Rte. 9" and led the way down a narrow, unlabeled side road, however, the thick trees rendered any light moot. Now, Willy's safe passage was solely reliant on his instincts and training.

Nevertheless, he began murmuring protectively to Mina, "Come on, girl, either drop back or turn off your lights. The guy's not *that* dumb."

As if having heard him, Mina did slow, letting the van pull far ahead, but to Willy's thinking, it was already too late. There were no houses on the road, its surface had quickly turned to dirt, and its condition was deteriorating, telling him that this was either private property or little enough traveled to have transformed the mere sight of a pair of headlights into a warning.

They continued for about one more mile before Willy grew aware of Mina's slowing to a crawl. At this point, he took a calculated risk, quickly pulled his car around so that it faced the other way, and left it to continue his pursuit on foot. Even if he was wrong, he reasoned, and the caravan kept going, he'd have time to run back and become mobile again.

But his instincts proved sound. Jogging down a few hundred yards brought him to Mina's car, dark and empty by the side of the road, within sight of a large, hulking, ancient building that blended with the blackness of the surrounding woods like a set designer's vision of No-ah's lost and abandoned ark.

Parked before it was the van they'd been following, caught in the halo of a single overhead light that looked like a cross between the rusty sculpture of a swan and a dinner plate-size showerhead.

There was no one in sight.

Willy soundlessly negotiated his approach to the building, pre-sumably an old factory left to rot, and surveyed what he was facing. The place was long and narrow, two stories high, and so pressed in by trees on both long sides as to make the exposure facing him the only way in.

It was also not empty, not that he'd had any doubts. But his gut told him that there were far more people inside than simply Mina and the van's driver. There was a muted sound of activity somewhere above him, and—now that he was close enough to see it—a leakage of light overhead from between the shriveled wallboards.

Finding at last a small side entrance just off the double doors, Willy worked its metal latch as stealthily as possible. True to character, it didn't occur to him to call for backup.

Once inside, he found what Lǐ Anming had discovered before him—a long, dark, neglected passageway running the full length of the building, leading toward a quasi-ghostly source of light. The wooden floor was covered in dirt and debris, including a scattering of small ob-jects plentiful and odd enough that Willy stooped to pick one up. It was, he recognized after a moment, a wooden bobbin.

Stepping carefully to avoid sending any of these artifacts skittering across the floor, Willy made his way past a series of closed doors and open overhead traps, pausing at each to rule out an attack from be-hind.

But he was becoming distracted by a growing commotion up ahead, seeing shifting shadows and hearing muffled voices, among which he could recognize a young woman's.

A couple of hundred feet farther in, he was able to distinguish a scene reminiscent of a horror show. Before him, gathered under the light that had earlier drawn his notice, and located at the base of what appeared to be a tower shaft at the corridor's end, Mina Carson was being held on the ground by the driver of the van, looking like a wife of Henry VIII being readied for execution. The light, supplied by two out-of-sight spotlights high above, shot down the length of a rusty guillotine worthy of the Dark Ages. Directly below it, right beside where Mina was being pinned to the filthy floor, there was a much-scarred and battered platform, where the huge blades were designed to drop.

Standing off to one side of the limelight was an elegant, slim woman, perhaps in her late thirties, and a slightly younger man, also skinny, well dressed, and looking distinctly ill at ease.

The man holding Mina down was speaking quietly to her. "Come on, bitch. Who the fuck are you?"

Willy took advantage of the action to slide along the shadowy wall to get closer.

He heard the well-dressed woman ask her companion, "Is that her?"

He nodded, his face pale.

"You better start talking, young woman," she said to Mina. "You're not going to like what Ed wants to do with this thing."

"I have nothing to say to you," Mina managed to say, half her face pushed into the floor.

The man called Ed knelt down, forcing his right knee between Mina's legs and jamming it up into her crotch, causing her to cry out.

"You know I saw you in the parking lot, right? Slumped down in your car like you were invisible? So, talk or I cut you. That simple. Who are you?"

"To hell with you," Mina said.

Willy slipped his cell phone out, shielded its screen with his turned body, and began sending a text message.

"Show her," ordered the woman.

"Oh," began the pale man. "Why do we—"

But she cut him off. "Go ahead, Ed."

Ed rose once more, flipped Mina over without effort, seized the front of her shirt, ripping it slightly, and dragged her up onto the edge of the platform. Keeping her clear of its center, he placed a chunk of nearby wood into the target zone, reached out for a lever, and let the looming bladed contraption high above drop with a thunderous crash. Its blades pulverized the stump of wood, sending shards flying in all directions, and making the two observers step back in reaction.

Ed merely laughed as Mina screamed out, having twisted her face away to avoid being hit.

Willy took that opportunity to step out into the light, his gun drawn. *"Do not move,"* he ordered. *"Police."*

All faces turned toward him in unison, including Mina, who was trying to hold her shirt together with one hand.

After a slow count of several seconds, Ed called out into the gloom, "That's it?"

"Want me to blow your fucking head off?" Willy asked back. "Get down on the ground, asshole, hands behind your head."

Ed slowly began to comply, talking as he went to his knees, one at a time. "Don't know, Holmes. You're sounding pretty lonely."

Willy couldn't argue with that. But he never got the chance. He felt more than heard the slightest movement behind him, began turning to face it, and caught a single explosive blow to the side of his head before everything vanished in a flash.

Ed returned to his feet at the sound of Willy dropping, smiling back at the woman in charge, whose eyes were wide and wondering at this sudden double turn of events.

"I had Miguel scout around after the little bitch dropped in," he explained. "I figured she might have company."

"But he's a cop," the woman's companion said in a cracked voice.

Ed laughed. "That he is. Or was." He called out, "Yo, Miguel. You do him?"

"He's done," came the response.

"And so are we," the woman said sharply, back in command, her shock already past. "Ed," she ordered. "Remember that evacuation plan we practiced and you hated? Now's the time. Everyone out; everything personal collected and removed. You got five minutes. *Now*."

Ed didn't hesitate, running upstairs to gather the workers, the piece-work, and whatever else they'd been trained to have ready for fast extraction. Despite her being a woman, the broad was okay in his book; she reminded him of the better sergeants he'd had in the service—organized, standoffish, and hard, but ready to be the first in a fight and tougher than anyone in the unit.

In the meantime, still standing by the guillotine, the timid man remained rooted in place. "He's dead?" he asked, incredulous. "He killed him?"

"It's over," the woman said harshly. "Get out to the car and wait for me. I parked it farther down the road, out of sight."

"You *knew* this was going to happen?" he demanded shrilly.

She took him by his shoulders and stared at him. "I knew the girl was in play, but not about him. It doesn't matter. We'll deal with it later. Get to the car and wait. Please."

She let him go, turned him slightly, and gave him a gentle shove toward the dark corridor and the front entrance beyond. "Go."

He walked in a daze, giving wide berth to Willy's motionless shape sprawled in the dirt, his head haloed in blood.

The woman watched him for three seconds, making sure that he was placing one foot before the other, and then took to the wooden stairs against the wall, calling down to Miguel as she went. "Take her to the van and tie her up. Gag her, too."

Miguel looked down at the wide-eyed Mina. "With pleasure."

It took barely five minutes, as planned, before everyone was headed toward the door, laden with whatever boxes and bags Ed had distributed. As they walked by Willy in single file, Lǐ Anming paused a half step to look down at him, only to be shoved along by Ed. "Step on it, Amy, or you'll end up the same way."

Ed made sure they were doing as told before stopping to look back at the boss. He gestured to the body. "What do we do with him?"

"Nothing." She gestured to him with a wave of her hand, stressing, "Keep going."

He looked surprised but complied. "We leave him here?"

"We don't have a choice. We have to assume that he called for backup, and that they're a minute or two away."

"But he's a cop. They'll go batshit finding him here."

"Ed," she said. "They'll go batshit anyhow. We planned for this—there is nothing in this building that connects it to us. That was the whole point. Would it be nice to plant him someplace neutral? Sure. Do we have time? No." She paused. "You hear that?"

Sirens were approaching from far off. Both the woman and Ed

broke into a run, she still giving orders. "We use the back way to get out. I'll lead. Drive normally. When you get to town, put the van in the garage."

"Where the hell're we going?" Joe asked anxiously.

Dan Siegel was in the front passenger seat. One of his officers, in black armored vest, was driving the SUV. Behind them were three more vehicles carrying a rapidly assembled and loosely organized response team.

"There's an abandoned factory down here. I don't even know if it's standing anymore. But that's where his GPS is signaling from."

"If it's still attached to either him or his phone," Joe said dourly.

"You thinking this is a diversion or something?" Dan asked.

"I hope it is," Joe said quietly, thinking back to the text they'd received minutes earlier: "Need you. NOW."

What Joe wasn't explaining was that Willy had never issued an SOS in all the years he had known him. It was a matter of pride. The man was a self-contained, self-appointed army of one—fearless and contemptuous of help.

What had gone wrong? He tried dialing Willy's cell for the twentieth time, to no avail.

"There's his car," Joe said as they passed by.

"And that's probably the Carson girl's," Dan commented as they drew abreast of it.

"Here we are," he said in the same breath, studying the screen of the tracking device in his lap. "We're officially on top of the phone, if nothing else."

The vehicles fanned out, and everyone exited tactically, guns drawn, running to cover as quickly as possible. Joe and Dan, also clad in black vests, kept to the middle of the pack, letting the special-weapons folks do what they did best.

Five minutes later, one of the entry team appeared at the front door they'd just breached. He looked directly at Joe. "We're still clearing the upstairs, but we found your man. I'm sorry."

Joe stared at him speechlessly for a moment before stepping through the entrance. "Where?" he asked, his voice strangled.

"Down near the end. Follow the light."

Joe ran, the implication unbearable, dread hitting like water breaking from a dam. He aimed for where he could see a couple of men kneeling in the darkness, their backs bent in hard labor, their outlines sharp against the bright light beyond.

He stopped beside them, breathing hard, not saying a word. They had a medical kit open between them and were working with cool dispatch.

One of them looked up. Joe's expression formed the unutterable question.

"We have a pulse," he said. "It's weak, but it's there."

Joe reached out with one hand as his legs grew wobbly beneath him, and he sat in the dirt like a marathoner on his last breath.

"Come on, man," he murmured, hoping that a whisper would somehow get through to both Willy nearby and his family, miles off. "Now's the time to be pigheaded."

CHAPTER TWENTY

"What're you doing back here?" Dan asked.

"Nothing I can do at the hospital. Not right now," Joe replied.

"You could catch some shut-eye. You look like hell."

"What've we got?" Joe said deflecting the attention from himself.

Dan picked up a set of keys from his desk. "Off to search Mina's hotel room. Wanna come?"

Joe didn't answer, instead levering himself off the chair he'd just occupied.

Dan collected two waiting detectives on the way out. They didn't bother with a car, being located so near the hotel. The town was almost deserted, the bars and restaurants having closed hours earlier. Northampton was never a place to empty out completely, however, so a few passersby paused to watch the foursome in ties and jackets, striding purposefully down the darkened street. Joe fantasized briefly about the long arm of the law that he'd read about as a kid, personified by men in plainclothes, intent on righting wrongs.

He was that, at least, even if freshly reminded of his own limitations.

They made quick work of serving the warrant and getting the master key, riding up in the elevator only minutes after entering the hotel.

"How's he doing?" Dan asked at last.

"I don't know what they call it," Joe told him. "It's like an induced coma. He's alive, anyhow. They want him out so the brain swelling can run its course."

"They give him a chance, though, right?"

"They don't know," Joe said tersely. "They're helping him to breathe."

The doors opened and Dan let it drop, leading the way down the hallway to the correct number. He worked the key card and pushed open the door.

The four of them paused, taking in the room. It was a standard layout, and Mina had done little to disturb it—aside from cluttering the desk near the window.

Dan turned to his men. "Greg, take the bathroom; Mike, the bed and night tables. Go slow and careful."

Everyone put on gloves. Dan and Joe moved to the desk. Scattered around an open but extinguished laptop computer were a pad, Post-it notes, several scraps of paper, photographs of Northampton, and a single pendant featuring a delicate cameo in its center.

"I'm going to leave the computer for the techies," Dan said. "There's no way I won't screw it up if I touch it."

Joe was already scanning the other material. "Works for me."

Dan read from the legal pad. "A hit list of dealers, pawnshops, art stores, and jewelers," he said. "From the check marks, looks like she contacted every one of them."

"Yeah," Joe commented. "But she only really liked one."

He showed him a photo featuring the Cone Heirlooms flagship store, adding, "About eighty percent of everything in her notes relates to Cone, including the receipt for this." He held up the pendant.

"He is the biggest player in town," Dan said reasonably. "We gave him the most attention, too."

"Not this kind," Joe said, displaying a list on which was written "Find covert factory. Who does the work?"

Both men looked at each other, the old building where they'd found Willy's near-lifeless body fresh in their memories.

"You said that your search team found a bunch of workstations on the top floor," Joe said.

"Maybe," Dan agreed. "There were cubicles that could've been used for that—signs of soldering, remnants of precious metals. I've got forensics in there now."

Joe poked at the pendant. "Old meets new. You think they could match whatever they're finding to the solder that was used to make that?"

Dan nodded thoughtfully. "I'll sure as hell ask them."

Joe stared at the desk for a moment before looking at his friend, his expression hard. "I need to talk to Cone again. I'm running out of patience with these people."

Sammie sat in the dark, listening to the sounds that a hospital emits with the regularity of the heartbeats within it. There were muted chimes, gentle announcements, the mutterings of nearby TV sets, the occasional phone, passing footsteps. Closer by, hooked to Willy's startlingly still body, were humming instruments, pinging now and then, wheezing in time with a bellows-type machine that looked better suited to the nineteenth century. By contrast, the dripping that she could see in the small IV chamber by his head was soundless.

Like the man she couldn't stop watching.

She hadn't been alone with him for long. Joe had been with her from the moment she'd arrived to when she'd virtually thrown him out to pursue who'd done this.

Now, at last, it was just the two of them. Three, actually. She'd brought Emma, after getting the okay from the doc. She was fast asleep at the moment, on the floor in a portable crib.

Sam was gauging her emotions as Willy's monitors were judging his vitals. How was she feeling? What was she feeling? For the most part, she was used to this solitary approach. Predictably, Willy was lousy at heartfelt emotional exchanges. In truth, she conceded, he wasn't much different now from when he was conscious—aside from the thick wad of bandages protecting the entire side of his head.

She was more inclined to explore the turmoils inside herself, anyhow. She felt strong emotions most of the time—anger, love, vengefulness, outrage, passion. And bewilderment. Especially the bewilderment.

What was she supposed to do now? Resign herself? Hold out hope? And if the latter, for what? Lately, Willy had been as much company as the chair she was sitting in, if less useful. He'd been stalking around, occupying rooms she'd just vacated, leaving the house as she'd arrived. His usual pent-up emotional confusion, always present in his eyes, had gone from sarcasm to gloom, and while the former could be homicidally irritating on occasion, the latter had left her feeling carved out and empty.

The man was no laughfest, but he was honest and straight and more loyal than a Doberman, and sensitive without being open about it. And so smart as to be scary.

But he was scaring her now.

What had he been doing? Why had he proceeded the way he had? He was impulsive—an iconoclast and a rebel. But rarely self-destructively reckless, especially since he'd curbed his larger demons of alcoholism and PTSD. And the man owned his responsibilities like armor—like others held a deity, or devotion to a cause.

Sammie glanced at their daughter. How could he have risked abandoning the love of his life? And how did Sam feel about it?

Or was she misreading it all, since the two of them had never openly discussed any of this?

She studied the slow mechanical action of his chest rising and falling like the machine it had become.

"Come back," she said, just loudly enough that he could hear her. "I miss you."

Joe gave Dan Siegel a lot of credit. This was his town, David Cone was his friend and occasional adviser, and Joe wasn't even a cop in Massachusetts. Nevertheless, when the two of them visited Cone's office once more, Siegel didn't hesitate to let Joe take the lead, nor did he complain at his hard tone of voice upon entering.

"Mr. Cone," Joe said. "We need to talk."

Cone looked up from his desk and smiled at them. "Of course. Good to see you again. I heard on the radio that one of your officers was hurt. Is he all right?"

"No."

"Oh." Cone hesitated as the two men remained standing, unsmiling.

He joined them awkwardly, pushing back his chair to do so. "Can I offer you something to drink?"

"It's not that kind of conversation," Joe told him. "And we'd like it to take place at the PD. You're free to refuse if you choose."

Cone's mouth opened. "Free to . . . No. I mean, of course. Why not here?"

Siegel's body language suggested hesitation, but Joe responded immediately. "There's something we want you to see."

"Well, then." Cone glanced back down at the paperwork he'd abandoned. "I guess this can wait. Sure." He shook his head slightly and then put his trademark smile back in place, spreading his hands. "Great. All right, gentlemen. I'm at your disposal."

It didn't take them long, even on foot. Nevertheless, Cone quickly realized from the general demeanor that the walk was going to take place in silence.

They escorted him to a room with no windows, three chairs, and a metal table bolted to the wall.

"Sit," Joe said. Not quite an order, but certainly no friendly invitation.

Cone sat, his expression by now openly concerned.

"Is everything okay?" he asked.

Joe sat opposite him as Dan remained standing by the closed door.

"What do you think?" Joe asked him.

"Well. I know you have a man hurt, like I said. I guess I meant with me. I'm a little confused."

"Mr. Cone," Joe addressed him. "How well do you know your business?"

Cone smiled wonderingly. "I've been at it long enough. Pretty well, I'd say."

"Your own business," Joe specified. "Cone Heirlooms. Are you aware of all its aspects?"

"Sure," he said. "I told you I was stepping back. Others run the day-to-day affairs. But I come in every morning."

"So it's safe to say that whether it's the Chinese factory or the flag-ship showroom, or a store in California or Florida, you have a good idea of what's going on?" Joe had been doing his homework—as well as working on Mina's disappearance, sitting by Willy's bedside, and avoiding sleep altogether. He was exhausted, anxious, and by now very angry.

Cone switched his gaze to Siegel. "Dan. Do I need a lawyer here?"

"Are you asking for one?" Joe demanded.

"I'm asking if I'm in trouble. I thought we were all on the same side. It sure felt that way before."

"Mr. Cone," Joe said. "You can put yourself on the other side of the fence from us and get a lawyer if you want to. You can walk out of here and stop being cooperative. It's your choice. We're looking for answers, and we're running short of time and patience."

"I'm happy to help," Cone stressed. "I just couldn't tell from your tone what was going on."

"To be clear, then, you do not want a lawyer?"

Cone's eyes moved from one to the other. "No. No, it's fine. I guess."

Joe pulled out the pendant that they'd discovered in Mina's hotel room, along with its receipt. He placed it on the table before the jew-eler. "Recognize this?"

Cone picked it up and studied it appraisingly. "It's well made. An antique piece married to a modern one. It's new, too, or rarely worn. You can tell from the chain and clasp. They pick up a worn quality from being rubbed against a woman's skin after a while." He smiled and added, "It's a kind of intimacy most people don't think about—the exchange between a woman and the gold she touches."

"Did you make it?" Joe's voice showed he wasn't feeling the romance.

Cone sat back and laughed briefly, the pendant still dangling from his fingers. "I don't know who made it. We might have. We mark our larger pieces with a tiny stamp, but something like this is so delicate . . ." He left the sentence unfinished.

Joe dropped the receipt before him. "That help?"

Cone picked it up. "It fits," he said. "Good price, too, if I do say so. It's a Cone Studio piece. That explains it. They tend to be more off-beat. They're all originals. Makes them a little more expensive, some-times."

"Tell us about the Cone Studio."

Cone looked a little uncomfortable. "It's just another branch of the business. You know, it's like any big operation. Who was it who had the Jane Seymour line? And the Jaclyn Smith line? It's kind of like that. We do contemporary, and classic—"

Joe chose to interpret the man's patter as a smoke screen and cut him off by slapping his hand on the tabletop. "Enough."

Cone bobbed his head several times nervously. "Right. Right. Sorry. It's something we do out of Northampton only—and through the In-ternet, of course, like everything else. Sort of honoring the tradition that I began when I was selling off the street corner."

Joe glanced at Dan before asking, "Where's the studio located?" None of the vastly enlarged forensic team they currently had scouring the abandoned bobbin factory—along with several more poring over the town clerk's files—had been able to connect the building or the workshop within it to anyone or anything yet.

But David Cone was not going to help there, either, it seemed. He was shaking his head, as if he'd just spilled water all over the floor. "I'm sorry. I know it sounds stupid, but I can't tell you."

Joe half-rose in his seat and leaned into the man's face. "David. I'm not interested in your little trade secrets—"

This time, the roles were reversed by Cone interrupting Joe with a frantic waving of both hands. "No, no. That's not what I meant. I've never been to it. I'm not involved. They won't let me."

There was a startled silence in the room, which Dan broke by speaking for the first time. "They won't let you? Who won't?"

Cone's face reddened and he stared at the floor silently. Joe took advantage of the pause to rethink some of the theories he'd entertained while taking his crash course in all things David Cone over the past twenty-four hours.

"Dave," he said in a softer voice. "I think I know what's going on. It's brutal when the people next in line put the founder out to pasture. You are Cone Heirlooms, after all."

Cone didn't respond, confirming Joe's guess.

"Except that you aren't, are you?" he added.

Cone shook his head without comment.

"Is it Donna?"

He sat back in his chair, looking tired and wan. "Partly."

"You introduced her as your companion and colleague when we met," Joe reminded him.

"More like my nanny," Cone said bitterly.

"How long's this been going on?" Dan asked, his voice betraying surprise.

"Years."

Joe compared this tidbit with his newly acquired knowledge. "She doesn't surface much in the company paperwork," he observed. "Not in any executive capacity."

"Leave that to Elizabeth Walker," Cone muttered, mostly to himself.

"Who?" asked Dan, who prided himself on knowing every mover and shaker in town.

"She calls herself Els," Cone explained.

Dan's eyebrows rose. "Els Walker? I thought she worked for the college."

"That's her day job," was Cone's terse response.

Joe scowled at Cone's misery, beginning to sense where this might be going. "Look at me, Dave," he ordered.

Cone glanced up without enthusiasm.

"You've been screwed," Joe said harshly. "We get that. You've been reduced to a figurehead in your own company, pretending to know what's going on and having no clue. Well, from where I'm sitting, that's probably a good thing, 'cause when the shit hits the fan and we start throwing people in jail, you can say you were totally ignorant. Am I right?"

Dan cast his colleague a look for perhaps saying too much, but David Cone underwent a change in expression.

"People are going to jail?"

Joe got up and began pacing the room, his mounting frustration pushing against his weariness. "Goddamn it, Dave, put it together. Do you honestly think they stuck you in a box because they wanted to start a jewelry line? Why the hell don't you know where the studio is? Didn't you ever wonder about that?"

In an abrupt, violent gesture, he strode over to Cone and shoved his face two inches from the other man's, giving in to pure, unbridled rage—visions of Lyn and Mina and Willy and even tiny Emma all floating in his head. "*Talk to me*, you stupid bastard," he yelled at him. "I got a man in a coma, hanging on by a thread. I don't give a flying fuck about your pride or your lost memories. You're an aging egomaniac being jerked around by his dick. Cry me a river. You're the one person who's gonna come out fine at the end of this mess. I need to know what the fuck is going on, Dave."

The options were there for the choosing—Cone could have hit him, pushed him away, yelled back, demanded to be let go, or even appealed to his old friend Dan, who was still standing by the door, by now staring, astonished, at a Joe Gunther he'd never seen.

Instead, Cone merely said, "It's my son."

Joe straightened to stare at him. "Your son? What son? I know you have family in the company . . ."

"Brandon," Cone explained. "He's a silent partner. Els came up with it. She's obsessed with secrecy, even when there's no need for it."

Joe, of course, was already thinking that she might have had all the need in the world for secrecy.

He sat down again, his temper back under control, and requested quietly, "Okay, so who really runs the company? In simple terms."

"My son Brandon, in theory, although not visibly in any public paperwork—which we can do more easily because we're family-owned—and Els Walker, who holds his leash. Els is the real power broker, even though she's not actually on the payroll. Donna just gets paid by them to keep an eye on me."

For all his anger moments earlier, Joe had a pang of sympathy at hearing Cone's choice of words. They really had reduced him to a show dog.

A dog with knowledge, nevertheless.

Joe shifted his chair, made himself comfortable, and crossed his legs.

"All right. Now that all the cards are faceup, take us through the deck."

CHAPTER TWENTY-ONE

Brandon Cone was seriously drunk. He sat unsteadily on a stool thankfully equipped with a back, his elbows on the pale wooden counter separating the ultramodern kitchen from the high-ceilinged, meticulously decorated living room in the house that he shared—or was sometimes permitted to share—with Els.

At the moment, she was stalking around the room in frozen silence, having just walked in on him in his inebriated state.

He knew that he was in deep shit—again—and was once more lost as to why.

But in a broader, more meaningful context, he was convinced that he would shortly be living in a prison cell—if he got so lucky. That explained the almost empty bottle of single-malt scotch before him.

"I don't believe you," he heard her finally mutter as she swept by within earshot.

He thought it best not to respond.

It didn't work. On her next rotation, she stopped across the counter from him and placed both hands on its surface—palms flat, fingers spread out. He noticed how perfectly her nails were painted and buffed, as always—complete with cuticles immaculately trimmed. He resisted the urge to reach out and touch them, as he might have the hands of a marble statue in a museum.

"Focus," she commanded.

He considered that for a moment.

"Look at me, Brandon," she tried, her voice as calm as the eye of a hurricane.

Wearily, he complied.

"What is your problem?" she asked.

That caught him off guard. "My problem?" he asked. He carefully reached up and scratched his hairline, too numb to actually feel the effect. "I guess it's that I'll be in jail soon."

"And why would that be?"

He studied her face, looking for signs of lunacy. Her affect was suspiciously measured, like a mother's giving counsel—hardly the woman he knew from long experience.

"We killed a cop?" he asked as a question.

"Who killed a cop?" she asked in turn.

He thought he glimpsed a glimmer of insight. "Ah. Right. Miguel killed him."

"No," she said with theatrical patience, drawing out the word. "Nobody killed him, or at least nobody they'll ever find." She leaned forward, so that he could feel her breath against his face, as she added, "*If we all keep cool and quiet. And*"—she cupped his chin in her hand—"*if we don't do stupid things like get drunk and cry in our soup about how we're going to jail. Right?*"

He tried nodding but found her grip too steely. "Right," he mumbled with difficulty.

But then he remembered something else amid the fog in his head and pulled free of her grip. "But what about the girl? And what do we do with the workers? And the safe house? What about the whole Cone Studio operation?"

Against his will, his voice had risen through the succession of questions, causing her to tap his cheek with what fell just shy of a slap.

"Be quiet," she ordered. "It's all under control."

He was beginning to rally from his stupor and straightened unsteadily on the stool. "It's not *feeling* under control, Els."

Her eyes assumed the slightly feline look he was used to as she said, no longer so maternally, "That's because, *Brandon*, you have no fucking clue what's going on. You never have. You're the brainless son of a minor street artist who compensated for *his* shortcomings with a good sense of timing and a taste for the jugular—before he turned into a senile lecher."

She paused to take a breath, dropped Brandon's chin, and pushed away from the counter to resume her pacing.

"Look in the mirror when you're sober again," she recommended. "And ask yourself if you or your dad would be where you are without me."

"I'm not ungrateful, Els," he protested. "That's not what I'm saying."

She stopped in the middle of the room to face him, her body tense. "It's not? Of course it is. You and everyone else. 'Els was born without a care in the world. She has looks; she must be dumb. You want to go to college? You want to major in art? You'll never find a good husband if you hang out with artists. Thank you, Els, now run along and get a life—Mommy's busy.'" Her face had become increas-

ingly red throughout, and now she shouted at him, "Well, *fuck you all.*
I have a life and I've done good work and I've made both David and
you a fortune, and it won't be long before I tell all of you to kiss my ass
good-bye."

Brandon rubbed his eyes with both palms, having heard all this before, many times, and hoping to ward off the rest of her familiar rant.
"I'm just saying we've done some superbad things here. This is not like
being blown off by your mom."

She bolted from her spot like a sprinter from the blocks and came
at him around the end of the counter with her arms extended and her
claws out. He lurched upright, pulled the stool out from under him,
and held it up to ward her off.

"*You cock bastard,*" she screamed. "After all I've done for you. You
lazy prick. I *made* you."

His tactic worked. She became tangled up in the stool's legs, giving
him enough leverage to twist her to one side and pin her against the
refrigerator, where, panting, she deflated almost as quickly as she'd
blown up.

He knew the signs. They'd been here before. In fact—he had to
admit even at moments like this—her violence was one of the things
that attracted him to her.

He slowly and carefully lowered the stool, placing it beside her so
that she could slump onto it sideways, bracing her back against the
fridge and propping one arm on the stool's curved back.

"You are a total jerk," she said softly.

"I know I am," he said appeasingly. "And I know what you've done
for us. But I don't always get the big picture, either. You kind of hang
on to that."

She sighed. "The bobbin factory might as well have been sterilized, for all we left behind. That was the plan from the start. Don't you remember? The whole idea of using someplace that could never be traced back to us? Same for the whole operation."

The alcohol was still fogging his mind. "But that was for when the authorities came to check for stolen jewelry, Els. Not a dead cop and a kidnapped girl. This couldn't get any more serious."

"The firewalls remain the same for us," she insisted stubbornly. "That's the design."

"So we keep the girl in some basement? For how long?"

She flared up at that, glaring at him and straightening her back. "You're a real asshole, you know that? Maybe we should put little Miss Mina and you on a desert island and you can figure it all out on your own. We all know you need the practice."

He remained silent, thinking that it was lowly little Miss Mina who'd burned right through the firewalls by driving up to the bobbin factory's front door, complete with cop in tow.

"We'll just get rid of her," Els said offhandedly.

Brandon rubbed his aching forehead.

"Aren't we going home?" Donna asked, looking out of the car windows.

"We will," David told her. "Time for that little surprise first."

She smiled and said in an artificially girlish voice, "Ooh. I forgot and I love surprises." After a pause, she added, watching King Street's unromantic and commercial landscape sweep by, "Kind of a weird neighborhood for it, though."

He pulled into the parking lot of a motel, grateful to be almost free of this imposed acting job. He might not have liked how Donna had entered his life, but he knew all too well that under normal circumstances at his age, he'd be hard-pressed to get a woman like her on his arm without paying for the privilege. It was yet another of his life's contradictions that while he'd rued how his handler had come to him, he now loved what they'd become.

She was obviously enjoying herself now, for example, and was clear in her chosen course. It had been her decision to make their arrangement work on all levels, to the satisfaction of everyone. Suggesting a steady diet of Viagra to David early on had only sweetened the financial pie being supplied by Els and Brandon, and had certainly made keeping him in line more pleasurable. And that had been just the beginning.

She reached out and rubbed his inner thigh with her hand. "Did you include a blue pill with dinner? You sly dog."

He pulled up to one of the numbered doors ahead, killed the engine, and said flatly, "Didn't see the point with tonight's menu." He then smiled at her. "But you have a one-track mind, don't you? Ready?"

She laughed. "Absolutely."

He didn't need a key. He turned the knob, swung back the door, and ushered her inside the room—in one gesture bidding farewell to the original premise of their relationship.

He didn't enter with her. With the abruptness of an unexpected blow, she found herself with the door closed behind her, David on the outside, and two men in ties standing before her.

She twisted around at the click of the latch. "What the—" She reached out to touch the door's flimsy surface, as if waving good-bye to a departing lifeboat.

"Donna Hawkins?" asked one of the men.

She turned back to face them, her heart beating rapidly, acting ignorant. "Who're you?"

"Good news or bad," said one of them. "You get to choose."

"We're the police, Ms. Hawkins," the other one said. "Don't you remember? And you're in deep trouble."

She did know them, of course, and worried for a moment that she should have said as much. Keep on your toes, she thought.

The first one, Joe Gunther, indicated a chair by the drawn curtains. The room's beds had been shoved against the far wall. The chair in question had been set up opposite a video recorder on a tripod, facing a bright light.

"Sit down."

It wasn't a request. She sat, the camera's presence at once unexpected and disturbing.

"Sure, I remember—Joe and Dan. What do you want?" she asked, looking from one to the other and squinting slightly against the light—purposefully positioned to make her uncomfortable.

They also sat, outside of the glare. "Well," said Joe, "this is for the record anyhow, so I'm Joe Gunther, of the Vermont Bureau of Investigation, and this is Chief Siegel, of the Northampton police. We are hoping you'll help us with some information."

She blinked. She liked his manner, and now that she was over the initial encounter, she was reading their approach as nonthreatening overall.

"About what?" she asked cautiously.

"First things first," Gunther explained. "You are not under arrest, nor are you being held against your will. Your coming here tonight was a surprise, I know, and we apologize for our methods, but please understand that we are doing this as much for your protection as for reasons of our own."

She processed that without comment. He talked fancier than any cop she'd met, and he had a slightly funny accent that she liked.

"You should also understand," he went on, "that you are free to go anytime you wish, or to call a lawyer should you want one." He kept talking without hesitation, pointing to the camera. "Is it all right if we use this, by the way? I'm not aging too gracefully—at least my memory isn't—and I don't want anything that might be said tonight to be misconstrued or overlooked."

She furrowed her brows slightly, to Joe's private satisfaction, and finally nodded once. "Sure."

Gunther settled back into his chair. "Great. Thank you."

"You said I was in trouble," she said to the chief, who hadn't uttered a word beyond that.

Joe answered for him, while Dan merely kept staring at her—good cop/mute cop. "You definitely could be. You're right on the edge. That's why we wanted to talk to you now, and why we had to talk to you off the grid, so to speak."

"'Off the grid'? I don't get it."

Joe gave her a sympathetic smile. "Well, of course. Or I should say, of course you'd say that now. What you can't be expected to know is that we found out about your arrangement with Els and Brandon." He gestured vaguely at the room's front door. "That's why David dropped you off." He lowered his voice to drive home his point. "You're only in trouble, Donna, if you keep saying things like 'I don't get it.' Now's the time either to come clean or go to jail with your pals. Not too complicated."

She studied them both, feeling the weightiness of her options. "I talk to you or I go to jail?"

"Yup."

"Meaning if I do talk, then I don't go to jail?"

"Could be."

Not the most comforting answer, but she didn't react to it, nodding instead as if she were reading reams of fine print.

"Okay. What d'you want to know?"

"First, a show of faith. Tell us what we've already learned. Describe the arrangement between you and Els and Brandon."

"You just did that."

"Humor us."

She made a face. "Can I smoke?"

"It's a no-smoking room."

She sighed. "It's like you think—I'm like the old man's baby-sitter. I keep him happy, I look over his shoulder, and I report back to them."

"In exchange for . . ."

Her eyes widened. "Money, of course. What d'ya think?"

"How often do they pay you?"

"Every two weeks." She smiled thinly. "It's like a real job."

"What kind of things do you report back?"

"Pillow talk, mostly. He's a real talker, and he gripes a lot, especially about them." She waggled her hand for emphasis. "He does not like that woman. That's for sure. Course, she is a bitch."

"Els."

"Right. The dragon lady. That's what he calls her."

"What's her story, anyhow?" Joe asked, encouraging her to open up.

"Real chip on her shoulder, if you ask me," Hawkins said. "Makes her scary. I wanted a raise once, 'cause the old man was asking for some kinky stuff in bed, you know? I called it, like, 'combat pay.' It was just the two of us—her and me—so I tried playing it friendly, girl-to-girl, 'cause I knew she was doin' Brandon, even though I figured there couldn't be much love lost there, right? And she nearly tore my head off. Grabbed my hair in one hand and twisted my neck."

"What did she say?"

"Some shit about 'Don't talk to me about combat pay, you whore.' Called me a whore. *Her.* Amazing. Woman's got balls. Probably really does, you know? Maybe you guys ought to look into that. She could be masquerading. Probably not, though, 'cause then she went on a tear about how it was about time women started doing some of the fucking from the top position. It was actually pretty crazy. She scared the shit out of me."

"I'm guessing you didn't get your raise."

She laughed. "I felt lucky she didn't kill me."

"Tell me about Brandon."

Her face soured. "Him I don't like. She may be nuts, but she's got brains. That company was going nowhere till she came on board. I learned all that later, of course, mostly through David. But Brandon's a real sleazeball—weak, whiny, lazy. And he cheats, too, which I really don't like. Not even David does that."

"How do you mean, 'he cheats'?" Joe asked, keeping her going.

"He put the moves on me—after they got me working for them. I mean, I was doing his father, on their orders, so I suppose creepy Brandon figured that gave him sharing rights or something. Comes up to me one night when we were alone and starts putting his hands all over me. It was revolting. Up to then, I wasn't even sure he liked girls. I'm still not convinced—I think he did it to get back at daddy and stick it to Els, both, if you ask me. But whatever it was, it didn't work. I told him that if he kept it up, I'd squeal to his girlfriend. That limped his dick."

"What else did David tell you about Els?"

"That she'd been born better off than him, so her cutthroat attitude was iron . . . something."

"Ironic?"

"Right. That. So he figured something must've gone wrong big-time between her and her daddy. I think he's right, 'cause he's a pretty smart guy—just old. Plus, I've known girls like her that got really messed up by their fathers' being weird."

"Okay," Joe told her. "I get all the personal stuff, but you implied earlier that she's doing more than just improving the business. Why else would she pay you to be a spy?"

"She was getting it both ways," Donna explained, by now so enthused that Joe imagined they could have conducted the rest of the interview by phone.

"I mean, yeah, she goosed up the legit business," she continued, "but her real deal was finding Brandon and working him up like a piece of art."

"Tell us about that."

"Brandon's a real waste of time. I even heard that from people besides David. He used to be, like, famous around here for drunk driving, doing drugs, getting laid, and blowing his daddy's money. Typical rich-kid stuff. David banned him from the business, wouldn't take his phone calls, stuff like that. But he still loved him, you know? 'Cause he's a soft touch, and the kid's his son, and the mom is long gone, and all the rest. So when Els came on the scene, she saw how to get Brandon under her thumb and use David's guilt to bankroll a whole new part of the business."

"That being Cone Studio?" Joe asked.

"Yeah. That was one of them. There were others. You hear about the Chinese factory?"

"Yes," Joe admitted.

She laughed, enjoying herself, oblivious of the camera. "That was another."

"It's not legit?"

"Oh sure—partly. It cranks out most of the shit that ends up in the malls, now that manufacturing has gotten so pricey in the U.S., but Els doesn't know that I figured out she was also using it to run illegal aliens."

Joe controlled his reaction to this. In part because of Donna's flamboyance, he'd forgotten that David had once introduced her as a functional part of his company. Her qualifications as David's baby-sitter had clearly been based on both her feminine charms and her ability to be a business spy—which, it now appeared, Els had undervalued.

"You know this for a fact," he challenged her.

She gave him a crafty look. "I wanted a little insurance after she almost ripped my hair out. I wouldn't trust that woman not to stick a knife in my guts, you know? She was using Brandon to get to David; so I used David and being in the firm to get to them a little, putting out feelers, getting access to some paperwork, and putting a tail on her once or twice, too. Call it job security."

She shifted in her chair and recrossed her legs, getting more comfortable. "It's not like she financed the Chinese connection or anything. Els is a practical girl. She just pitched the factory idea to David and his money people. But once it was up and running, she used all those trips out there to research how to round up a little free labor, which she arranged to have close by so she could keep an eye on it. It was a win-win for her—she made money from the people who paid to come here; she made big bucks turning out jewelry with free labor; and she covered her tracks by making sure that labor changed over all the time, which also kept the money flowing from the immigrants. Cool, huh? I'll give her that much—no heart, but she's got brains."

Joe smiled despite himself, caught by her matter-of-fact outlook on virtually everything. "What about the production side of the Cone Studio?" he asked, hoping for some insight on the one aspect to all this that had first caught his attention. "How did she make the supply end work?"

But here, Donna gave a shrug. "I'd bet my bottom dollar she had a scam working there, too. I don't know what it was, though. You'd have to ask Brandon. I only found out what I did about the labor thing 'cause I dug for it, and maybe got lucky. But the Cone Studio's day-to-day operations were, like, top secret. That was one of the reasons I was hired to keep an eye on David—he was supposed to *never, ever* get involved with the Cone Studio." She laughed and added, "Which is exactly why I got interested in it. It did frustrate him sometimes—I can tell you that. Like I said, David's not a dummy, and he didn't like what Els and Brandon were doing—whatever it was. If it hadn't been for me, he probably would've done something, sooner or later, but I kept him distracted."

"I bet," Joe complimented her.

She smiled brightly at him. "Thank you. Plus," she suddenly added, "nobody was complaining about the money. I may be good at what I do, but the cash flow helped."

Joe nodded, going back over what he'd learned. He cast a glance at

Dan, who finally spoke, asking Donna, "You said you put a tail on Walker once or twice. How did that work?"

She laughed and tapped the side of her head. "I hired a private eye, duh."

CHAPTER TWENTY-TWO

"You look terrible."

Sam woke up, to see Willy's one unbandaged eye blinking at her, his head turned on his pillow. The covered eye was functional but had been hurt in the assault.

She smiled slightly. "You're such a turkey."

The smile was returned, along with "How's our girl?"

Sammie was nestled, cross-legged, amid a pile of pillows shoved around an enormous armchair that had been dragged into the room for her. Willy's surfacing propelled her from its embrace, her eyes tearing, to throw her arms around him and kiss his exposed cheek. They had removed his plastic airway earlier, once they'd determined he could breathe on his own, and had declared that from now on he was master of his own fate when it came to awakening from his coma.

"Hey, hey," he said hoarsely, one hand softly patting her. "Little sore here and there."

"She's fine," Sam kept saying. "We're fine."

He finally moved his hand up to her face and laid it against her cheek. "I heard you," he said.

She pulled back a couple of inches to focus on that one eye. "What?"

"I heard you. When I was under. I couldn't move. Couldn't speak. But I heard you when you talked to me. And you read to me, too, right? The newspaper or something?"

She was laughing. "I did. That's right. I can't believe it. They told me you might be able to, but I thought it was kind of a movie thing."

"But you did it anyhow."

She kissed him on the lips this time, quickly. "Of course I did."

He smiled again. "Did you have to read the *Reformer*? Such a rag."

She stuck her tongue out at him and climbed off the bed. "I got something for you," she said, dropping briefly from sight.

She reappeared holding Emma, whose eyes were shut tight in slumber, her round cheeks enacting the details of a happy dream.

Willy tapped his chest silently so that her mother could place the baby there, where he could feel her warmth against him and the scent from her feather-soft hair could fill his nostrils.

He took a deep breath. "I missed you guys."

"You're feeling better, then?" Sammie asked, her expression serious. "About us?"

He gave her a rueful look and tried to explain. "You know I'm made up of spare parts, right? Not all of them exactly functional."

She nodded, not wanting to interrupt. This kind of conversation was rare enough to be unique.

"I'm sorry I put you through a lot."

"It's okay," she barely whispered.

"Yeah, but it's not right. I feel things one way, I can't get them out, and when I do, they're all wrong anyhow. Then I figure it's just such bullshit, and I give up. . . ."

He paused, and she let him struggle with his thoughts, grateful for the effort.

"It's been tying me up in knots, looking forward to seeing you when I head home, then getting angry because I feel crowded and threatened by your being too close, then feeling guilty because I'll turn into a dad like all the losers I knew growing up."

He shook his head angrily. "Like I said, stupid stuff—no point talking about it."

"Good to hear, though," she told him hopefully. "I knew something was eating at you."

"Probably won't get any better," he said.

"She's a kid," Sammie acknowledged. "She's going to do kid stuff. And I can do more to stay out of your hair. We'll work it out, even if we have to make parts of the house out of bounds, so you won't feel totally invaded."

"It's idiotic," he repeated. "It's not normal."

She twisted around to sit on the edge of the bed, her hand resting on his good arm. "Is that why you took that risk, almost got yourself killed?"

His eye rested on her thoughtfully. Her voice had been quiet and encouraging, with no accusation in it.

"What?" he protested without fervor, almost to maintain face. "For the insurance or something? I'm not *that* wacko."

She touched his chin with her thumb and smiled sadly. "Of course not. And you wouldn't be that selfish to her."

He studied her for a second and then bent his neck to kiss their child.

"Right," he said softly.

. . .

Debbi Culbertson looked up when there was a knock on her office door. She was located on the third floor, above the bustle of Northampton's Main Street, almost directly across from the old courthouse. She loved the location, despite a rental rate that had forced her to do some pro bono work for the landlord. Dog-eat-dog, she told herself, happy she had the skills to make such a deal possible.

Two older men were standing in her doorway. Dan Siegel, she knew all too well. She'd worked for him back in the day. The other was unknown to her, despite having *cop* stamped on him like a designer label.

"Hey, Debbi," Dan said. "You got a minute?"

She rose and circled her desk to greet them both. "Sure. Long time, Dan."

He nodded and made the introductions. "Debbi Culbertson, Joe Gunther, from the Vermont Bureau of Investigation."

Debbi appraised the visitor as she shook hands. "No shit? Vermont. What brings you down here?" She retreated back behind the desk, waving at two guest chairs, "Sit, sit."

They did as invited.

"You get a call from Donna Lee Hawkins?" Dan asked, getting straight to business.

"I did," Debbi admitted, looking at Joe. "She told me to share everything I had. I didn't know it involved Vermont, though."

"Maybe it doesn't," Joe said cautiously.

Debbi smiled and raised her eyebrows at Dan. "Doesn't like private cops, does he?"

"Did you when you worked for me?" Dan asked in turn.

She shrugged. "Didn't have much to do with 'em. They do have a reputation."

"'They'?" Dan asked.

The smile widened. "Who's looking for a favor here, Dan?"

"My apologies if I was rude," Joe conceded.

She waved it off. "Nah. I'm just jerking you around. Stands to reason we don't like each other much. Necessary evils, like they say. I will tell you this, though, Dan: You may not think much of my profession, but I would never go back. When and if you ever retire, drop by and we'll shoot the shit. I'll tell you what I mean."

"Okay," Dan said doubtfully. "In the meantime, can you tell us what Hawkins hired you to do?"

Culbertson got comfortable. "Sure. She wanted the lowdown on Elizabeth Walker, who calls herself Els. She was also interested in anything I might pick up on Brandon Cone, although she didn't want me making him my primary focus."

"And?"

"And it was tough," she admitted. "Very hinky woman. About as paranoid as I've bumped into. I started slow, which turned out to be a good thing. If I'd just tucked in behind her off the bat, she would've pegged me, and that would've been that. But there was something about her—all skinny and wound up and neat as a pin—that put my guard up. So I kept my distance and never pressed too hard. There was someplace up north of town that she went to regularly, but I finally just gave up on that."

"Around Leeds?" Joe asked.

"Yeah. Guess you found it. I never did. Never dared get that close when she headed that way. I figured if she didn't see me in the rearview mirror, then she probably had cameras or people along the route to pick me up without my knowledge. I got to the point where I wasn't putting that past her. There were other places where I dropped back, too, like when she went up to the Summit House once—on Skinner Mountain, across the river—in the middle of the night. Who knows what that was all about. She was dressed in black, like a wannabe ninja. Brandon was with her then, too, complicating things."

"They carrying equipment that time?" Joe asked.

Culbertson gave him an analytical stare before asking, "If you know all the answers, why're we talking here?"

"We know some of them, Debbi," Dan reassured her. "Not all."

"Yeah," she said, addressing Joe. "They were carrying equipment. What, I couldn't tell."

"What did you find out in the end?" Dan asked.

"Enough to satisfy Donna. It wasn't like she was looking for a cheating husband, complete with photographs. She just suspected dirt, and I supplied it: Els was definitely running illegals."

"How'd you get that?"

"She'd visit a place on King Street—one of the dumps you don't look at twice when you pass by. But it also wasn't in the boonies like whatever she had up in Leeds, so I could hide myself in traffic or in a building nearby and not get made. It wouldn't have been enough to justify a warrant in the old days, but I'm here to tell you that she's got illegals stored there. After she'd come and go—which she'd do real fast, by the way, never staying long—I'd sometimes hang around to see what was up. She had handlers pack those people into a van every day and drive 'em off, and they'd change every now and then—new ones coming in, old ones disappearing. If you could get into the place, I'll guarantee you'd find a dormful of people. Mostly Asians, from what I saw."

"Did you take pictures of any of it?" Joe asked. "Or was it all reports?"

Culbertson pulled open a filing cabinet behind her. "Nope. I took a few shots. I'm guessing you already know what Walker looks like."

"Yeah," Dan said. "I'd like to see the King Street operation."

She pawed through the drawer and removed an envelope, dropping it where they could reach it on her desk.

"All yours, according to what Donna told me on the phone—including a copy of the final report. You must've put some kind of squeeze on her."

Neither man responded to that, concentrating instead on the photos that slipped from the envelope into Joe's hand.

They were in large part predictable—a surveillance subject crossing the street, walking down the sidewalk, conversing with people here and there. There were pictures of Els taken through windows, at the wheel of a car, and sharing lunch at a restaurant with an unimpressive man, whom Dan identified as Brandon Cone. Eventually, there came a small collection of images showing Walker standing on the sidewalk before a run-down building, looking over her shoulder furtively, and wearing a light sweatshirt with the hood up, an apparent stab at disguise. Subsequent shots, taken in rapid succession, showed her approaching the building's door, speaking with someone in the shadows, and immediately being ushered in.

"Let me see that one," Dan requested, taking hold of the last of the series.

Holding it in the light from the window, where Joe could see it also, he pointed to the black rectangle representing the open doorway.

"See that guy?" he asked.

Joe leaned in closer and noticed the face of the man who'd greeted

Walker and let her in. It was in dark shadow, to be sure, but discernible.

"You know him?" Joe asked.

"Ed Young," Dan said. "Nasty guy. Haven't heard from him in a while; thought he might've left town."

He returned the picture to the pile. "Guess I got that wrong."

Joe held up the whole packet to Debbi. "We keep these?"

She shrugged. "Far as I know. Donna said the works."

The two men exchanged looks, knowing that they had things to discuss, and knowing that here and now wouldn't work.

Joe stood up first, tucking the photos under his arm and extending a hand. "Debbi. It's been a pleasure."

She smiled ruefully. "Don't hear that much anymore. Happy hunting, boys."

As they hit the sidewalk outside of Culbertson's office, Joe paused to respond to his cell phone, which was vibrating deep inside his pocket. Often, he would merely peer at the caller's ID and then put the phone back. But not this time.

"Sam?" he asked.

"He's awake," she said.

"And all right?"

"Cranky as ever. He's also got something to tell you."

There was a pause before Willy's husky growl came on the line. "You catch anybody yet?"

"Been waiting for you. Welcome back."

"Yeah. Whatever. I didn't see who clocked me, but I broke up a torture party in the making—least I hope I did. Some big bastard with a shaved head, a goatee, and built like an over-the-hill bodybuilder, working a guillotine contraption on your Beacon Hill girl."

"Mina Carson."

"Yeah. Two others were there, too. Stuck-up broad with fancy clothes and an eating disorder, and a nerdy guy, also well-heeled, who looked like he was about to puke. The broad was giving orders and pushing the nerd around like she had him by the balls."

"He's David Cone's son, Brandon."

"*Brandon?* Please. Perfect. Why hadn't we heard of him?"

"Father/son fallout. The skinny woman is Elizabeth Walker, who put the whole operation together, using the son's access to the company to make a bundle smuggling illegals, running a burglary operation, and undercutting the jewelry trade by stealing her raw materials."

"What happened to Mina?"

"Vanished," Joe told him, "But we just got a lead on where they may be keeping her, or if not her, then some of the illegals. How're you holding up?"

"Like a fucking fool deserves to."

"We'll talk about that later. Tell Sam she's on paid leave till I get back to make sure you stay strapped into that bed. Understood?"

Willy made a buzzing noise on the phone. "You're breaking up."

The line went dead.

"Crazy bastard," Joe murmured, pocketing the phone.

"Willy?" Dan asked.

"Yeah. He ID'd Els and Brandon as being there, and gave a good description of Ed Young. Mina was alive when he last saw her, but he said they were using that chopping machine to torture her, or were about to."

"We didn't find any blood," Dan said comfortingly.

"True," Joe agreed. They began walking back toward the police department. "Did you recognize the building in Culbertson's photos? The ones showing Young?"

"Yup," the chief said. "It's on King Street. One of a string of flop-house rentals. You want to kick in the door?"

Joe looked at him as they walked. "I do, but at the right time. Given what Debbi said about how often Els drops by the place, wouldn't it be nice to hit it when all our chickens are in the coop?"

Dan considered that before countering, "In theory. What about the torture reference? If we find out they were inside, working on Mina while we waited to pounce, I'll be looking for a new job."

"It's your town, Dan," Joe told him. "Your call. But I'm thinking we might be taking Willy too much to heart. Why would they want to torture her?"

"To find out how she got to them?" Dan suggested.

"Maybe," Joe agreed. "But that's kind of null and void, now that they've pulled up stakes. They have to move or hide their workers any-how; if I were them, I'd just throw Mina into the mix for the moment, and see how things developed."

Dan wasn't happy. "Let's split the difference. We'll start by watching the building to see if we can corroborate what Debbi saw, update her information. Then, depending on that, we'll either wait or move in."

CHAPTER TWENTY-THREE

Mina opened her eyes slowly, staying absolutely still. Her head hurt, and her body was sore, her clothes torn. She remembered being at the old factory, the man with the limp arm appearing out of the dark, holding a gun and shouting, and finally, after he was knocked down, the bald giant, as she'd come to see him, bending over her menacingly.

After that, nothing.

She shuddered, recalling the one they'd called Ed, and reassessed how she was feeling, running one hand down the front of her, feeling the waistband of her jeans. He hadn't assaulted her—she knew that much—but had he tried to, perhaps after she'd lost consciousness?

Her jeans were fastened, which mitigated the memory of his tearing her shirt at the factory—and of finding her bra out of place now. She reached up and at least put everything back where it belonged, sensing that the damage had been more related to the way he'd hurled her around than to any sexual assault.

She slowly propped herself up on her elbows and took inventory of her surroundings. It was very dark, but with the little light leaking in from under the door, she could make out the confines of a small room with a double bunk bed lining the other wall, matching the one she was occupying. There was a window as well, blocked by a sheet of heavy plywood.

She swung her legs off the lower bed and touched the floor, immediately feeling dizzy. She placed a hand against her head, as if this might somehow help stabilize the tilting room.

What the hell had happened?

She thought back to following the van from the store, then arriving at the factory and seeing light from its second floor, and she remembered wanting to discover what was going on. . . .

What a dope she'd been. That cop—the older one, named Joe, who'd bought her coffee at the hotel—he'd told her that he didn't want to have to investigate her death. And she'd known from his eyes that he'd meant it.

Was that where this was headed?

She rose unsteadily, holding on to the bed's upright for balance. Her head hurt much worse as a result, and she fended off a resulting surge of nausea.

"Oh boy," she muttered, blinking to focus on the strip of light beneath the door.

She took a step or two in its direction, when, as if blown open by a blast of wind, the door flew back on its hinges with a crash, flooding the room with light, and confronting her with the oversized dark outline of a towering man.

"You're up," Ed said in a voice slurred by alcohol. "That's good. No fun fucking a zombie."

He stepped into the room, reaching for her.

. . .

Lǐ Anming heard the door bounce off the wall beside her, making her jump up in bed.

"What was that?" Wú Méi asked from below her, her voice sharp with fear at the accompanying female cry.

Lǐ Anming didn't answer at first, listening instead. "It is the woman they brought in. Next door."

"From the work place?"

"They locked her in the empty room. Later, after you went to sleep."

They both paused to listen to the muffled sounds. It seemed like a struggle.

"She was tied in the van," Wú Méi said plaintively.

"I heard them move her a while ago," Lǐ Anming explained. "I think it is Ed."

"Now?"

"Yes. He is raping her," Lǐ Anming said, slipping out of her bunk in the darkness. The others in their room were still asleep or, more likely, pretending to be.

Wú Méi reached out and grabbed Lǐ Anming's hand as she landed silently on the floor. "What are you doing?"

Lǐ Anming eased her hand free. "I will not let this happen."

Her companion protested, "No. Please. He'll hurt you, too."

But Lǐ Anming wasn't listening. It was time to do something.

Past time.

Outside, on King Street, Joe sat in an unmarked cruiser beside Ruth Constantine, one of Dan Siegel's detectives.

"Any movement?" she asked. She'd just joined him, walking up wearing cargo pants and a light sweatshirt and sliding into the still-warm seat just vacated by her predecessor.

"Movement, yes," he told her. "But nothing illegal. We did confirm that Ed Young is inside. Saw him go in about an hour ago with what looked like a case of liquor—at least it was labeled that on the outside."

Joe had been on stakeout for ten hours already—not a record for him, but no string of laughs, either, given that what he'd just described amounted to the sum total of their target's activity.

"What exactly are we hoping for?" Ruth asked. Dan Siegel had set up a rotation for this duty, but without going into much detail.

Joe kept it simple. "Anything that'll get us legal entrance. We're pretty sure the place is full of illegal workers, headquarters for a bur-glary ring, and maybe the hangout for a murderer or two, but we can't prove it."

Ruth frowned at the news, thinking of how unlikely it was that this stakeout would be successful. "What do you expect them to do?" she asked. "Throw a body off the roof?"

He smiled broadly while keeping his eyes locked on the building. "That would be nice, but all I really need is for a certain well-dressed, slim woman named Elizabeth Walker to use the front door, so that I can connect the house with the person."

With "well-dressed" hanging in the air, Constantine eyed the whole neighborhood doubtfully. "You sure about that?" she asked.

"We're hopeful," he said, holding up a thermos. "Coffee?"

"Step on it," Els said angrily.

Brandon didn't respond. He kept his eyes on the road, his hands on the wheel, and his mind off the headache that was threatening to split his cranium. As hangovers went, this was a trophy winner.

"It's not like there's traffic," she insisted.

"You really want us to get pulled over?" he asked reluctantly, not able to resist.

It didn't work, of course. She glared at him. "How many times do we have to go over this? It wouldn't matter." She enunciated the last three words slowly, as if taunting a child. "The cops don't know shit."

He retreated to his previous silent mode, shifting his concentration to how he was going to get out of this nightmare.

Throwing his hand in with her had been as satisfying emotionally as it had been lucrative. He'd enjoyed the money and reducing his selfish, narcissistic father to puppet status within the confines of his own company. Even Els's violent temper and imperious manner had held their weird appeal, at least giving him a steady diet of highs and lows he'd never known, along with the occasional over-the-top aggressive sex. He'd come to envision the entire experience as a journey comparable to his teenage years—another hellish passage survived because of its brief life span and excessive fringe benefits.

That had been the case, at least, until about twenty-four hours ago, when he'd seen a girl threatened with a guillotine and a cop left for dead.

At that point, he'd realized—as if emerging from one of the chemically induced comas of his youth—that the world might have taken a new direction during his inattention.

He now understood that he'd linked his fate not with an exciting opportunist but with a psychopath, and that there didn't seem to be any likely extraction from her company, at least not one that he would survive.

In that way of thinking, whether because of his self-indulgent ways or despite them, Brandon Cone had always been a fatalist.

Joe and Ruth, even from their vantage point in the weed-choked parking lot across the street, almost missed the car's headlights as it shifted suddenly from conventionally moving down the street to abruptly going dark, like a stealth fighter hitting its invisibility button. It then veered into the building's driveway and straight into a garage, the door of which immediately dropped down behind it.

"Wow," Ruth said. "Like friggin' Batman."

Joe pulled out his portable radio. "Yeah," he said to her. "Batman driving Brandon Cone's car." He keyed the mic to call for backup.

Brandon and Els entered the building through the garage's connecting door and immediately headed for the cellar. There, they found Miguel sitting on a bedraggled couch, watching TV.

"Where's Ed?" Els demanded. "We had a meeting."

Miguel stood up nervously. "I know. He's here. I'll go get him."

But Els stopped him. "What's wrong? You look like a cat on a highway."

His eyes grew large. "What?"

Her scowl deepened. "What're you hiding? What's Ed up to?"

Two flights up, Ed had staggered into Mina's room, managed to get his arms around her, and forced her back onto the bottom bunk. He was now simultaneously trying to unzip his pants and unbutton hers as she shoved and punched at him wildly. It was a scene filled only with the sounds of her blows, the creaking of the bed, and the awful sound of his efforts to tear off her clothing.

Neither one of them noticed Lǐ Anming's entrance or her desperate search for a weapon.

All she found was a broom with a wooden handle.

Taking a wide stance, she aimed carefully and jabbed at Ed's ear, using the handle like a spear, hoping to penetrate his skull.

She hit his temple instead.

He let out a scream of pain, rolled away into the wall, and allowed Mina to twist the other way and fall out of the bunk bed, pulling at her jeans as she scrambled to her feet.

She stared wildly at Lǐ Anming. "Who are you?"

Lǐ Anming pulled at her, still holding the broom in the other hand. "Come. Come now."

Ed was kicking away the blanket, which had become tangled in his legs, and he yelled at them as he struggled to get free of the lower bunk. "You fucking bitch. You're gonna die now."

Lǐ Anming took an overhand downward swipe at his neck as he emerged, whacking him across the nape and shattering the handle, before both women fled from the room, running for the staircase.

The door at the top of the stairs was generally kept locked, but as Lǐ Anming had left her room to help Mina, she'd seen that Ed had left it ajar in his hormonal, drunken state.

Ed fell off the bed with a grunt, hitting his face on the floor and rolling onto his back, yanking on his pants.

"You bitches. You're gonna die now."

. . .

In the basement, Els turned at the muffled commotion and twisted around to confront Miguel. "What the hell is going on?"

Miguel burst forth, "Ed got drunk. He said he was going to fuck the girl—get something out of this mess before we all got busted."

"You morons," Els exploded, including Brandon in her gaze. She gestured angrily to Miguel. "*Upstairs*. Get that son of a bitch."

Miguel ran past them, with Els and Brandon on his heels.

In the lobby just above, Lĭ Anming and Mina half-fell down the stairs and careened toward the front door, with Ed tumbling after them, still yelling. As the three from the basement reached the first floor, Els pushed past Miguel angrily and ran down the hallway as Lĭ Anming yanked open the door to escape into the night.

"There," Joe said, pointing.

Light had spilled from the building's interior, outlining two women, hand in hand, moving fast. As they hit the three steps leading to the ground, however, a large man burst out and tackled one of the women, causing all three of them to go sprawling into the dirt.

As Joe and Ruth bolted from their car and began running across the street, more people began appearing. Joe called into his portable radio, "People are running from the building. Get here as fast as you can. We need help, people."

He'd just seen a gun appear in the hand of a second, smaller man in the doorway.

Almost as soon as Joe had exchanged the radio for his own weapon, he saw strobe lights bearing down from the far end of the street.

"*Do not move*," he yelled as he and Ruth reached the other sidewalk. "*Police*."

On the ground, the three were slugging it out like barroom brawlers, rolling around and screaming at one another.

Joe kept sprinting, drawing close now, and saw Els Walker emerge and furiously grab the smaller man's pistol, pushing him away.

"Put the gun down," he ordered loudly as, instead, she leveled it at the threesome before her.

Joe stopped dead in his tracks, as did Ruth, and they both fixed their weapons on Walker, just as Brandon Cone shouted, *"Enough,"* and, facing Walker, swung his body before her to block her shot.

Her gun went off with a muffled, high-pitched crack, and Brandon crumpled at her feet.

Without hesitation—almost calmly—Els Walker then shifted her aim toward the two cops, just as the scene became inundated with light from several arriving squad cars.

Ruth Constantine fired first, placing two rounds into the center of Walker's chest. She fell lifeless against the small man, who instinctively caught her under the armpits before setting her down gently.

After which, for the slightest fraction of time, Joe noticed an almost jarring moment of utter stillness, as if the world were holding its breath.

CHAPTER TWENTY-FOUR

Jimmy McAuliffe smiled as the headlights died at the end of the alleyway and he saw two figures emerge from the car. He brought up his night-vision binoculars for a better look.

"That them?" his companion asked.

"Yeah," Jimmy said, still watching. "And James White is even carrying a bag of something. You gotta love it when these losers cooperate."

He reached over to the receiver resting on the console between them and adjusted the volume slightly. Up to now, they'd just been eavesdropping on a conversation between Jill Dean and Tony Leto's mother, who owned the Dorchester Avenue store they were watching. The women were waiting for Tony and James to arrive bearing the haul from their latest "shopping expedition."

Jimmy punched the TRANSMIT button on his radio and updated the rest of the team about the newcomers, followed by instructions to be ready to move fast on his command.

They heard over the receiver the heavy footfalls of the two men descending the building's staircase as they neared the basement room where Jill had told Jimmy earlier they met to plan their raids and divide the spoils afterward.

Jimmy wasn't feeling cocky exactly—he'd been at this for too long not to know that Murphy stood ready to screw things up at a moment's notice. But unlike some cases, this time he was confident that he'd considered most of the more obvious stumbling blocks.

Jill had been the biggest hurdle, of course. Once Mina Carson had told him about her—and he'd concluded that hanging around Northampton wasn't going to add much—he'd made turning Jill into an informant his mission in life.

Especially after Willy Kunkle had almost been killed. Jimmy McAuliffe might not have been the most ambitious cop on the force, but he took the law-enforcement brotherhood seriously. He was a tribesman, and he'd pegged Willy as one, too. You take on one of us, you take on all of us. That was his credo.

In theory, Jill should have been open to suggestion. She was scared, self-serving, and feeling guilty about compromising her aunt Pam in the first place by revealing Billie's treasure trove to her boyfriend. But James White scared her, and the idea of spilling her guts to the cops and then wearing a wire to a post-robbery divide-the-loot party had become a hard sell for Jimmy.

Still, here I am, he thought with satisfaction—a pleasure enhanced by the news that he'd just received about the shoot-out in Northampton. Being able to match that success with one of his own wouldn't hurt in the least. Mina Carson's finding Jill Dean first had made Jimmy feel bad about his initial poor showing.

The conversation over the speaker became more animated. They heard the men being greeted, the sound of the pack being dumped on the central table and its contents strewn across its surface. Both women began commenting on some of the jewelry.

Jimmy had to hand it to Jill. She was a good actor, laughing and praising the boys, admiring their prowess and its end results. He listened to her as she extracted from them all the details of their heist, including the address and the methods employed for the break-in.

Finally, with a nod from his partner, Jimmy decided that he'd captured what he needed. He keyed the radio once more and released his team.

Mina picked up the phone reluctantly, enmeshed enough in her own sorrow that it had become her place of preference, where, unlike in the so-called real world, she at least knew the territory.

"Yes?" she asked dully.

"Miss Carson? It's Detective McAuliffe."

That surprised her. "Oh. Hi."

"Hi. I wanted to give you an update on your grandmother's case. I also heard about your close call in Northampton and wanted to tell how happy I am that you are all right."

She didn't answer, startled and unbelieving that anyone might consider her "all right" in any form.

Jimmy paused, confused by her silence. "Miss Carson?"

"I'm here."

"We got the people who did it," he said. "Got one to turn against the other, and then got a confession from that guy. The prosecutor was part of it all, of course, offering deals to make it happen, but even I am happy with the outcome. The ringleader'll be locked up for years and years."

She still didn't respond.

"I know it won't bring your grandmother back," he tried, losing steam, "but I thought you'd like to know anyhow. Sometimes it helps. Least that's what I've heard."

"Thanks, Detective," she finally murmured.

"Are you hanging in there?" he asked, immediately regretting how it sounded.

"Sure," she said. It seemed like the entire structure of her life before the attack had simply turned into mist.

He paused. "I'm sorry we got off on the wrong foot, Miss Carson. We lose touch in this job—how this sort of thing hits people who aren't used to it."

"It's okay. I gotta go. Thanks."

The phone went dead.

Jimmy sat back in his chair, the phone still dangling from his hand.

"You okay?" a colleague asked, walking by.

He shrugged. "Yeah. Dealing with a citizen. You know how that goes."

The man laughed. "They ain't like us, man. Have no clue."

Joe sat next to Willy's bed. "You're lookin' better."

In fact, he was. The bandages had been reduced to a fat patch over one temple, leaving the once-covered eye to blink next to its companion, even if surrounded by puffy, bruised skin.

"Yeah. I wanna get out of here. Drivin' me nuts."

"Tomorrow, from what I heard." Joe scanned the food tray that Willy had rejected.

Willy pushed it toward him. "You probably like this shit. Feel free."

Not being shy, Joe reached for a small plastic pot of dubiously colored Jell-O and a spoon.

"Everything wrapped up?" Willy asked him, watching Joe eat, as if the Jell-O might suddenly spring forth and lash out at them both.

Joe slithered a spoonful down his throat with satisfaction. "Yup. Pretty much of a clean sweep. Els and Brandon didn't make it, but the other two're behind bars and the feds got everyone else."

"What about Cone?" Willy asked. "Seems like he should do some time just for being stupid."

Joe laughed. "Once the IRS is done looking at his books, his bankers might be agreeing with you."

Willy shook his head. "I doubt it. They take care of one another at that level—assholes unite."

Joe nodded in sympathy, adding, "I thought Sam might be here."

"Just missed her," Willy told him. "She wanted to get some groceries. She'll be back in a couple of hours."

"She been here a lot?" Joe asked neutrally, knowing Willy to enjoy his solitude like few others he knew.

His friend's benign response, therefore, surprised him. "Yeah. It's been nice."

Joe put the small tub back on the tray, along with the spoon. "So things are better?"

Willy cast him a glance and smiled ruefully. "She talk to you, too?"

Joe raised an eyebrow. "You know how it is."

"Yeah. Father Joseph—leaning post for the walking wounded. What would we do without you?"

. . .

Dan Siegel stood on the sidewalk outside Northampton's town hall, feeling like a western sheriff looking down the center of town with a paternal air. He should have been wearing a six-gun, of course, instead of looking like a rumpled and oversized accountant. No one would have commented.

The beaming, buoyant presence of Lǐ Anming by his side didn't hurt. She'd been talking nonstop since they'd met up two hours ago, so that he could help her through some of the bureaucratic steps on her way to securing legal status. She'd been making him feel like a minor deity with her ongoing praise and thanks.

"So, what do you think you'll do first?" he asked her now that they were about to part ways.

"I have money," she replied in her careful English. "Thank you to Miss Carson. And to both of you as my sponsors." That came following a broad smile. "I think I will enjoy your beautiful city for a while. I will rent a new apartment."

He laughed, seeing Northampton in a somewhat more jaded light. "Well, we're certainly unique. But you should thank yourself. You earned your own good fortune, helping to stop a crime like you did. I think you'll be fine in this country."

They shook hands then and exchanged a few more polite words before separating. She watched him walk away toward his office, until his figure blended in with the other people perpetually crowding the town's sidewalks.

She thought back to when she'd first caught sight of this place through a small rusted-out hole in the side of Ed's van and had felt its pull on her.

She smiled at the memory and stepped off the curb, into her new life.

. . .

Later, at the other end of the same street, David Cone stood at his top-floor office window, holding a glass of scotch and admiring the scenery. There was a Gay Pride Parade going on—Northampton at its exuberant best—and he was enjoying a ringside view of a team of co-op grocery employees executing an intricate, close-order shopping cart drill.

Donna came up beside him and looped her arm around his waist. "Having a good time?"

He smiled, keeping his eyes on the goings-on. A lesbian motorcycle team was coming into view, leather-clad and pumping the air with their fists. "I haven't missed one of these in thirty years."

She shook her head and glanced up at his profile. "Everything back to normal, huh?"

He glanced at her quickly. "Regrets?"

"I'd think you'd have a couple. Your son died."

"My son was out to destroy me."

"*She* played a small role in that."

He turned from the window to take her in fully. "True," he conceded. "But if it hadn't been for your telling me about them, they both would've eaten me up and spat me out—regardless of what they had planned for each other later."

"You were the one who told me I should hire that private eye. Plus, I fell in love with you," she said simply.

He kissed her forehead. "You're a practical girl."

She didn't take offense. They were kindred spirits, and had acted as such to turn the tables on Elizabeth Walker's ambitions, albeit to a slightly more bloody conclusion than anticipated.

Still, as a result, they were now facing a virtually clean slate—having played the total innocents in a grilling by the IRS, and having made a few phone calls to Els's erstwhile offshore bankers.

There had been a couple of details that Donna had instructed Debbi Culbertson not to share with the police about the fruits of her investigation.

Cone nodded thoughtfully. "You hear how he died?"

Donna dropped her arm and took a half step away. "Brandon? What do you mean? He was shot by the cops."

He settled comfortably into a leather armchair by the window and crossed his legs. "He stepped in front of Els's gun, just as she was about to shoot someone. Sacrificed himself for another."

Donna's hand hovered near her mouth. "Oh."

David stared sadly into his glass. "But was it redemption? Or had he just grown sick of it? Christ—how little we know. . . ." He looked up at her. "Or maybe, how little we ask."